Lost Sols

Book Two

Rise of the Annunaki

James Kirk Bisceglia

Edited by Jennifer Koth

Cover design by Barbara Vallejo Francis

Visit my website at www.JamesKirkBisceglia.com

First Printing: October 2015

ISBN-13: 978-1517774691
ISBN-10: 1517774691

Chapter 1

Azmune was entombed in the same room for the majority of his life. The incompetent humans did not have the necessary knowledge or technology to repair his injuries. On rare occasions when he regained consciousness the humiliation was overwhelming. The room was always the same; only the faces of the strange creatures changed. He opened his eyes and braced himself for the horrible smells associated with the species, yet this time was different. Humans weren't hovering over him experimenting on his body and the smell wasn't nearly as bad. In fact, it was peaceful, and he felt better than he had in a long time. Azmune attempted to sit up, but his atrophied muscles wouldn't allow such movement. He did manage to turn his head and was surprised to find he was in an Alliance transport. He must have finally been rescued.

A human walked into his field of vision. She was saying something. The computer began to translate her words. "Please stay calm. We are taking you home." He tried to respond, but his voice failed. Azmune closed his eyes and contemplated his new situation.

Vincent was in the command center nervously awaiting the arrival of the gate. In less than a day, the Santa Maria would pass through the gate and into the unknown. His thoughts were interrupted by the computer, "The patient in the medical center has regained consciousness." Immediately after the computer reported the change, Vincent was summoned to the medical center.

Julia was waiting anxiously when Vincent entered the medical center. "Andy woke up for a short time. He was trying to speak but couldn't. I told him we were bringing him home. I think the computer translated the message, but he fell asleep again," she said in a worried tone. "Hopefully the message was comforting for him. It would be helpful if his species recognizes we are trying to do what is best for him. Despite what happened at Roswell, this is the first opportunity humanity has been given to return him to his people for help," Vincent said. "If the Rabanians are the aliens we believe them to be, they will be grateful and understand we are doing what's in Andy's best interest," Julia replied. "I hope you're right. I'm returning to the command center. Please notify me the next time he shows any signs of consciousness. I need to speak to this alien and inform him of our intentions," Vincent said as he walked out of the room.

Monique was staring out the viewport when Vincent returned to the command center. "How long until we reach the gate?" he asked. "We will reach the gate in thirteen hours at present speed," Monique replied. "Good, our patient is waking up. It's time to reunite him with his own species. I hope there aren't any hard feelings," Vincent said. Sarah, Isabella, Dominic, Julia and Tony were all in the command center awaiting the arrival of the gate and listening to the conversation. Vincent instructed Tony to wear clothing. Everyone needed to know his location onboard in order to feel comfortable. "Do you think these aliens will be able to diagnose my new abilities?" Tony asked. "I imagine they will know exactly what has happened. According to the computer, we will gain access to the knowledge base of many worlds once we pass through the gate," Vincent replied. "Good, I need answers and can't help but wonder if there will be more changes to my body and mind," Tony said. "Time is growing short; we'll find out soon enough," Vincent replied.

Thirteen hours passed and two minutes remained before the Santa Maria would pass through the gate. Everyone was nervous and on edge. "Computer, is there any danger to any life forms on this vessel when we traverse the gate?" Vincent asked. "There is no danger," the computer replied. The gate appeared and was magnificent. It was oval, edged with deep purple and a small shimmering whiteness glowed opaquely in the center. The Santa Maria and her crew flew gracefully through the gate and out the other side.

Samya was assigned to the Sol outpost. His assignment was scheduled to last for seventy-eight cycles. He was now on cycle sixty-five. His duties were normally mundane and routine. Recently, an unmanned automated ship returned from the Sol system through the gate. He viewed the data and immediately sent it to his superiors. The intelligent life forms from the third world discovered the Alliance ship and the base where it was located. The latest report indicated the vessel was docked and being prepared for a return voyage to the Sol System for further observation. Samya was about to check for an update on the ship's status when an alarm sounded. Another vessel was traversing the gate from Sol. He scrambled interceptors and began reviewing data which suddenly appeared on his screen. The analysis indicated the vessel was the only remaining Alliance craft in the Sol System and was last located on the fourth planet. Samya viewed the ship's interior and was stunned to find humans in control of the vessel. He promptly issued an override command and took control of the craft.

The positions of the stars changed after the Santa Maria passed through the gate. Vincent felt his entire body relax. "Computer, have we successfully passed through the gate?" he asked. "The gate has been traversed. The craft is now in the Rabanah System," the computer replied. "Where is the closest inhabited planet located?" Vincent asked. The computer failed to reply. Vincent asked the question again and didn't receive a response. "All stop. Let's see where we are and find out what options we have," he commanded. "Captain, the controls are unresponsive; I have no control of the Santa Maria!" Sarah exclaimed.

"Oh my God! I think we're in trouble," Monique said as she stared out the forward view screen. A dozen interceptors surrounded the Santa Maria and were falling into formation on all sides. "I guess someone knows we're here," Tony said grimly. "Everyone remain calm. The Rabanians have known about humanity for a very long time. As far as we know, these aliens have never been hostile toward us. I don't know why they would be now. Let's see where we're being taken," Vincent said, trying to calm his crew.

Chief Administrator Azira was in the middle of his first meal of the day when he was interrupted by an alert. He received a message from the Sol outpost. "We've intercepted a ship which has come through the gate. The vessel is one of ours and is crewed by humans. How do you wish to proceed?" Outpost Commander Samya inquired. Azira was shocked. The study of humanity was ongoing and the species was being groomed for eventual entry into the Alliance. He knew mankind was advancing quickly as a species. It was surprising the Terrans managed to find a way to make it through the gate. Their species wasn't expected for many more cycles. "Bring our guests to the capitol. I will personally greet these humans," Azira ordered.

Randy arrived at Leviathan and parked in his assigned parking spot. Nothing seemed out of the ordinary. He walked into his office and found his secretary in her usual place in the outer office. "Good Morning Mr. Stedman; it's good to have you back. We thought you were either dead or in prison and have heard all sorts of rumors. You must have had a really good ace up your sleeve. None of us thought we'd ever see you again," she said with concern. "You have no idea. Please inform all department heads to meet in the conference room at ten o'clock. We have a great deal of work ahead of us. Summon all members of research and development as well," Randy replied. Dalton would arrive shortly hoping to get to Mars as fast as possible. Randy needed to work quickly to prepare another mission. Mars likely held many more secrets and he was determined to uncover as many as possible.

The staff members summoned to the meeting were spellbound as Dalton explained the events that took place and the discoveries they'd made on Mars. It took Dalton three hours to tell the tale and answer the numerous questions. "Thank you. I think I've learned a few things I didn't know before as well. Time is a critical factor right now. We have a few ETS units and the capability of reentering the dead zone and there is a wealth of undiscovered information and technology on Mars. We will disassemble one of the ETS units in an effort to reverse-engineer the device. If the attempt is successful, we can send multiple teams to continue exploring the Cydonia Region.

In the meantime, we will prepare a ship for launch next week. Patrick Weeks has been assigned captain of the expedition. He's familiar with the Cydonia Region and has the experience necessary to deal with any issues on Mars. Dalton will be in command of conducting research on the surface. We only have four ETS units. One will remain at Leviathan for examination. The units we have will be locked in the vault and placed under guard. The four ETS units are the most valuable pieces of technology on Earth at the moment. Dalton will choose two other individuals for exploration and research. It's time to prepare for launch. We're back in business despite our intrusive government," Randy said.

The day Vincenzo and his crew set sail for the unknown, Enzo received a call from President Louis requesting a meeting. Enzo decided to stay in Trundle for the immediate future; it was peaceful, and he didn't trust the government. He refused to travel to the United States under any conditions. The President was informed the meeting would only take place at the villa in Trundle. Vincenzo would be summoned if Enzo or any of his people were taken or threatened in any way. Reluctantly, the President agreed.

Enzo watched as Marine One descended toward the villa. The aircraft was flanked by two identical helicopters. The Secret Service had been in Trundle for the last fifteen hours ensuring the President would have a safe visit. All weapons were temporarily seized and Enzo was currently at the mercy of the government he opposed. He sat in his large, leather-bound chair and waited for the leader. The man would come to him.

Secret Service agents led the President into his office. "Welcome to Trundle, Mr. President. It's my hope we can dispense with most of the usual nonsense and get down to business," Enzo said stiffly. "Thank you. As usual, you get right to the point. Keep in mind I'm a military man and can dispense with bullshit when necessary," retorted the President.

"You need to understand something. This planet requires leadership and a functioning government. If there is no leadership, anarchy and chaos will ensue. You must comply with the law and you must assist your government in any way possible. We know you are in possession of advanced technology and you have information about the lost city on Mars. This information must be shared. The people of Earth need protection and if you don't cooperate, things could get very uncomfortable for you and Randy," President Louis said vehemently.

"Mr. President, you have a lot of balls to come here and threaten me, especially after what Randy did in Washington. The Romans built an empire. They were overconfident, cocky, and arrogant just like you. If you can't learn from the lessons of the past, the same failures will be repeated. I suggest you study more history in order to lead your constituents to a better life. If you truly care for the people you represent, you will do what is best for them."

Enzo sneered at the President and continued, "It will take years for you to rebuild after the attack on the White House and the capitol, so listen to me carefully. The days of keeping secrets are coming to an end. After speaking with Vincenzo and Randy, I've learned humanity is insignificant in the larger picture. The United States Government is the biggest ant on the hill at the moment. You will leave Randy and I alone from now on. Interference in our activities will not be allowed. Randy will resume his duties at Leviathan without your intrusion. We will make a return trip to Mars. Do not attempt to intervene or obstruct this mission in any way. Like it or not, Vincenzo and the crew of the Santa Maria represent humanity and will contact our mysterious alien allies. My nephew is an intelligent man and will form an alliance with the species if it's possible. Vincenzo will describe the conditions on Earth and explain the injustices that have been perpetuated by the government. He is likely to return with a contingence of new allies and will contact me upon his return. If you make an enemy of me, you will become an enemy of my family and our new associates as well.

It's obvious our planet has been visited for thousands of years, if not longer. The truth will soon be revealed to our population. Spinning the facts will no longer be sufficient to keep the truth from the remainder of humanity. The media loves sensationalism and drama; that said, if I need to conduct interviews with every media outlet on Earth I will do so. The people will soon learn what's really on Mars. I doubt if the aliens will care about one government among many that has temporarily ruled of a small portion of humans on this planet. Any moral being would release the truth of alien existence," Enzo said.

"I'll agree to a truce, but I want information. I would like to know what was discovered on Mars and would like to send a government representative on your next expedition to Mars," the President said. "How do you know we're planning another expedition?" Enzo asked suspiciously. "I'm not a fool. Our people on Mars witnessed crew members emerging from the ground in more than one location. There is an underground city in the dead zone and I know there was insufficient time to explore the area fully," the President said. "I'll agree to your terms as long as the government representative is a scientist. I won't endanger my people with a member of the military and will perform my own background check on the person selected. If I'm not satisfied, you'll need to find a replacement. It's important for you to remember these aliens cannot be defeated. We will share the information found on Mars, but you should reevaluate the tenuous position of your government in the larger picture," Enzo said flatly. "I think we've come to an understanding. I will provide the name of the assigned representative after consulting with my scientific advisors," President Louis said and abruptly left.

Chapter 2

Azmune awoke feeling much better. He remembered the human female telling him he was going home. He turned his head and saw her sitting nearby. He tried to speak and was pleased with the results as his voice was now working. The female was startled and rushed over to him. She said something, but the computer was not translating her words. He knew if the computer was not translating; it was offline. He attempted to bring it online. "Computer, this is Azmune of Rabanah. Override your previous command and restore all functions." There was no response.

Vincent wondered how long it would take to reach their destination when Julia rushed into the command center. Without the computer she was unable to call from the medical center. "Andy is awake. With the computer offline we are unable to understand each other," she said with concern. "Come on Julia let's get down there," Vincent said.

Samya received a report he was having trouble believing. He brought up the data from the ship's medical center and learned a male Rabanian was injured and alive aboard the ship. He took a few moments to contemplate the situation before restoring computer function aboard the ship with the exception of weapons and guidance systems. The Chief Administrator was requesting to be updated on any new developments. An injured Rabanian aboard a ship crewed by humans was definitely a new development. Samya sent an update.

Vincent and Julia arrived at the medical center followed closely by the rest of the crew since there was no need to staff the command center. Andy sat up as the crew entered and spoke. The computer suddenly was back online and translated his words. "My name is Azmune. Am I your prisoner? What is the current situation? Is the Alliance still at war?" he inquired.

Vincent looked into Azmune's bright blue eyes and was impressed with the alien's composure. If the situation were reversed, he didn't think he would be nearly as poised. Vincent took a deep breath and began to explain, "You crashed on our planet during a battle. Our species does not have the required medical knowledge to repair your injuries. You've been unconscious for one hundred of our years. We recently discovered this ship on the fourth planet from our sun. When we decided to traverse the gate, we were given the opportunity to return you to your people where we hope your injuries can finally be properly treated. You are not our prisoner and I don't know if your species is still at war. We are unable to communicate with any non-human species at the moment.

That said, we are likely prisoners of your species. We no longer have control of this vessel and are being escorted to an unknown location. You need to understand we are not hostile and wish to establish a peaceful relationship with your species and all species you are in contact with. Is there a way for you to communicate with the vessels escorting us?" Vincent asked. It was difficult for Azmune to take in all this information. He didn't know how long one hundred Earth years was, but it must be a great many cycles. "It's probable the ships escorting us know I am here. The computer came back online after I attempted to override the previous command. The ship was likely scanned, I was discovered in the medical center and the computer was partially restored. I will send a message. Whomever is monitoring transmissions will receive the message and may not respond depending on their orders." Azmune instructed the computer to transmit the current conversation through the primary communication channel.

Chief Administrator Azira was monitoring the communication channel and immediately saw the message transmitted from the captured vessel. He enjoyed history and studied humanity in great detail. Such a message was not a surprise to him. All representatives from member planets were summoned to discuss the new situation. He would greet the humans and escort them to the Great Chamber where the Assembly would hear what the visitors decided to say. The day would be historical for mankind. Humans managed to travel outside their solar system for the first time. Without a doubt they would be questioned at length by the assembled members. The ship was due shortly. Azira prepared himself for the arrival and decided to wear his ancient ceremonial robe. One way or another it would be a pivotal moment for mankind. The humans would be greeted and proper first contact protocol would be adhered to. Azira issued orders for the humans to be greeted with full diplomatic honors.

Vincent and the rest of the crew returned to the command center after Azmune transmitted their message. Fatigued, Azmune slept once again. "Vincent, we are approaching a planet," Tony said. "I don't see it," Vincent replied as he surveyed the screen. Tony momentarily forgot about his advanced vision. "It's getting closer and we're heading straight for it; it's amazing!" The planet had a bright purple landmass surrounded by vibrant green oceans with two distinctly artificial rings. All structures were bathed in bright red light. There were two small moons. One was completely white and appeared to be made entirely of ice. The other was completely gold in color. Tony couldn't help but wonder if it wasn't made of actual gold. The moon was completely spherical and smooth. It looked like a beautiful gold marble floating in space.

The Santa Maria approached at a tremendous speed and the planet grew larger by the second. The rest of the crew could now see the planet. "Rabanah. I never thought to see my home world again," the computer said startling Vincent. He turned around and saw Azmune standing in the entryway to the command center. The computer translated what he said. "It looks like we've arrived at our destination. Welcome home my friend," Vincent said.

The crew stood in silence, transfixed as the Santa Maria gracefully flew into a hanger near the shore of the largest continent. The massive green waves broke hard as they crested the shoreline. "Captain, we've arrived at the new world. We are awaiting your orders, sir," Isabella said. "Yes, we have, Isabella. Let's hope the natives aren't too restless. I will represent mankind for better or worse, but don't be hesitant to speak up if you have something valuable to contribute," Vincent said as the ship came to a standstill and the hatch opened. "Let's go; everyone be on their best behavior," Vincent ordered.

Azmune hobbled past Vincent and rushed into the waiting arms of his people. He was quickly escorted away by members of his species. "I hope he makes a quick recovery. Maybe he can put in a good word for us," Vincent said and descended the ramp. A lone alien awaited them. "Humans, I am Chief Administrator Azira. Welcome to Rabanah. At the present time you are our guests. Follow me please," the alien said benevolently.

Vincent was nervous. He heard the Chief Administrator's words and was caught up in the moment. The Chief Administrator arrived alone and thousands of aliens viewed the proceedings from the massive buildings behind Azira. The crew of the Santa Maria followed the Chief Administrator as he walked towards a large golden pyramid. The walk was short, and Vincent marveled as he approached the entryway. It was marked with the Eye of Ra. The crew of the Santa Maria entered the pyramid, climbed a flight of stairs and found themselves in a massive chamber. The sight was overwhelming. The chamber was filled with aliens of all sizes, colors and shapes. The varied creatures were grouped by size. On his left, Vincent saw an alien resembling a large cat from Earth. As he looked around the room, he was taken aback by the different lifeforms and the various vibrant colors of their bodies. The largest species was on his right. The representative was the size of an elephant and his large six-legged frame was topped by a massive horned head. The eyes of the life form were looking directly at him as Vincent and his crew arrived at a singular raised platform. Chief Administrator Azira was at the center floor of the chamber and began to speak. "Welcome to Rabanah, humans. Please explain how you managed to traverse the gate in an Alliance Transport," he said.

The moment was at hand; it was time to represent mankind. "Chief Administrator, my name is Vincent Moretti. I am here to speak on behalf of humanity. We've struggled in the past and the search for proper morality is ongoing for our species. My crew and I represent those who wish to attain a higher level of enlightenment."

Vincent continued, "The Alliance has observed humanity for thousands of years. Our species has interacted with alien species throughout our history. We have documents and records that prove the fact. Our purpose is to establish a peaceful relationship with the assembled world members gathered here. We are curious and wish to know why there has not been any recent communication and why an offer of membership has not been made to the people of Earth. As a representative of mankind, I respectfully request planet Earth, and the species known as human, be added to your membership. We have much to offer," Vincent humbly requested.

"If humanity were ready to join the Alliance, we would have made contact and asked your leaders to join us, but your species is not yet ready. You are too primitive; your time has not yet arrived. Your species must still pass certain tests in order to be considered for membership. A species must be at peace with itself before it can be at peace with others. Mankind has too much internal turmoil," a pink-skinned representative opposite of Vincent flatly stated.

"It's true we have our differences and at times we do not get along with each other. As you are most likely aware, we've waged bloody wars in recent times. A great many humans have died representing a government or a religion that doesn't always provide the truth to the people it claims to represent. Our wars have been horrible and have always been started by religious differences. A unifying voice is necessary in order to combat the ongoing, petty and religious arguments. We need a reason to quit fighting with each other. Membership into the Alliance would provide humanity a greater perspective and a reason to unite," Vincent replied.

"Mankind must find its own answers regarding faith. We will not assist in your request. Explain to this assembly why humanity deserves a seat in this chamber and representation." Vincent didn't know where the question originated from, but he had an answer. "We have made great advancements as a species in our recent past. We've discovered your existence, your involvement in our past and Alliance involvement in the fourth planet in our solar system. Your presence can no longer be ignored by the leaders of humanity. I am here to move our species forward and to ensure mankind will survive. We know of the gate and have traversed it. We are curious explorers and more of us will make this journey in the future," Vincent said.

Chief Administrator Azira rose and addressed the Terrans. "We know your species very well. You have been under observation since you learned to walk on two legs. We always believed a time would come when humanity would join us, but the decision is not mine to make alone. This assembly will debate the issue in your absence; it is not a quick process as such an important decision must be thoroughly debated with all facts and opinions taken into consideration. This assembly has already debated this issue on a previous occasion due to your advancements. When a species discovers how to travel in space, it is mandatory for a vote and a decision to take place regarding contact. In the previous debate it was decided not to offer membership to humanity. The vote was close. You will be our guests until the debate concludes. I cannot provide a specific time as membership debates are complex and do not conclude quickly," Azira said.

Vincent knew a simple yes was unlikely and was satisfied with the answer. He hoped his questions would be allowed. The crew discussed what to ask on the way to Rabanah. "I have some questions; may I ask them?" he said. "You may ask, but we may decline to answer," Azira replied. "We know an intelligent indigenous species once lived on the fourth planet from our star. Can you tell us what happened and do any individuals still exist?" Vincent asked. "A war took place between the Alliance and the Annunaki. We were able to successfully relocate a very small percentage of the population to a planet outside your solar system. Mars was left uninhabitable after the war," Azira replied. "Is the species from Mars a member of the Alliance?" Vincent asked. "The Martians were members until recently," Azira replied. "They are no longer represented?" Vincent asked. "Unfortunately, the species no longer has a voice in this assembly. I know you will ask why the Martians are not represented and I will give you an answer at the end of your questioning. Please proceed with your next question," Azira replied.

Vincent found the response curious. He was getting some answers and didn't want to pursue the issue at the moment. "We found two data recording devices. In one of the recordings we observed humans from an island we call Atlantis; they were removed from the area after a volcanic eruption. The humans did not appear to be relocated within our solar system. Can you tell me what happened to them?" he asked.

Suddenly the chamber erupted in conversation and many of the members appeared agitated. Vincent apparently learned more than the Alliance expected. "Atlantis was a unique situation. The humans were safely relocated outside your solar system. Any additional questions on this topic will be answered at the end. Next question please," Azira said solemnly.

"We witnessed a great battle near our planet after recovering data from the craft of Azmune. Who was your enemy?" Vincent asked. "I offer our gratitude for returning Azmune alive. Information regarding this battle will be provided with my last response; please ask your next question," Azira replied. Vincent was growing increasingly frustrated. "While we were exploring Mars, we observed an image of Martians interacting with an extinct version of man known as Neanderthals. You previously stated you've been observing us since we were able to walk on two legs. I must ask, were Neanderthals removed from our planet, and if so, have any other species been relocated from our solar system?"

"Our duty is to safeguard all forms of life. The majority of life forms that have evolved in your solar system have been preserved at the genetic level. There are four life forms with the potential for supreme evolvement and have been placed alive outside your solar system. The four are Martians, humans,

Neanderthals and an aquatic species from the Jupiter moon, Ganymede," Azira answered.

The information was almost more than Vincent could comprehend. A species from a moon orbiting Jupiter? It couldn't be true. His head was spinning as he tried to process too much information too fast. Vincent could only think of one more question. "Where are the four species that were relocated from our solar system now? Can we visit any of them?" he asked. "This will be your last question today and I will now revisit your earlier questions as well. The four species from your solar system were relocated to a planet named Vandi. All four are able to live comfortably on the planet due to acceptable atmospheric and gravitational conditions. Neanderthals and what you consider 'modern day humans' have successfully interbred. The two species are now one.

The battle that downed Azmune's craft is called The Great War. It was a miracle Earth survived the encounter. We abhor violence and war. The Alliance will always take the necessary steps to protect member worlds and potential members as well. The Great War occurred in your year of 1947. The name of the enemy species is Annunaki. We saved Earth during the war but lost the Vandi system. The four species of Sol are now slaves to the Annunaki. We have placed a blockade at the gate to the Vandi system and do not have access to the planet. You cannot visit the relocated people of Sol as the citizens are inaccessible. This session is now concluded. The assembly will return in the morning and our guests will be escorted to acceptable Earth-quality living quarters," Azira ordered.

The crew of the Santa Maria was immediately led to their quarters. The room was large with multiple beds. Looking around the room Vincent saw a VHS player, a cassette player and a very old television set. "They've done their research but, they missed the mark by about seventy years," he said. "Look, there's an antique Donkey Kong arcade game in the corner," Dominic said.

"The information is unbelievable. Neanderthals, modern humans, Martians, and a species from Ganymede all on one planet," Sarah mused in astonishment. "And all slaves to the Annunaki," Monique replied. "The Alliance was attempting to preserve intelligent life from our solar system. Life from Sol was enslaved. We need to know more about the Annunaki. How long has this war been going on? Why is the fighting intermittent? Has the Alliance or any of the member worlds attempted to take back the Vandi system? I don't like the thought of humans and other intelligent life from our solar system being enslaved. It's a repulsive situation," Julia said. "I'm going to request a meeting with Azira. I will try to talk to him alone.

Maybe he'll open up and give me more answers," Vincent said hopefully.

The crew settled into their quarters and began watching an old movie. Vincent went to the door which opened automatically as he approached. A guard was stationed outside. "The Chief Administrator has requested you remain in your quarters." "Please inform Azira I'm respectfully asking to meet with him. I need to ensure the physical and mental needs of my people are met," Vincent said. "I will relay the message to the Chief Administrator," the guard replied.

Vincent was beginning to enjoy the bizarre old movie as he fell asleep. "Wake up, the Chief Administrator has arrived," Monique said. "Tell him I'll be right there," he responded groggily.

Azira observed as the human was revived from his rest period. He knew the Terrans would have questions and felt bad he delivered the news regarding the planet Vandi. The one who called himself Vincent approached. "Chief Administrator, can we take a walk and have a private conversation? I have some additional questions I'd like to ask," Vincent asked respectfully. "Follow me. I will answer your questions provided they don't violate our protocol as it relates to non-member species," Azira replied.

Azira led Vincent to an area away from the structures. There were no buildings and the two of them were surrounded by purple foliage. He couldn't help but wonder why all the vegetation was purple, but more important questions were on his mind. "Chief Administrator, has an attempt been made to recapture the Vandi system?" he asked. "There has not been an attempt to recapture the system to date. We are planning to recapture the system but must wait until we have the best possibility of success," Azira replied. "Do you have an estimate as to when the possibility for success will be highest and the effort will be made?" Vincent asked. "The most recent report states we will be ready to launch an offensive and retake the Vandi system in approximately seventy Earth years. The timetable is unfortunate. You must understand we will only attempt to retake the system when we're confident it can be retaken successfully. If we fail, the entire Alliance could fall. The Annunaki are highly intelligent. We paid a heavy price when our military leaders underestimated their ability to wage war. The Annunaki control another alien species known as the Krace; they are ruthless and follow the orders of the Annunaki without question. The best possibility of success lies in the future when we have sufficient military resources to retake the system.

We don't prepare for war, we prepare for an extermination of the Annunaki and Krace in the Vandi system," Azira replied. "How long have the hostilities between the Alliance and the Annunaki been going on?" Vincent asked. "The hostilities commenced approximately five hundred thousand years ago. Humans have trouble understanding such timelines. In that time, there have only been a few dozen major battles. Neither side will engage in warfare unless victory is guaranteed. The Annunaki have established a base that is difficult to access. We were at peace until they arrived. Our primary advantage is the manner in which the Annunaki consume resources. The Krace multiply quickly and need large amounts of food to keep their species flourishing. Our best method of attack right now is to let them consume their resources and prevent them from gaining new ones. When they overpopulate and their food sources become scarce, the more desperate our enemy becomes. The Annunaki consider the Krace inferior and utilize the species to conduct many of their military operations.

We were unprepared and overconfident in the Great War of your year 1947. We believed we were prepared, but the Annunaki and Krace overpowered us with their combined military force. It's not a mistake we will make in the future; we will retake the Vandi System. I know many lives will be lost and many lives will not be worth living for those on Vandi until we are ready. We may be able to save the children of those on Vandi now," Azira said.

Vincent thought over the chief administrator's information. Seventy years would pass before the next possibility of freeing the members of Sol on Vandi. The thought was frustrating and infuriating. He had one more question for Azira. "You stated my solar system has four intelligent species which were relocated to Vandi. Are there any individuals from those species remaining on any Alliance worlds?" Azira paused thoughtfully and replied, "There is one. Her name is Mox. She is a Martian and represented Vandi when The Great War took place. When the planet was lost, there was no longer a society to represent. She has remained on Rabanah and continues to take any action that might free Vandi." "I would like to meet her if it's allowed," Vincent replied optimistically.

"You've said a decision to admit Earth into the Alliance could take a long time. My crew and I cannot stay in the room assigned to us for such a period; we need to travel outside our quarters. I request time for my crew to explore this planet. At the very least, my crew must be allowed to exit our quarters. We didn't expect to be detained indefinitely," Vincent requested. "I will make arrangements to ensure your crew has a varied schedule and will not feel like prisoners. You will all have limited access to nearby areas," Azira said.

"Thank you, Chief Administrator. Please do what you can to arrange a meeting between myself and

Mox. The opportunity to speak with a Martian who has knowledge of Alliance operations is an opportunity I must pursue," Vincent said. "I will forward the request to Mox. She is isolated and has become withdrawn in her advanced years. She may very well deny your request. I will take my leave of you now provided you have no additional urgent matters to discuss," Azira replied.

"One of my crew has a medical situation; as you've probably observed, there is an abnormality with Tony. His body, and possibly his mind, has been altered by an alien substance. I request he be diagnosed and given any assistance he might need. Doctors on Earth were unable to explain his condition and how it might affect his future," Vincent said.

"You were all scanned when you arrived. I was alerted to the man's condition. I expect to hear results of the medical diagnosis shortly. Normally, I have the results immediately, but our medical experts were perplexed and required additional time. Once we have a proper diagnosis, we will help Tony any way we can," Azira said. "Thank you, Chief Administrator. I appreciate the time you've given me. It's my sincere hope humanity will have the opportunity to contribute to the effort of the Alliance," Vincent replied. "I hope mankind can alter the tide of battle and help the

Alliance in the future. Your species certainly knows how to wage war," Azira responded solemnly.

Randy didn't like what Enzo was saying. "We shouldn't have agreed to let the government send a representative. We're only going to have three ETS units and now we will have to commit one to the government. Regardless of who the President selects, I won't trust the representative," he said. "President Louis could have made the expedition troublesome. One missile will end the mission. It's best this way. Make sure you keep an eye on the government representative. Above all else, guard the ETS units. If the President can get his hands on one all bets are off. How soon until you're ready to launch?" Enzo asked. "We'll launch in five days, so you better let the President know. I seriously considered going on this mission myself. We've made the most amazing discovery in the history of mankind," Randy said. "You made the right choice. You're the only person capable of ensuring additional missions will take place and has the will to stand up against the government. I'm not qualified to do your job and anyone else would be corrupted and bribed by the corporations President Louis represents," Enzo said. "You're right of course. In my heart I want to go, but I'll stay and take care of my duties here. It may not be as exciting, but it's necessary," Randy said resignedly. "I will need your council and advice my friend. I'm glad you've decided to stay," Enzo replied.

Chapter 3

Two days passed since Vincent requested the meeting with Mox. He hadn't received a response and figured he probably wouldn't. Azira was as good as his word. The crew was allowed to visit a wilderness area and ate at various locations throughout the sprawling city. The food tasted horrible, but nobody became ill. Vincent wondered how long he could wait for a decision, when the door chimed. A guard stepped into the room. "May I present the former Ambassador of Vandi." The Ambassador entered the room in a mechanical suit which assisted her muscles and allowed her to travel. "You are dismissed, I will speak to the humans alone," she told the guard.

"It's a great honor to meet you, Ambassador," Vincent said offering his right hand. Mox shook his hand. "I'm nearing the end of my life and I'm tired. Let's sit and talk. I haven't spoken with people from Sol in a very long time. Your arrival could very well change the timetable of the Vandi invasion. The situation on Vandi is something all of you must comprehend. Working together you can make a difference," Mox said.

"We learned of your existence only recently and believed your species was extinct. It warms my heart to know you have survived. It was upsetting to hear about the situation on Vandi and I can't imagine how terrible it was for you. My crew and I will do anything we can to assist those who are enslaved," Vincent said.

"The Vandi issue is the reason I left the Assembly. I understand the need for patience and planning in military operations; however, the Alliance takes too long to act. Individuals from our solar system are killed, tortured and treated horribly on a daily basis. I made every effort to generate any argument I could think of to get the Assembly to retake the Vandi System. Eventually, I ran out of arguments and was encouraged to retire. I will likely be long dead before any action is taken. I can only hope the planet will eventually be freed," Mox said.

Vincent admired the Martian's courage and conviction. "Have any forces been sent through the gate? Have attempts been made to decipher the tactical situation?" he asked. "Some of the probes sent through the gate were destroyed quickly. About half make it back through the gate with limited information. We do receive some tactical information from the returning probes.

Manned ships have been sent through the gate with disastrous results. The Annunaki scan Vandi for any non-indigenous DNA. Any foreign life forms are hunted down and killed. We can change the appearance of various species to resemble Martians, humans and almost any species. We cannot change the DNA of a person without altering the individual. Approximately fifty cycles ago, the Alliance sent a ship through the gate. As expected, the vessel was immediately destroyed. The ship contained a small craft designed to survive the destruction of the primary vessel. Nanotechnology transformed the exterior of the craft. The small ship appeared as an ordinary asteroid and traveled to Vandi unnoticed. Inside were four Rabanians altered to look like Martians. Once on the surface, the Rabanians were quickly hunted down and killed; it took very little time for the Annunaki to identify the invasive species.

After I retired, I attempted to return to Vandi to mount a rebellion. The Alliance intercepted my ship and refused me entrance to the gate. Until your arrival, I was the only individual who possessed DNA acceptable to the Annunaki on Vandi. This crew represents a new opportunity to make such an attempt.

There is only a small number of Annunaki on Vandi; they control a species known as Krace who conduct the majority of operations on the planet. Without the Annunaki, the Krace could be easily defeated. They are incompetent. This has been a long day for me and I must excuse myself. Please consider what I've said. Our people are being massacred, tortured and worked to death. I will return, and we will discuss the situation again," Mox said as she summoned the guard and left.

"She wants us to go to Vandi to start a rebellion," Isabella said. "Yes, she's made her position very clear," Dominic added. "We won't make any rash decisions. It will be quite some time before the Assembly acts on our membership request. In the meantime, we need more information. I'm sure Azira doesn't want us to have access to technology and information until we are granted membership. I'll meet with him again and do everything I can to get as much intel as possible regarding Vandi. We won't go through the gate on a fool's errand to be immediately killed. If there is a chance of helping the people on Vandi we must seriously consider taking action," Vincent said.

Azira instructed the Assembly to prepare for debate, one that would likely be heated and lengthy. It was time to discuss the membership request made by the humans. Adding a member species was a serious matter and a vote from every member was required. Adding a new species to the Alliance proved disastrous in the past. In the history of the Alliance, four new races were ultimately removed; two of the instances were war related. Unless someone could make a persuasive argument to change his mind, Azira would vote to allow Earth's entrance into the Alliance. He knew mankind's many internal issues needed resolution and was confident they would overcome their shortcomings eventually. Earth contained many valuable resources which would strengthen the Alliance. He would have felt more comfortable if their request came after their internal issues were resolved. Azira called the proceedings to order and didn't have to wait long for the arguments to begin.

Randy scrutinized the President's information. The government representative selected for the expedition held degrees in geology, archeology, information technology and advanced robotics. Her name was Kathy Shivel. She could really cause trouble if not watched closely. Randy didn't find any disqualifying factors. His research indicated she didn't have any military or special operations training. Kathy Shivel's selection was made by President Louis who hadn't earned any of Randy's trust. Kathy wouldn't be given any leeway and the entire crew was directed to watch her closely.

Randy looked out the window as his employees worked tirelessly to prepare the Intrepid for a launch that was nearly at hand. His crew was ready, and Kathy would arrive just hours before tomorrow's launch. Randy planned to send Leviathan's own research and development team on the Intrepid. When necessary,

Dalton would lead them to any discoveries requiring their expertise. Dalton selected Jose Velazquez, another experienced archeologist, as the third member of the Cydonia ground team. Jose would stay with the ship and analyze new discoveries and information. Randy couldn't help but wonder if the real treasure on Mars was yet to be discovered.

A week passed since the commencement of the debate. Rabanah was a magnificent wonder. The crew of the Santa Maria was treated well and escorted to selected parts of the world by various chaperones. Vincent arranged another meeting with Azira. "How is the debate proceeding?" he asked. "You would be familiar with the format. The debate is much like those on Earth. There are ambassadors for and against your acceptance into the Alliance. Whichever side can make the best argument will likely sway the undecided votes," Azira replied. "I asked to meet with you about a far more serious situation. Ambassador Mox was gracious enough to pay us a visit. She explained the situation on Vandi quite thoroughly. The information was very disturbing; I understand why she resigned her position in the Assembly. She asked for our help," Vincent said. "Did you agree to help her?" Azira asked. "We haven't made a decision yet. I've given my crew time to consider what the Vandi Ambassador said. We will soon have our own debate about a potential course of action. What we require is more information. We've heard her side of the story. I'd like to hear yours," Vincent said.

Azira normally avoided the topic of Vandi, feeling terrible about the entire situation. The Alliance failed and intelligent life was suffering as a result. "I certainly sympathize with Mox. I understand her position and her frustration. We lost the Vandi system because we were unprepared for an engagement with the Annunaki and our defensive strategy was flawed and insufficient. Our tactical leaders and what you would consider a military force have worked tirelessly to develop a strategy which best allows us to retake the system. Acting too quickly could be disastrous and lead to more decades or centuries of enslavement for those on the planet. When we invade the Vandi system, it's the intention of the Alliance to keep it permanently," Azira said.

Vincent carefully considered the words of the Chief Administrator. "I've learned eighty-nine of your cycles have passed since the Great War. While you look for the best possible chance of retaking the system, your enemy is likely preparing forces to invade the Rabanah System. The Annunaki are likely reinforcing the Vandi System and preparing for all-out war. The Alliance prepares for battle but lacks vital intelligence regarding the enemy. At the present time, you have little or no idea what the Annunaki are preparing for. Humans may not be as advanced as the races represented in the Alliance, but we do understand warfare; probably much more than we should," Vincent stated solemnly. "Are you offering the services of your crew?" Azira asked. "I am not. I will not order my crew to undertake a task we don't completely understand and aren't prepared for. My crew and I will discuss the issue and we will likely have additional questions. It's possible my crew will refuse such a mission. We have virtually no knowledge of the Annunaki or the Krace. My crew and I will not undertake a suicide mission that may preclude our success and salvation." Vincent responded.

"I understand. There is one more issue we need to discuss. I've received the diagnosis from our medical experts regarding Tony. The flowering plant was found on a dying planet. It removed damaged cells from the species that used to inhabit the world. The plant is called thoki and the biology is difficult to explain. Imagine stem cells on steroids. Waste is removed while the body is enhanced. Results vary from species to species. The reaction was very strong with Tony. The biology is still not completely understood.

The medical team concluded the flower slowly enhanced and expanded the brain of the indigenous species. The symbiotic relationship was ongoing and quite miraculous. However, the plant affected Tony much more drastically. He is now using parts of his brain no human has ever been able to access. His abilities will most likely continue to evolve, and it is unknown what additional changes might occur in the future. The medical staff continues to work on the issue. Unfortunately, the only known specimen of thoki was left in the biological vault on Earth. Our records indicate there are no more samples of the plant within the borders of the Alliance and we don't know if the flower was relocated to any other worlds," Azira said.

The Chief Administrator considered the human's words as he returned to the Assembly. Vincent made an intelligent and compelling argument for the inclusion of humanity. The vote would likely be close again. After speaking with the Terran, he was now certain of the position he would take. He'd make one last argument and call for a vote. The members of the Assembly were beginning to repeat themselves and no new arguments had been forthcoming for quite some time.

A day on Rabanah lasted thirty-three hours. The crew of the Santa Maria didn't know when to sleep, but the majority of the crew was sleeping when a foreign alarm sounded in their quarters. Shortly after, two guards entered the crew's quarters. The lead guard spoke, "Your presence is required in the Great Chamber immediately. A decision on your request has been made."

The guards waited patiently and observed as the crew prepared themselves. The human leader spoke. "Let's go. One way or another, we finally have a decision. It's safe to assume if the vote is against us the Alliance doesn't want our help and we will return to Earth. If the decision is in our favor, we have our own decision to make regarding the situation on Vandi." Vincent turned and led his crew to their fate.

The Great Chamber was completely silent as Vincent and his crew entered. All illumination was extinguished except for one purple light cast on the Chief Administrator. "Welcome back to the Assembly, humans. A decision on the request of humanity has been reached. Display the vote," Chief Administrator Azira commanded.

At the far end of the chamber, a graph was displayed, but Vincent couldn't decipher the foreign language. Suddenly the chamber was awash in noise. Every member was making a clamor. He looked at his friends who were just as confused as he until the noise finally subsided. "The species from Earth has been granted membership. One cycle from today we will send a delegation and meet with the leaders from the third planet of Sol. At this time, you are required to select a temporary ambassador to represent Earth. Whom do you choose?" Azira asked.

Vincent was overwhelmed and surprised he was required to make an immediate choice for ambassador. A name came to mind; one individual possessed the experience to adequately fill the position. "If she is willing, I choose former Ambassador Mox of Vandi to represent Earth," he said. The chamber once again erupted in shouts and noise. "Silence!" Azira demanded. "The individual you've selected is not indigenous to Earth. Mox is of a different species," Azira said. "The words you speak are true, Chief Administrator; nevertheless, Mox is the best choice for humanity in the Assembly. I have confidence she has the wisdom and experience needed to successfully guide us into the future. She also belongs to a species native to Sol," Vincent said.

Azira was really beginning to like the human called Vincent. He was unpredictable; a quality missing in the Alliance. "So be it. If Ambassador Mox accepts the position, she will be the temporary ambassador representing Earth in the Assembly. I recommend finding an alternative choice, as Mox may not accept the position and may find she no longer has the energy to conduct the required duties of an ambassador in a satisfactory manner," Azira dismissed the assembled members and Vincent and his crew were led back to their quarters.

"I can't believe it. You did it!" Monique hugged Vincent. The crew was celebrating when the door chimed. Vincent expected Mox heard the news and wanted to talk. Instead, he opened the door to an empty corridor. No guards were in sight; he glanced down and found several champagne bottles with a note attached. "Congratulations humans. I believe this beverage is consumed when there is reason to celebrate," Vincent smiled. The note was signed by Azira.

"This is one hell of a night for humanity. Let's raise a glass to the men and women who made this possible. We wouldn't be here today if it weren't for those before us who helped advance our species. In particular, I would like to mention Albert Einstein, Marie Curie, Aristotle, Abraham Lincoln and Stephen Hawking," Vincent said. "What about Vincent Moretti?" Tony asked. "I think your first drink went to your head, Tony; I'm simply a messenger. My grandmother Maria did all the hard work. I appreciate the thought. Her name should be remembered, not mine," Vincent said.

"Do you believe selecting Mox as Earth's Ambassador was the right decision?" Isabella asked. "I hope so. I didn't know the Assembly would ask for an ambassador immediately. I only had a few seconds to think about it. I'm sure anyone in this room would have done the job to the best of their ability. Mox knows how the Assembly works and she has experience; I have faith in her ability to represent humanity," Vincent said.

Mox hadn't seen an official messenger from the Assembly in a very long time. One was now standing in her entryway. "My business with the Assembly has been long concluded. You serve no purpose here. Please depart immediately," she demanded. "I'm required to fulfill my duties. A response is required as quickly as possible, so I will leave you to review the information," the messenger said as he handed her a data pad and departed. She activated the data pad and couldn't help wonder what official business the Assembly needed her for. The official request in the corner of the screen was shocking. Mox watched the video in which the human requested her to be mankind's first ambassador. Mox was filled with mixed emotions. She never intended to return to the Assembly under any circumstances and would only consider a return if there was a chance to help her people. Perhaps her time was finally at hand. This opportunity would likely be her last chance to make a difference. She would speak to the humans once more before deciding, but first she needed to sleep.

Vincent woke with a headache. The champagne came with a painful cost. His shared quarters were empty. Apparently, everyone else decided to explore their new-found freedom. He discovered a data pad on a nearby table. The Alliance apparently trusted his crew enough to allow them to have access to some data and to communicate. Vincent activated the device, found the contact list and called Monique. She was at a nearby waterfall and invited him to join her.

As he approached the waterfall, Vincent heard Monique talking with someone. He turned the corner and was shocked. Monique was nude in waist high water with members of two separate alien species. "It appears I'm missing the party," Vincent said. "No, it's nothing like you think. This is a communal bathing area. I've been learning about some of the social aspects of the Alliance. Most of the member species aren't hung up on appearances and many don't normally wear clothing at all," Monique stated. "I'm not sure if I'm quite ready to run around naked yet," Vincent responded coyly. "We all need to acclimate to radically unfamiliar cultural situations and throw our predispositions out the window," Monique said. "Yeah, but such radical changes will take a little getting used to." Monique began putting her clothes back on. "I think you're right. We better return to our quarters; I'm sure Mox will be paying us a visit soon," Monique said.

Patrick enjoyed his new role as captain. He no longer needed to worry about enemy ships hunting him down. The change was welcome, and he could focus solely on the upcoming mission. The Intrepid was halfway to Mars and his crew was getting anxious. Dalton and Jose constantly lingered in the command center requesting updates on an arrival date that never changed. For the most part, government representative Kathy stayed in her quarters. None of the crew trusted her. "I hope we don't experience any problems on this mission. We have so much to explore in the Lost City. Just trying to decipher the gold walls will take a long time. Unnecessary delays and distractions are unacceptable," Dalton said. "I don't anticipate any potential problems and as long as we keep an eye on Kathy everything should be fine. We will hide any advanced technology we discover from her as necessary," Patrick said. "I hope you're right; it was agonizing leaving Mars last time knowing so much more was left to be discovered. It will require a great deal of time to properly explore the Cydonia Region," Dalton replied.

The hours of exercise should have left Tony exhausted. He couldn't remember ever feeling as good as he did now. His developing abilities were far from normal for a human. In addition to improved vision and his ability to blend in with his surroundings, he was now gaining new physical attributes. He ran a mile in two minutes and fifty-eight seconds, far exceeding any previous record on Earth. Before the transformation, his hand-eye coordination was terrible and he was generally considered a klutz. Now Tony completed multiple complex tasks simultaneously. In solitude, he ran as fast as possible while counting his steps and juggling nine sticks. His ability to think clearly and solve problems was also improving. He knew the answers to many questions which perplexed him in the past. Without taking any tests, he knew his intelligence was improving. The answers to mathematical and scientific questions he pondered in the past were suddenly clear. For reasons unknown, Tony was becoming more advanced than any other human in history. He began to meditate when the Santa Maria left Earth. Inner peace was something he could never attain in the past. As he closed his eyes and crossed his legs, he felt he found it for the first time in his life. Tony was at peace with himself and contemplated the future. How he was supposed to use his abilities, and to what purpose, was the only question he didn't have an answer for. He felt energized and ready for any challenge.

Vincent and Monique returned to their quarters and found Mox waiting for them. She was fast asleep in one of the beds. Monique called her name and she groggily woke up. "I must apologize. The journey here wore me out," Mox mumbled. "No apologies are necessary, Ambassador. You've heard the news about our request to make you the Ambassador for Earth?" Vincent asked. "Yes, the news came as quite a shock. Why would you want to make me Earth's Ambassador?" Mox asked. "You have experience with the Alliance and likely more wisdom than all of us combined. None of us have the experience and knowledge to succeed in the council. Both our species originated from Sol and we all have a shared interest and common goal to see Vandi liberated. In the future, we will choose a human to represent Earth. I'll begin the process of grooming a candidate to replace you. At the present time, you are without a doubt the most capable and best candidate," Vincent replied.

"I've spent a great deal of time considering your request. You must understand I'm declining both mentally and physically and don't have much life left. I will accept the position and advise you to find someone to replace me as soon as possible. My first order of business is to revisit the Vandi situation. The timetable for an invasion must be altered. I will need your full support and you will need to decide on a course of

50

action quickly," Mox said. "We will meet tonight, and I will have an answer for you tomorrow. Thank you for accepting the position, we are all very grateful and in your debt. I hope that working together will make a difference," Vincent said. "Don't thank me yet. I'll likely be asleep most of the time we are in session. I will need one of you to function as my aide and fill me in on anything important I might miss due to my excessive age," Mox said as she headed toward the door. "We will have an aide assigned to you by tomorrow as well. Thank you, Ambassador."

Vincent summoned everyone to the shared quarters immediately after Mox left. It took two hours for his crew to return from their various locations on the planet. "It's time for us to choose a course of action. We've all been given ample time to make a decision. Mox has agreed to be our ambassador and she will pursue a course of action to free Vandi. I've made my decision; I'm volunteering to go to Vandi to help free the people of Sol. What have the rest of you decided?" Vincent asked. Monique, Dominic, Tony, Isabella and Julia all agreed they would travel to Vandi. "What about you, Sarah?" Vincent asked. "It's just all so overwhelming. I haven't decided for sure, but I think I'd rather stay and return to Earth as soon as possible. I'm trying to adjust to the changing conditions and I don't think I can handle traveling to another new world," she said honestly. "Mox is looking for an aide; I told her we would provide someone. Will you stay here on Rabanah and perform the necessary duties for Mox?" Vincent asked. "Yes, I accept the position and wish to return to Earth within a reasonable time," she conceded. "I will make sure you are on one of the first Alliance ships when we return. Vincent replied. "I will do everything I can to assist Ambassador Mox," Sarah said.

In the Great Chamber, all ambassadors were present. Azira decided the first order of business was to call on Ambassador Mox. She requested an emergency debate regarding the situation on Vandi. He knew circumstances were now different with the arrival of the humans. The tactical situation was no longer a constant. "The Ambassador from Earth has the floor," Azira said.

Mox slowly stood and the Great Chamber erupted with applause. After retirement she wasn't expected to return. Nearly all of the ambassadors still had a great deal of respect for her and her reception was warm and welcoming. As the Ambassador for Vandi, she'd been a worthy adversary in a great many debates. "Thank you, Chief Administrator; I will get directly to the point. You are familiar with my position as it pertains to Vandi's plight. The strategic situation has now changed. Vincent and most of his crew have agreed to go to Vandi. The new arrivals will provide as much intelligence as possible and send the information back to Rabanah. At the present time, we have no information regarding the Annunaki's plans or Vandi's military situation. From a strategic and military standpoint, sending the humans to Vandi is the correct action. In addition to gathering intelligence, it's possible the humans could incite a rebellion and undertake other activities to distract and disrupt the Annunaki. The unique human Tony, has exceptional abilities which will prove useful.

There will never be a better time to gather intelligence to defeat our enemy and reclaim the system. The people of Vandi can be freed and it's time for action. The atrocities against the citizens of Sol must come to an end. Thank you for your consideration in this matter," Mox said wearily and sat down. "That's all you're going to say?" Sarah whispered. "I've said everything there is to say before. Everyone knows my position and past arguments. Presenting new facts is our best chance of success. Rehashing old debates will do nothing to help our cause," Mox replied. Sarah opened her mouth to ask the Ambassador another question, but quickly closed it. Mox was fast asleep and snoring loudly.

"She definitely gave them something new to think about. The decision will have a major impact on all our lives," Sarah said to another aide sitting next to her. Later that day she tracked down Vincent and the rest of the crew and gave them the report from the Great Chamber. "When will the Assembly vote on the issue?" Vincent asked. "I wasn't given a timetable, so I'm not sure. Mox told me what really matters is the Tactical Council's opinion. The council will make a recommendation in the chamber after all facts are taken into consideration. A vote will immediately follow with most members following the military's advice," Sarah said. "Did Mox make a compelling argument?" Vincent asked. "She made a quick argument which was presented well. After she spoke she immediately fell asleep. I feel we may be asking too much of her. I don't know how much life she has left in her," Sarah responded. "Mox wouldn't have accepted the position if she didn't think she could make a difference. Make sure you fill her in on anything relevant she misses," Vincent commanded.

Chapter 4

"Mr. President, we have a report from NASA requiring your immediate attention," an aide relayed. President Louis was in the process of courting the leaders of major U.S. corporations in his bid at reelection. He didn't appreciate the interruption. It wasn't a quick or easy process to buy votes. "Bring me the report," he demanded. The folder was black which meant it hadn't been seen by anyone else in his administration. He rarely received a black folder from NASA.

President Louis dismissed his aide and opened the report. The Hawking Space Telescope located an armada of over three thousand alien vessels on a direct course for Earth. The fleet's expected arrival was eight months if the velocity of the ships remained the same. President Louis assumed Vincent Moretti found the aliens and was returning to Earth triumphantly. He wondered how the son of a mafia boss was suddenly the most important human in the history of mankind. Enzo would likely call soon to make more threats against the United States and to gloat. The mafia boss would probably be in contact with the aliens first. President Louis would arrange a welcome for the aliens making them forget all about Enzo and Vincent. It was time to reveal the aliens to the people of Earth. A welcome would be arranged, and millions of people would meet humanity's new allies. The President scheduled a meeting with his cabinet. Sharing the existence of aliens with the people of Earth would be a momentous event, but first he needed to score political points and ensure the proclamation would define his presidency and guarantee reelection.

Mox summoned Sarah. A decision was at hand and she was to report to the Great Chamber immediately. Sarah arrived just as Chief Administrator Azira began to address the council. "We have a recommendation from the Tactical Council and the odds of victory improve substantially if we send the humans to Vandi. The council's vote was unanimous. We will now vote on whether or not to send the humans to Vandi to gather intelligence," he said. Sarah watched as Mox voted in favor of the resolution. After a few moments, Azira spoke again. "The majority has voted in favor of sending the humans to Vandi. There are five votes against and the motion has passed. A mission will be planned immediately. The human leader will coordinate with the Tactical Council to ensure all precautions and all aspects of the mission have been considered. An attempt to gather intelligence and liberate Vandi will commence at once," Azira said.

Sarah was stunned. She hadn't expected an overwhelming vote in favor of their position. "Why was the vote so lopsided?" she asked Mox. "The opinion of the council is enormous. Every possible variable is taken into consideration when a recommendation is made. I've recently conducted research on the various political processes occurring on Earth. The Alliance operates differently; there are no special interests here. No members of the Alliance Council can be bought with outside influence. This situation also involves torture and mass genocide on Vandi. If a possibility of success exists, the members know it must be pursued as quickly as possible. You must tell Vincent immediately. Once a decision is made, action will follow quickly. It's likely the operation will begin in the next few days," Mox said.

The crew of the Santa Maria gathered in their quarters after receiving a message from Sarah. "The vote was overwhelming?" Dominic asked. "Yes, Mox told me there are no special interests involved. She essentially told me the council always does what is morally right," Sarah said. "We will be leaving shortly. Sarah, it will be your responsibility to explain what happened to us if we don't make it back. You will need to talk to Enzo; tell him the situation and why we undertook the mission. He will understand and might be able to help someday. We will do our duty for the

Alliance and Earth. The mission contains a great deal of unknowns and there are many variables. There are never any guarantees in life and we are taking on a great deal of risk. Everyone get some rest. We will meet with the Tactical Council shortly," Vincent said.

It was a long day for Chief Administrator Azira. He was pleased with the result of the vote and was about to begin his regeneration cycle when a message arrived from Vincent. The human wished to meet immediately. Azira sent a message stating he would arrive shortly.

Vincent couldn't sleep. They would be leaving for Vandi soon, and he wanted to ask more questions. The barely audible door chime sounded. He went to the door knowing it could only be Azira. "Thank you for meeting me after such a long day Chief Administrator. If it's alright with you, I'd like to go for a walk and ask you a few questions," he said. "A walk sounds fine. Exercise is good for the body and mind. I will answer your questions to the best of my ability," Azira said.

Vincent led Azira toward the waterfall where Monique liked to bathe. "There are two pyramids the Alliance placed in our solar system I'm curious about. One on Earth, and one on a moon of a planet we call Jupiter. We found a vast quantity of biological specimens on Earth's pyramid. What is the purpose of these pyramids?" he asked. "It's standard operating procedure. We store copies of every biological specimen within the Alliance in the event a catastrophic event takes place. Should such an event take place, we have redundant automated systems in place to reanimate the biological specimens. The life forms we are responsible for would thrive again in time. There are many more such depositories in other solar systems," Azira explained.

"Why didn't you previously announce your presence to the people of Earth and why did you visit us in the past?" Vincent asked. "Every species must grow and mature in their own way. If we announced our presence in your past, we would have unduly influenced the growth of humanity and robbed you of your ability to discover what you could accomplish on your own. We would have been an arbitrator for every internal conflict your species experienced. We visited your species in the past to point you in the right direction. Far too often, those in power are more interested in retaining their power and wealth. In such situations, we intervene and give those in power something to think about beyond themselves. Moral leaders truly care about their society and govern for their people. We were never interested in the treasures of your world.

Your ancestors needed to discover new ways of advancing as a civilization. We assisted the ancient leaders to encourage the brightest minds to develop and teach the young. We provided tools, not answers," Azira continued.

"Humanity has reached a point where we are now able to construct artificially intelligent life forms, yet we have not seen any artificial life forms here. Why doesn't the Alliance make use of artificial intelligence?" Vincent asked. "In our distant past we did utilize artificial intelligence. There is an inherent issue of self-preservation with all life forms, including artificial ones. Any intelligent life form will place self preservation as their first priority. Regardless how artificial intelligence is programmed, it will eventually reach a stage when it becomes self aware. The Alliance was nearly destroyed in a protracted war with artificial intelligence. No member worlds are allowed to introduce any such technology; it simply isn't allowed. Even the Annunaki don't utilize the potential resource. It's far too dangerous," Azira replied.

"Why did you relocate people from Earth and Mars?" Vincent asked. "We relocated the remaining citizens from Mars at the end of the war. Your Sol system was invaded by the Annunaki. The citizens of Mars were more advanced than you are now. The Annunaki struck quickly at Mars and butchered most of the population. The EMT attacks wiped out all electrically-stored historical records on Mars. We now transfer all planetary records into Alliance data bases once a species has been accepted as a member. A great deal of history was lost.

The Annunaki weren't interested in Earth at the time. We arrived with considerable numbers, but unfortunately it was too late to save the fourth planet. The majority of the inhabitants on Mars were killed before we defeated the invading Annunaki. We rounded up the few thousand remaining Martians and relocated them to Vandi. Many were disabled after the battle and required medical treatment. The Annunaki's attack left Mars uninhabitable and contaminated. Our only choice was to relocate the remaining survivors.

Mars taught us a lesson. When your species began to advance on Earth, we brought specimens to Vandi. The Neanderthals were being hunted to extinction and we wanted to preserve their unique lifestyle. One of the primary missions of the Alliance is to safeguard potential intelligent life forms. Relocation of life from Earth was necessary according to our beliefs.

Atlantis was a unique situation. We'd been assisting the leaders of Atlantis and guiding the people to create a working infrastructure. We planned on making Atlantis the center of knowledge and advancement on Earth, but the volcanic eruption changed our plan. It was decided the Atlanteans would be relocated, taught and eventually returned to Earth. Sadly, the eruption killed four of the five leaders we selected to help your species advance. At the time, we didn't have any modern day humans on any Alliance worlds. The eruption gave us the opportunity to relocate members of your species onto an Alliance world and preserve the human race should something happen to your home planet. Unfortunately, we did not return any of the Atlanteans to Earth after we brought them to Vandi. It was an oversight we failed to reverse. Once the Atlanteans established a functioning society on Vandi it didn't make sense to return them to Earth.

"Why did you lose the Vandi System and nearly lose Earth in 1947?" Vincent asked. "We were unprepared for multiple attacks and thought the Annunaki were defeated. They launched a massive attack from their side of the Vandi gate. Our enemy conquered the Vandi system. Alliance leaders believed we amassed enough forces to repel any attack. Unfortunately, we were wrong. The Annunaki sent unmanned ships which targeted and destroyed the majority of the vessels protecting the gate and the system. Manned ships followed and destroyed our remaining forces. After the attack and loss of the Vandi system, we refocused our effort to protect the remaining worlds of the Alliance and potential member planets, including Earth. The Annunaki armada invaded your solar system after the Vandi system was secured.

The gate leading to Earth was unprotected at the time. We were barely able to hold on to the Sol system. Only a handful of our people and ships made it back. Guarding the gate to the Sol system has been one of our top priorities since the war. Since 1947, there has been no military action.

You and your crew are now responsible to provide the Alliance with as much intelligence from Vandi as possible. I recommend you listen to the advice from the Tactical Council carefully. We are counting on you. Vandi is a wondrous planet. If you enjoy birds, the planet has an abundance of beautiful creatures in the sky. The dominant bird species on Vandi are called Strithu and they are moderately more intelligent than apes on your planet.

You will meet with a council representative tomorrow. If you have any questions, now is the time. This is a pivotal moment for the Alliance. Have a safe and prosperous journey, Vincenzo," Azira said as he left. Vincent couldn't help but wonder how Azira knew his birth name was Vincenzo.

Monique slept well. She knew she was in the right place at the right time. The CIA meant nothing to her anymore. She was first to the door when the chime sounded. A messenger informed her the crew had two hours before meeting with the Tactical Council. It was time to wake everyone. She poured a cup of coffee and noticed Vincent hadn't stirred. "You need to get up Vincent; we have much to learn today," she said. He barely moved. She needed him awake, alert and ready for the day. There weren't many options left, so she pulled him off the bed and he landed on the floor with a thud. "What the hell?" he said. "It's time to get up, sleepy. We have much to do today," she said with a smile. "You suck at waking people up. Is there any more coffee?" Vincent asked.

Mox and Sarah observed from above as Vincent and the rest of the crew of the Santa Maria arrived at Tactical Council headquarters. "I feel guilty. The mission ahead will not be easy and our future hangs in the balance. I hope the faith the Alliance has placed in Vincent will be rewarded," Sarah said. "He appears to have common sense and will not make any decisions harmful to the people under his command. If he can remain hidden and gather intelligence, we will surprise our enemy. I need you here to assist me. When I'm asleep, I only remember about half of what I hear. Your duty here is not insignificant. My age is catching up with me," Mox replied.

The remaining crew of the Santa Maria entered the headquarters of the Tactical Council. The group was quickly escorted underground to a small room. Only one individual was present. "Welcome, my name is Denzar. I have been assigned the duty of explaining the mission to you. I've studied the history of Earth. I imagine you are all familiar with the story of the Trojan Horse and how the Greeks used it to gain entrance to the city of Troy?" he asked. "I believe we all are familiar with the story. If anyone here does not know the story, I will fill you in later. Please continue," Vincent replied. "You will be leaving for the gate in thirty minutes. Additional information will be provided on your way to the gate. Communication will be possible until you pass through the gate. You will have twenty-two days to ask any questions.

The Alliance often sends ships through the gate to gather as much intelligence as possible. The ships are quickly destroyed, normally within minutes or hours. The Annunaki also send ships and probes through the gate to gather intelligence. We destroy their crafts immediately as well. The vessels passing through the gate are almost always unmanned. The craft you will be onboard will be destroyed after it passes through the gate. You will all be placed in reinforced stasis tubes prior to your entrance. When your ship is destroyed, the stasis tubes will continue the voyage to Vandi. The tubes have limited functionality. Automated thrust and guidance systems will ensure you arrive safely on

Vandi. What you call nanotechnology will redesign the exterior of the tubes to appear as small rocks or asteroids. An additional piece of the craft will remain in orbit and act as a communication satellite. The satellite is advanced and will randomly switch communication frequencies; therefore, communication should be kept to a minimum. The Annunaki scan all frequencies constantly searching for something that doesn't belong. If you decide to communicate, it could give your position away to the enemy. Communication should only take place when absolutely necessary.

The stasis tubes disguised as asteroids will appear small enough to burn up in the atmosphere. The Annunaki will not consider them a threat to damage the planet and are unlikely to destroy them. This course of action is the only way we can get each of you onto the planet safely. Each tube will parachute safely into an unpopulated area during nighttime hours on Vandi. Mass of any larger size would be destroyed before it entered the atmosphere," Denzar explained.

"So, we will be rendered unconscious before we reach the gate, unable to wake up until we are on the surface of Vandi?" Vincent asked. "Yes, it's the only way. It will be disorienting and something you should prepare for. Let's get to the ship; the time has come," the alien said.

Denzar led Vincent and his crew onto an old mining ship. The spacecraft was nothing like the Santa Maria. The interior was dirty, and the ship looked like it was falling apart. "I don't see how we can survive an attack on this craft. It's a piece of junk," Vincent said. "Follow me, I will provide you an answer to ease your mind," Denzar said with assurance. The group traveled to the center of the ship. A new keypad was recently installed on an unmarked door. Denzar entered a code and the group entered the room. "This area has been designated as a safe zone. This chamber has been reinforced and fortified to withstand anticipated Annunaki weaponry. You can survive any weapon unleashed by simply staying here. The stasis chambers within offer another level of protection. I will now depart. The ship will leave in ten minutes. The computer will begin providing mission details in one hour. Transmit any questions you have as soon as possible." Denzar turned and left abruptly.

"He's not very chatty," Isabella said. "The Alliance doesn't waste much time after a decision has been made. We volunteered for this and we will do the best job we can to save the Vandi system. Everyone must pay close attention to the mission details. Mox is counting on us, so we need to provide our new ally a reason to invade and liberate the Vandi System,"

Vincent said. "I think we're in over our heads. We'll be lucky to survive," Isabella replied.

Enzo watched as Sandy caught another fish at his lake in Trundle. The troubled woman recently became withdrawn and politely refused his council. She beat the fish mercilessly until the animal stopped moving. He knew Sandy couldn't continue taking her anger out on animals. She required the satisfaction of knowing she was acting against the enemy who killed her family. She walked up the hill with a pile of bloody, mangled fish. "Bring those to the kitchen and meet me in the dining room. I would like to speak with you," Enzo said. "I'll be there shortly," she replied.

Sandy walked into the dining room with blood stained clothes and hands. "You have refrained from seeking my council. Instead, you wish to beat the hell out of fish and other animals. I'm assigning you a task to help you satisfy your need for vengeance. In the meantime, you must regain your focus. Your personal vengeance is a secondary consideration to the responsibility you have to help others. I've kept you safe from the authorities in the United States and I don't understand why you won't listen to my advice," Enzo said. He honestly didn't have a task for Sandy yet, but he would find one. The government was full of corruption, dishonesty and ruthlessness; it was only a matter of time.

"I haven't been speaking to anyone. It's been difficult coming to terms with the loss of my husband and children. It's hard for me to think of anything else and I haven't wanted contact with others, but I'm grateful for your protection and will perform any task you assign me to the best of my ability. You are my friend, Enzo," she said. "Your gratitude is appreciated Sandy. You are part of my family now and always will be. As part of my family, you have new responsibilities and a duty to protect what we wish to accomplish," Enzo said. "What do you wish to achieve?" Sandy asked.

"We must advance mankind as a species. We've accomplished much in our short existence, but if we can spread throughout the galaxy, our potential is unlimited. Humanity must discover what we are fully capable of in the future. If only we could replace our current leaders with the patriotic men and women from the past. Unfortunately, we're stuck with a perverted, corrupt government. We're in need of a new revolution and new patriots," he replied.

Enzo was returning to his study when the phone rang. The call was from President Louis. "What can I do for my country today?" he asked. "Have you heard from Vincent? We have reason to believe he will be arriving on Earth in approximately seven months," President Louis inquired. "No, I haven't heard from him. Why don't you tell me what you know instead of beating around the bush?" Enzo asked. "We've located an armada of over three thousand alien vessels traveling towards Earth. I thought Vincent would have contacted you by now," President Louis replied. "I haven't spoken with Vincent since he left, but I'll attempt to establish contact and get back to you." Enzo said and hung up the phone.

President Louis wondered if Enzo was bluffing and was aiming to take a position of power when the aliens arrived. The man was sly and quietly ambitious. It was critical to try and make contact. He called a cabinet meeting and began strategizing.

Enzo found the call from the President very curious. It wasn't like Vincenzo not to establish contact if possible. Returning with thousands of ships seemed excessive. A show of power and strength didn't make any sense. If the aliens wanted to take the planet, it could be done with just one of their spacecraft. It was time to take a trip. He texted Randy to let him know he'd be arriving in New Mexico the next day.

All reports indicated the government was going to allow the Intrepid to land on Mars without incident. There were no forces on the perimeter of the dead zone and all ships in the area were on regular patrols. Randy hoped additional technology would be discovered on Mars. If the government was kept in the dark, he would be light years ahead in research and development, but his thoughts were interrupted as Enzo entered his office.

"You have an obsessive personality. You need to learn to relax once in a while," Enzo stated. "I wouldn't be where I am today if I didn't pay close attention to detail. What is so urgent you needed to come to New Mexico immediately?" Randy asked. Enzo relayed the President's message. "Vincent will make contact if he can. Sending so many ships is completely unnecessary. I don't like the sound of it. Did the President give you coordinates or pictures of this armada?" Randy asked. "No, I didn't ask. Is it important?" "Yes, if we can identify the type of vessels we will know which side they're on. I'll ask the President for the information. If Vincent is on one of the ships, he'd attempt to communicate," Randy said. "I agree. You better contact President Louis quickly," Enzo said.

"First, I have a personal matter I'm hesitant to bring up. It's a delicate situation and you're the only person with the resources to handle it properly," Randy said. "You've done so much for Vincenzo and me, so if there's anything I can do to help, I'll do it," Enzo replied. "When the CIA arrested me, my relatives were taken into custody and interrogated. I received a call from my fifteen-year-old niece this morning. In addition to being interrogated, she was raped by an agent. She said there were no witnesses. I was planning to contact the President, but I'm not sure if it will do any good," Randy said acidly. "It won't do any good. Ask her for the name of the agent. If she doesn't know his name, get a description; I'll handle the rest."

An hour later, Randy and Enzo met with Leviathan's senior staff. "After a short negotiation, we were able to obtain information from our government. We have reliable data indicating an alien species will arrive on our planet in less than seven months. The President and his staff believe Vincent Moretti has made contact and is returning. There has been no contact with the incoming ships and the armada is on a direct course for Earth. If it is Vincent, he hasn't transmitted a message. I've sent a message to the armada requesting contact and haven't received a reply. We're here today to get your opinion on the government's data." Randy displayed the information on the conference room screen. A blurry image of the alien armada appeared. "Is this the best detail possible?" someone asked. "Yes, the only useful data is the fact that all the ships are massive. These ships are not like the interceptors involved in the battle of 1947," Randy said. A new voice spoke out. "Spacecraft of this

72

design is intended for long voyages. Large craft indicate the vessels are designed to sustain a crew for years, decades, or even centuries." Apollonia Morris was given the task of researching the data received from the president and possessed one of the best intellects at Leviathan.

"What are you saying?" Enzo asked. "I believe this armada was launched a very long time ago. There simply isn't another explanation for sending such large spacecraft. Unless of course, the ships contain a large invading force. Either way, it's not good news for us. I strongly advise we consider the armada hostile," Apollonia contributed.

"Thank you, Apollonia; I interpreted the data in a similar way and needed to hear confirmation from a team member. Until we hear otherwise, we will assume a hostile force is headed for Earth. What is the status on the ETS units? Has there been any progress with reverse engineering the devices?" Randy asked. "We've made some progress and I think we will be able to perform tests fairly soon," Apollonia said. "I want the work on the ETS units to be our top priority. If we can send more people to Mars before the armada arrives, perhaps we can learn what the Martians knew. Our second priority is to manufacture effective weaponry with Tratium. Work is to begin immediately. All future launches are cancelled. It is my expectation that the next time we launch a ship it will be destined for Mars with a large crew and a large number of ETS units," Randy said.

Monique studied the Vandi information given to the crew, but most of the data was out of date. Oceans covered eighty-three percent of the planet. There were two main continents on opposite sides of the planet and before the invasion, Martians occupied the largest of the two. Humans and Neanderthals occupied the smaller continent. For the most part, the people of Earth and Mars stayed on their own continents. It was a peaceful arrangement before the Annunaki arrived. The Martians and humans traded with each other and managed to coexist without hostilities. The species relocated from Ganymede, known as Volmer, was reclusive and lived in the polar regions. Volmer were completely white and lived both on land and in the ocean, much like penguins on Earth. The species wasn't interested in technology and was placed on Vandi long before Martians and humans. The Alliance asked the Volmer if it would be permissible to place additional intelligent life on the continents of Vandi prior to relocating the other species of Sol. The Volmer weren't interested in the continents and didn't object, provided they were left alone.

"Most of us are going to the Martian Continent," Vincent said. "Why?" Monique asked. "I asked Denzar the same question. The Martians always represented Vandi in the Alliance and were more advanced than the humans on the planet. Denzar believes the Martians would have more intelligence and be better able to assist us. I've spoken with Dominic and Julia, they will travel to the continent occupied by humans to gather intelligence. We will coordinate any subversive efforts between the two continents together. Dominic and Julia will establish contact with the local human leaders. We will do the same on the Martian Continent. These people are slaves, so there won't be any easily identifiable leaders. We must contact people who have more respect and wisdom than others in their local communities. These people will have influence over the local population. Our primary objective is to gather intelligence and send it back to the Alliance," Vincent said. "It's a good plan and makes sense. It would be a good idea to contact anyone who might have access to any records which survived the Annunaki invasion. Perhaps we can uncover useful information from the past," Monique pondered.

Maxis watched in anger as Tissa tried her best to repair the severe wounds again inflicted by the guards on his son Zanther. His son recently reached working age and was subject to initiation by the Krace. The initiation was violent and often led to death. Krace guards beat and humiliated new workers. If the young were unable to overcome the beatings or continue their duties, they were killed. It happened countless times in the past and Maxis vowed he would not lose his only son. "It looks like you are doing better. You'll come through this just fine. Do you want me to tell you a story tonight?" he asked. "No, I just want to sleep and for my pain to go away," Zanther moaned. "Very well my son. Get your rest, I'll tell you new stories later," Maxis replied.

"He's asleep now." Tissa entered their sleeping chamber. "My son is a slave. It's not right. Our people were proud once and now we are nothing but a defeated race. I've been researching how to disarm the bracelets with the ancient informational device. I think it's time to try," Maxis said. "Do you think it's wise? Vandi is a prison without sanctuary. Where would we go if we can escape?" Tissa asked. "Our child will not undergo a lifetime of pain and suffering as we have. If I were given a choice at his age, I would have taken the chance at freedom. The only reason I continue with this existence is the possibility of improving the life of my family. It is time to try. If we can successfully get outside the boundary, we will flee to the caves in the mountains to the north," Maxis replied.

Chapter 5

Martino tracked the depraved and overconfident CIA man for three weeks. Agent Spivey followed a well-established routine. He went to the same dive bar almost every night looking to get lucky. Normally, the agent would leave the bar with a woman who could barely walk. Martino discovered the agent possessed a large quantity of ketamine in his hotel room. The man drugged women at the bar and brought his victims back to his hotel room barely conscious. Enzo asked him to observe and assist Sandy with the murder of the CIA rapist. He observed Sandy as she entered the bar. She followed his instructions and looked like an easy mark. A microphone was placed on her bracelet so Martino could listen and intervene if the situation got out of control.

Sandy was nervous as she entered the bar. The agent was engaged in conversation with a large breasted blond woman. She needed to find a way to get rid of the voluptuous tramp. A table was available next to the couple. The woman was talking about her new car and how fast it was. Sandy sat for ten minutes trying to think of a way to get rid of her. The tramp finally stopped talking when her phone chirped at her. "Son of bitch! Someone just broke into my car. I have to leave," the woman said. Martino was an efficient fellow Sandy thought.

"Hello there; I see your friend left. I don't understand how she could leave such a handsome man like you. Would you like to buy me a drink?" Sandy boldly asked Agent Spivey. "No, I wouldn't. How about you buy me a drink?" the agent replied. Sandy immediately despised the arrogant asshole. "How about we play some pool? Whomever loses the most games buys the drinks," she said. "It's fine with me. You'll still be paying. What's your poison?" he asked. "I like everything. Bring me whatever you're having." she said. "Sounds good, we'll start with White Russians," he replied.

Martino could barely listen to the conversation. The agent spent much of the evening bragging about himself and paid little attention to Sandy. "Will you order another round while I go to the ladies' room?" he heard Sandy ask. "Absolutely, after the next round I think we should make this party a little more intimate," Agent Spivey suggested. "You think so? Maybe it's a good idea. I think I'm getting a little tipsy," Sandy said. With Sandy in the bathroom, Agent Spivey used the opportunity to lace her drink. Martino told Sandy when it would happen and explained how to turn the tables on the perverted agent. Sandy took a deep breath and prepared herself for what needed to be done.

A new White Russian was waiting when she returned to the table. "Drink up and let's get out of here," Agent Spivey forcefully directed. "One more game. It's your turn to rack 'em," Sandy said. "Fine, I'll kick your butt one last time," he said with reluctance. With his back toward her, Sandy took the opportunity to switch her drink for his. She was tired of letting him win all night and quickly ran the table. "Wow, I've never done that before. Finish your drink, sexy, it's time to go have a different kind of fun," Sandy said coyly.

Enzo told Martino what happened to Sandy's family. He understood her need for vengeance and knew she would have to do this on her own. Emotions led to mistakes and it was important to be cautious. He rented the room next door to the agent and could intervene in seconds if necessary. The two of them would arrive at any moment.

Sandy was laughing at something stupid the agent said as she entered his room. "Why don't you lie down, big boy? I'll help you get your clothes off. I've got a surprise for you," she said as she removed a set of handcuffs from her handbag. "I'm not feeling very well all of a sudden," Agent Spivey said as he collapsed on the bed. "I can't imagine you would be you disgusting son of a bitch," Sandy said. She was tired of putting up with the cockiness of the man and it was getting late. She jumped onto the bed and stood over Agent Spivey.

He groaned and tried to grab her leg. His coordination was gone, and his arms flailed in the air. "How's does it feel to be on the other end?" Sandy asked as she kicked him in the face as hard as she could. The agent lost consciousness for a few seconds and began screaming when he came to. Sandy stood on his arms, put duct tape over his mouth and kicked him in the face three more times. The agent was out for the night. She rolled Spivey over, handcuffed his hands behind his back and put a gag in his mouth. He was heavier than expected she thought as she moved him to a chair. She carefully removed the handcuffs, taped each of his limbs to the chair, ran duct tape across his chest and wrapped it around the back of the chair.

Martino preferred jobs which ended quickly. If this was a professional operation, the agent would be dead by now. Sandy needed to exorcize her demons however. Agent Spivey would be granted a few more hours of life. Martino listened throughout the night and into the morning. After Sandy fell asleep, he entered the room to ensure the agent wouldn't be able to escape when he woke. Sandy did an excellent job of restraining the agent. When he returned to his room, he heard nothing but snoring for the remainder of the night. He would call Sandy at eight and wake her up. The effects of alcohol would be mostly gone by then.

Agent Spivey woke up with a splitting headache and found himself bound to a chair. He tried to scream and could only make a muffled moan. His body was completely immobilized and he couldn't shout for help. The woman from the bar was nude, snoring loudly and sleeping peacefully on the bed. He couldn't remember a thing from the previous night. The last thing he remembered was the two of them leaving the bar.

He spent the next five minutes trying to free himself, but his efforts were futile. Spivey was completely immobilized. The phone rang, waking the woman on the bed. She picked it up and immediately put it back down. Five minutes later, she got out of bed and approached him. "You were great last night. I'll be back in a minute," the woman said and kissed him on the forehead. He breathed a sigh of relief. Apparently, he was bound for sexual purposes only.

Sandy prepared herself as she left the bathroom. It was time to kill the son of a bitch. "Is this how you like your women? I know you like them naked, but you like them helpless as well don't you? Maybe I should untie you, so you can drug me and have your way with me. Isn't that what you like? You aren't man enough to get women the old fashioned way, are you? You must resort to chemicals in order to have a woman or rape a helpless fifteen-year-old girl. You drug women because you're an asshole and have a shitty personality." Sandy continued as she went to her handbag and removed a knife. "I'm going to take the tape off your mouth. If you scream, you'll no longer be a man…as if you ever were one,." she said and placed the point of the knife on his crotch.

"What do you want? I'll give you anything you ask for," Agent Spivey sputtered. "Can you offer me a high paying job in the government and a large amount of money?" Sandy asked. "I can get you millions of dollars. I know of a secret government account we use to send arms to the Middle East. I can get you anything you ask for," blurted Spivey. "What I really crave is a simple answer. Can you tell me why the corrupt government you work for killed my family?" Sandy asked.

Agent Spivey was struggling for an answer. He didn't know who this naked crazy woman was. She was definitely pissed off and wielding a knife. "I would be more than happy to investigate the circumstances of anyone who was killed. I don't rape women; someone has provided you incorrect information," he said.

Sandy listened to Agent Spivey's lies. "You are so full of shit. You're an immoral asshole and a waste of life," she spat. He was about to speak again, but Sandy couldn't take it anymore. She plunged the knife into his chest, stabbing him over and over as her arm weakened. Blood was everywhere.

Martino was impressed with Sandy. The most important aspect of the operation was to keep things quiet. She performed well until now. Sandy apparently accomplished her mission. The agent wasn't making a sound, but Sandy was screaming obscenities, crying and making way too much noise. It was time to intervene.

Sandy was in a blind rage and covered in blood. She raised the knife to strike again, but the knife wouldn't come down. Someone was preventing her arm from moving. "No matter how many times you stab him, you can't bring back your family," Martino said. Sandy began sobbing uncontrollably.

Martino cleaned up as Sandy cried. It was a cathartic moment which would finally free her. After ten minutes, he picked her up and put her in the bathtub. "Clean yourself and clear your head. Enzo wants us to return to Trundle as soon as possible. He has reason to believe the world might be ending," he said grimly.

The team was fast approaching the gate leading to the Vandi system and it was time for the crew to enter their individual stasis tubes. "Good luck my friends. Make smart decisions and stay out of sight. Observe all you can and proceed to the rendezvous point as quickly as possible. Remember, we are working with outdated information. If necessary, we'll meet at the secondary rendezvous point. Patience is imperative; don't make any rash decisions that could draw attention or endanger the mission," Vincent cautioned. "I hope we are put to sleep quickly. I'm claustrophobic," Dominic said. "You're a big, tough guy Dominic; I think you'll be fine. Dream well my friends, let's prepare to meet our brothers," Vincent said as he entered his stasis tube.

Patrick circled Cydonia twice searching for any forces along the perimeter of the dead zone. There were none. The Intrepid would be able to land without any interference from local authorities on Mars. He chose the initial landing location the Constellation used. Seeing the Constellation brought back the memory of how perilous his first trip to Cydonia was. The crashed vessel was mostly intact and served its purpose. The Intrepid landed nearby without incident. "Here we go! Let's see what's out there. We're going to have a hell of a good time, so let's get moving. I can't wait to get back in there!" Dalton exclaimed. "I won't bother to tell you to slow down and have some patience. You wouldn't listen to me anyway. Just make sure you take everything you need and please be careful. Remember to send someone out every other day for a status update," Patrick said. "Yes, of course. I will follow the mission guidelines. You won't see much of me. I plan on living in one of the Martian rooms we found. I will send out one of the others for supplies and to give you updates," Dalton said. "You will see more of me than you think. Unless I'm desperately needed here, I will spend a day or two every week in Cydonia as well. You don't get to have all the fun," Patrick said. "Just know you won't be replacing me," Dalton said as he gathered his supplies and activated his ETS suit.

Bazor was getting excited. She spent her entire life preparing for the mission which was finally about to begin. She assumed command of the fleet after the death of her mother. The mission was simple; conquer the third planet and destroy any ships attempting to enter the Sol System through the Rabanah gate. She was told the tales of the Great War from her mother. It was now her time to satisfy the needs of her species and ensure her family name would be spoken of proudly on every Annunaki world. After the Great War, the Empress decided to send a fleet of ships to the Sol System through normal space. Rabanians controlled the one gate which led to the Sol System. The third planet was abundant in resources and the trip through normal space was deemed necessary regardless of the duration. The long voyage was nearing an end. Bazor was ready for action and her first taste of human blood. She'd been savoring the moment far too long. Her offspring would rule the planet long after she was gone. The Empress would keep Mars for herself.

The fleet was nearing the star the humans called Sol. Bazor gave her first operational order as the armada approached. She would board a smaller ship in the hanger and arrive on Earth before the rest of the fleet. The first aspect of the plan was to confuse and disorient the dominant species on the planet. Bazor was bringing a few guards in the event she needed protection. She still didn't feel entirely comfortable with the sheer number of humans on the world.

The species needed to be thinned considerably; Earth was overpopulated. She was determined not to lose any of her personnel. The indigenous species on the third planet was intelligent, emotional and easy to manipulate. "Increase speed now. Destroy all vessels and satellites in the vicinity of Jupiter as we pass," she instructed as she activated the device which bent light around the craft. The ship was now invisible to all human technology. A recent report indicated humans discovered how to bend light as well. Mankind only recently learned how to do so, and their methods were crude and easily detected. The humans were naïve and broadcast all their activities into space. She brought up the most recent image of herself on the screen. Bazor was disgusted with her appearance. She was physically altered to appear as a male human. The thought of standing among them as a male was revolting.

Vincent was disoriented. He didn't know what time it was or where he was. Looking up he saw a dark blue sky. He sat up and took in his surroundings; it was all very strange. A small unrecognizable animal scurried past and reality suddenly crashed down upon him. He was on Vandi. It took a minute for his muscles to work and for him to stand. A small cave was nearby and he ran inside. He took a few minutes to compose himself and gather his thoughts. There was no immediate threat as far as he could tell. The safety of the cave afforded him time to think. Peering out, he could see a valley below. Unbelievably, he saw a pyramid surrounded by primitive housing.

To the north, an advanced city was easily recognizable. It was similar to a city on Earth with towering buildings and an advanced infrastructure. He retrieved his rations from the storage compartment of the stasis tube and found a dry creek bed to follow down the mountain and into the valley. The hills and vegetation would conceal his journey down the mountainside. Vincent navigated his way down the mountain after covering the stasis tube with vegetation. He hoped to reach the primitive housing and the pyramid by nightfall, but he didn't know when it would occur. The two stars Vandi orbited were amazing. He didn't know how long it would take for both of them to set., but he could see that the first of the two stars was approaching the horizon.

After six hours, Vincent made it to the base of the mountains. The pyramid wasn't far away. He navigated the dry creek bed and was able to remain hidden. He could go no further without risk of being spotted. The second of the two suns disappeared behind the mountain he descended. Light slowly gave way to darkness and stars shone brightly in the alien sky. A moon brighter than Earth's provided enough light to see nearby. The housing around the pyramid appeared abandoned; there was no one in sight. His long trek down the mountain was made in vain. Just as he was about to travel to the rendezvous location he saw movement. A group of aliens were traveling in the direction of the housing and the pyramid. Some were Martians. He knew due to information and pictures provided by the Tactical Council. A young Martian child was being whipped without mercy as he walked toward the pyramid. Vincent was instantly enraged; slavery was unacceptable under any conditions. He couldn't help but wince with each crack of the whip. It was difficult for him to maintain his composure. A century of such torture was unthinkable and had to be stopped.

The emotional pain was unbearable for Maxis. He could only watch as his son was whipped over and over on the journey home. The innocence of childhood was no longer inside his child. The hope he'd seen in his son's face was replaced by pain, agony, and surrender. Zanther was bleeding heavily as Tissa tended to his numerous wounds. All members of the village were beaten much more than normal during the day. The guards claimed production was falling and those who didn't produce more would soon be killed. Maxis was scared for his son. Zanther worked as fast as possible with tears rolling down his face from the pain the guards inflicted. His son believed he might be killed at any moment. Maxis couldn't watch any longer and went out to the nightly fire. He was immediately surrounded by nearly everyone in the village and knew he could not help his friends. "I don't have any answers for you. We are still alive for the moment and I must take care of my own family. My son will be lucky to live through the night. Tend to your own families," he said. For the remainder of the night, Maxis was left alone. He sat in solitude staring at the fire as his friends returned to their homes. There would be no sleep for him. He needed time alone to come to terms with his failure. Zanther would live the same life he was forced to endure. Maxis stared into the fire as the last of his friends left. He would have to accept the same ugly fate as his son and give up all hope. There weren't any other options.

As he rose to leave, he heard someone approach from the opposite side of the fire. He was in no mood to explain how he was powerless to act again. Panic overtook him as he looked up and saw a human. He'd never seen one in his lifetime.

Vincent observed as the Martians converged on their leader as he emerged from his dwelling. The villagers were turned away quickly. If there was a leader in this community, it must be the one who sat alone after everyone else left. The air temperature was cold and the fire would provide some warmth. It was time for action anyway. He activated the translation device and approached the fire. The suddenly panicked Martian looked for a weapon to use against him. "I'm from the Alliance and here to help," he said.

Maxis was scared and picked up a large rock. He was about to attack the human when he heard the man's unbelievable words. He put down the rock and sat down again and stared into the fire. The human stood waiting for him to speak. He studied all available Alliance files on the ancient device and knew humans occupied the landmass on the opposite side of the planet. Maxis knew all member species of the Alliance and according to the records he uncovered, Earth was not a member world. "You lie and are not from the Alliance. You come from the opposite side of this planet. The Alliance abandoned this world long ago," he said.

Vincent was glad the Martian put the rock down. He didn't want to be injured by someone he was trying to help. "Humanity has recently been admitted as a new member in the Alliance. Your species and mine shares a special connection. We come from the same star. We are from the third planet. Your species originate from the fourth planet. We are brothers. I'm here to gather information that will free you and your people," Vincent said.

Maxis was overcome with emotion. He couldn't believe what the human was saying. "You've come to free us? My people have been enslaved for far too long; we have never received a visitor. I will listen to your words and will do anything necessary to free my family and friends. You must earn my trust, however. I will not lead my people on foolish endeavors," he said. "I'm not here to free you. The reason we're here is to gather information. Freedom will come, but not soon. Tell me everything you know about the Annunaki and Krace," Vincent asked sternly. Maxis would have a long day tomorrow. Sleep wouldn't come this night. At great length, he told the human everything he could think of. His species led a tormented, yet simple life. It was difficult for him to describe a lifetime of pain, submission, and humiliation.

Julia awoke from her stasis tube and immediately covered it with fallen vegetation as instructed. She began to search for Dominic. The two of them needed to find a human settlement as quickly as possible. The plan was to land close together and work as a team. As the only two crewmembers which would be visiting the Human Continent on Vandi, they would have to watch out for each other. She landed in a lightly forested area with amazingly bright, yellow trees next to a river. Birds flitted everywhere. She found a game trail and followed it. Dominic shouldn't have landed more than a hundred yards away in any direction. Suddenly, she heard a mechanized sound overhead traveling in her direction. It was a flight capable vehicle of some kind. She ran away as quickly as possible from the noise.

It took Julia another five minutes to locate Dominic. He was still sleeping in the stasis tube. She unsealed the tube and dragged him out. She quickly checked his pulse and heart rate; he was fine but was having difficulty regaining consciousness. The vehicle in the sky approached closely again. She slapped Dominic hard in the face. "Wake up! We have to get out of here!" she screamed as Dominic slowly came around. Julia was about to hide the tube when she saw the airborne vehicle. It would be over their location in a matter of seconds. There was no time to hide the tube. She yanked Dominic up and pulled him toward the nearby river. "Come on! We're in danger. Move your ass!" she shouted. Dominic was now fully awake. "Where are we and where are we going?" he asked groggily. "We're on Vandi and we're about to be discovered and killed if you can't pull yourself together. We're going to hide in the river," she said. "Why are we hiding in the river?" Dominic asked. "If we have heat-sensing technology, I'm sure our enemy has it too. Hopefully they don't have anything more advanced or we're screwed," Julia explained with frustration as the duo scrambled into the water. "We'll go downstream as quickly as possible and put as much distance as we can between us and them," she said.

The sky began to lighten, and Maxis finally stopped talking. "I will leave you now. I appreciate what you've told me and I'm sorry for what you've been forced to endure during your lifetime. Do not take any action at this time. There are currently only a few of us on Vandi. Be patient and know my friends and I will return," Vincent said. "Thank you; I will wait," Maxis said and placed both of his hands on Vincent's chest. Vincent didn't know what to do, so he placed his hands on the Martian's chest. "Thank you, my new friend. I hope to see you soon. We will work together as brothers," Vincent said as he turned and traveled in the direction he originally came from. He hadn't walked more than twenty feet when he heard a distant noise coming from the direction of the city. Maxis quickly came running. "What is the sound coming from the city?" Vincent asked. "I've only heard it once before in my lifetime. If it's the same as last time, guards and soldiers will be here in a matter of minutes. You must travel quickly," Maxis cautioned. "I think our presence has been discovered. Don't do anything to bring attention to yourself," Vincent said as he ran toward the dry creek bed.

He knew someone had been discovered. The timing was too coincidental for an alarm to go off the same day his team arrived. Vincent decided to head directly to the rendezvous point hoping the rest of his team was still alive. He couldn't resist taking one final look back at the Martian village. Dozens of aircraft converged and landed. Krace soldiers rushed into the primitive dwellings. Villagers were brought outside clothed or not and Vincent couldn't help but wonder if he would be the cause of more torture and death on Vandi. Maxis stood in the center of the village and tried to speak to the soldiers. A Krace leader whipped him severely. The last thing Vincent saw was Maxis looking in his direction.

Tony was given a special mission suited to his unique abilities. He landed near an isolated outpost and discarded his clothing. He hoped the small translation device he was required to carry wouldn't be seen. His mission was to gain access to the facility and gather as much intelligence as possible. The small facility was on top of a mountainside and likely contained only two or three small rooms. Tony observed the structure for thirty-eight hours. He never saw more than two Krace and approached the facility with caution. There wasn't any activity during the night. His abilities were improving, but he didn't blend in with his surroundings instantly. Sunset approached again. It took an hour to traverse the last hundred yards while remaining hidden. He finally reached the entryway to the facility. The most dangerous part of the mission began as darkness fell. Tony entered the facility and hoped to remain unseen.

After thirty minutes, a female exited. She was so close Tony could have touched her. He scurried through the doorway and found a dark corner. A male in the back of the room was viewing a data pad. After a few minutes, the female returned. She went to the male and touched him on his ears. The male immediately rose and followed the female to a chamber further back in the facility. The data pad was still active and illuminated. Tony wanted nothing more than to grab the data pad and run as far as possible; however, his mission parameters stated he was not to remove any technology. Any missing technology would alert the Annunaki to their presence. He took the data pad, activated the translation device and returned to the corner of the room. All data was to be captured if possible. Information on the screen was translated to English. Tony was confused. The translation was only partially successful; much of the information was translated poorly or not at all. It was an alien technology and it took an hour before Tony was able to start accessing files. He didn't have time to review every file. He copied each file as quickly as he could. After four hours, he couldn't find anything else to copy. It was still dark and quiet. Tony returned the device where he found it and quickly exited the facility. He ran for ten minutes before he was able to compose himself. He felt good having successfully completed the mission. After a brief nap, he jogged toward the rendezvous location.

Monarch Reltith was not pleased with the information she received. She immediately summoned her council which consisted of nine of her most trusted advisors and one token Krace representative. As the Supreme Annunaki Ruler of Vandi, it was her responsibility to ensure there were no threats against the kingdom. A stasis tube was found which meant the Alliance had at least one agent and possibly more on the planet. She immediately called for a two-day lock down. No slaves would be allowed outside their village, work would be temporarily suspended, and villagers would be tortured until information regarding the invaders was provided. "I want the area where the stasis tube was found searched again. Send in as many teams as necessary; we must find the intruders quickly. It is imperative we find out if more Alliance members are here. We can only get this information if we capture and extract information from the person who landed near the human colony. Nothing else is as important as this task and I expect results immediately. Once we are certain all valid information has been extracted, the Alliance member is to be killed. I want patrols across the planet to search for additional intruders and I expect results. That is all for now. You are dismissed," she commanded.

Reltith made her way to the grand chamber with her aide, Priex, in tow. "We should have more of our own people here. The Krace are incapable of conducting a proper search. The soldiers are ruthless, but stupid. If we hadn't been able to control them, their species would have been outsmarted and killed by now. We must remain vigilant. Oversee all operations and report any progress to me as soon as possible," she commanded. "It will be done, Monarch," Priex replied.

The river slowed and emptied into a small lake far too soon. "Now what do we do?" Julia asked. "We need to put as much distance as possible between us and them. Let's see if this lake empties out on the other side," Dominic replied. "It's too late! I hear more aircraft coming this way. We're out in the open and are going to be found!" Julia shouted. Dominic quickly surveilled their surroundings. "Over there. It looks like an entrance to an underwater cave. If we're lucky, we'll find a gap above the surface inside," he said. Julia took a deep breath and swam as hard as she could through the entrance. There was nothing above her but rock. Just as she thought she would pass out, she surfaced. She jumped onto a ledge with Dominic right behind her. "If the Krace didn't see us, how long should we wait?" she asked. "We'll wait as long as we need to. It's likely the stasis tube was found, and soldiers know we're in the area. It is very cold in here. Hypothermia is a real possibility if we can't get out of here in the near future. We won't be able to wait too long. I'll swim out every hour or so to see if it's clear. Let's plan to leave at dusk," Dominic said.

Roughly an hour later, Julia was shivering uncontrollably. "I think hypothermia is setting in. We're going to have to leave soon." "Let me go take a look. I'll be back in a few minutes," Dominic said as he submerged and swam toward the lake. When he surfaced at the cave entrance, he saw activity at the opposite end of the lake. About a hundred yards away he noticed an area where the rockface gave way to a small clearing with a forest beyond. He went back and retrieved Julia.

Julia was cold and exhausted. She swam hard with her dwindling strength. At last she was finally out of the water. She quickly clambered up the hillside and made it to the clearing. A large Strithu was startled and jumped up as she breached the hill. "Damn those birds are massive. I need to get some sleep. I can't go on much longer," she said. "You're going to have to make it a little while longer; I hear more aircraft approaching," Dominic replied. He was sure they were about to be captured and tortured. Aircraft were approaching from all directions. "I think we're screwed. We're surrounded and are out of options. It's time to take the pills," Dominic said.

Each person on the mission was given a poison that would end their life if necessary. Denzar instructed them to take the pills if capture was imminent. If captured, the Annunaki would surely inflict extreme torture to extract information before killing them. "Hang on, I have an idea. Come with me," Julia said.

She approached the sleeping Strithu. "We need to get in the pouch. It's our only chance," she said. "Are you kidding me? That huge bird will kill us in an instant!" "We 'll die for sure if we're captured. Do it now!" Julia commanded. Dominic was disgusted. "Look at all this mucus. I don't think I can handle this," he said. "You lived for the first nine months of your life in a womb. You'll be fine," Julia replied. She didn't know what to do next and screamed as loud as she could into the face of the sleeping Strithu. The bird stood abruptly and took to the skies joining others of its kind.

"Well, this isn't bizarre or anything," Dominic said. "We're safe and it's nice and warm in here," Julia replied. Dominic hated heights and was feeling queasy. The Strithu cocked its head and looked at him quizzically. He was momentarily scared when the beast bent its head down. The giant animal opened its mouth and licked his face. "A fitting end to the day," he said to Julia, but she was fast asleep and didn't respond.

The flight lasted longer than Dominic expected. The giant bird decided to travel a great distance. He was grateful for Julia; she thought of a plan he never would have considered. They were miles away and moving quickly. There were so many Strithu in the skies it would be impossible for the enemy to track them. Many of the birds had young in their pouches. The journey took place over land so far. Dominic saw a coastline and an ocean appeared on the horizon. All the birds suddenly descended in unison. Looking more closely as the bird pitched downward, he saw a village guarded by soldiers around the perimeter. The birds were heading directly for it. Dominic pounded on the underside of the animal trying to get it to change course. The Strithu poked him in the head with its beak and blood dripped into Dominic's eyes. "Wake up, we're about to land," he whispered loudly and nudged Julia. "Where are we?" Julia muttered as the opiate of sleep stayed with her. "We're still on the mainland and nearing the coast. We will be surrounded by soldiers when we land. Duck down and try not to be seen," Dominic replied urgently.

The bird landed in the center of the village next to four other Strithu and immediately began licking Dominic and Julia. The perimeter was two hundred yards away. "The guards haven't noticed us. I'm done with this animal, let's go," Dominic said. It wasn't easy getting out of the pouch. Dominic clambered out and helped Julia to the ground. "It sure was sticky in there," she said. "Do you have your translation device?" Dominic asked. "No, I lost it somewhere at the lake," she replied. Their Strithu stood up and began to walk among the other giant birds. The duo was in plain sight and vulnerable. "Follow my lead," Julia said. She approached the closest individual she could find. The woman appeared completely human. "We need help," she said. The woman immediately walked away. "Now what?" Dominic asked. "I don't know. We are among people from Earth. Let's go stand by the fire and stay quiet. Try to blend in," Julia replied. Nobody spoke to them, but they were watched with great curiosity.

Grice prepared for his evening meal. The village was returning to normal after the alarm sounded the previous day. The guards searched the village thoroughly and didn't find anything amiss. Tomorrow would be a good day. The Krace declared a lock down and it would be a day of rest. His thoughts were suddenly interrupted by his wife. "We have newcomers. Two unknown people arrived in the pouch of a Strithu. One of them tried to communicate, but I do not understand her." The information caught Grice by surprise. "Bring them to me and don't draw any attention," he said. "It's too late. Everyone in the village has already seen them," she replied.

The woman Julia originally spoke to returned to the fire. She slowly approached and took both Dominic and Julia by the hands and led them in the direction of the dwellings. A man was waiting as they entered one of the structures.

"Where do you come from?" Grice asked. The female spoke and gestured. The words were unfamiliar. "We will take this couple to Athos. He is familiar with strange and primitive languages. He might be familiar with this one," he told his wife.

Julia was relieved to be in the company of other humans. Dominic almost convinced her to take the pills and death had been a very real possibility. The village leader escorted them to a new dwelling. The man inside was older than anyone she'd seen thus far. The leader spoke, and the elderly man retrieved paper from underneath a floorboard. He approached Julia and put both of his hands on her cheeks. After touching her lips, he said one word, but she didn't understand. "My name is Julia; we are here to help," she replied with a reassuring smile.

Athos studied the antique documents he'd carefully spread out on the floor. Eventually he shrugged his shoulders and put the papers back under the floorboard. He produced a writing instrument and began drawing pictures. Julia knew it would be a long night. It took the remainder of the night and most of the early morning before Athos understood who she and Dominic were and why they were on Vandi.

Chapter 6

Bazor and two guards arrived on the third planet. Her ship returned to orbit immediately after they disembarked. The time was at hand to thin the human population and put the species to work. The sole purpose of humanity would be to serve the Annunaki. She prepared a message to be broadcast from the ship on her command before she departed. Her guards were now in place. Bazor contacted her ship and the message was broadcast across the entire planet.

President Louis relaxed after a long day of courting corporate leaders. He watched the evening news and was having a glass of champagne. The news anchor reported on the unrest in Miami where citizens protested and fired guns on drones whenever the aircraft came within range. The incident was sparked when a drone lost power and crashed through the window of a school bus. The driver lost control of the vehicle and it was struck by a garbage truck. None of the children survived. The story was suddenly interrupted and a man in a white robe appeared onscreen. "Gentle believers around the world, my name is Malachi. I'm the Son of God and have arrived to save the chosen ones. Many have forgotten the ways of the old world. Evil is now rampant on Earth and God has decreed the time for evil on Earth is at an end. I'm announcing my presence in this manner so you will all know He still exists and is forever omniscient. This will be my only communication through this medium. Your leaders will attempt to discredit me, but if you are to be with God you must also be with me. Choose wisely and be saved; I can be found at the Church of the Holy Sepulchre in Golgotha. Evidence of my power will be demonstrated soon."

President Louis watched as the anchorman attempted to regain his composure. "I apologize for the interruption. Apparently, we have a developing story. Stay tuned we'll be right back." Aides rushed into his room and his phone rang simultaneously.

A mass of Terrans traveled uphill toward the church. "Humans are so easily manipulated. You are not to speak unless necessary. Watch and learn," Bazor commanded her guards. People were arriving in air machines, ground vehicles and on animals. The first to arrive began to ask questions. "Remain patient; I will address all those present in one hour," Bazor said.

President Louis watched as thousands of people converged on the church. "How the hell was he able to broadcast on every channel and social media site at once?" he asked. "We don't know yet, Mr. President. We're working on it," an aide said. The man who called himself Malachi stood up and walked toward the crowd and the cameras. "God must know you have faith in His actions and are true believers. Each of you must be prepared to give your life to save yourself and your soul. You must decide which path to take. Your leaders represent evil and nothing more. The time has come for God and his faithful servants to punish the evil-doers in His kingdom. The governments of Earth believe their strength will save them, but there is only power in God. The time has arrived for all to be judged," Bazor abruptly turned and entered the church. She issued a command to her ship. Masquerading as a human male was barely tolerable. The end result was all that mattered.

President Louis was impressed with the audacious man. "Whoever this person is, he has resources. I want him taken alive, captured, questioned and killed quietly. We don't need a religious martyr. Find a way to discredit him." The President knew what to do and was annoyed when his secretary rushed in and interrupted him. "Turn the television back on," she said. "We've already seen what he had to say. We don't need to see it again," the President replied. His secretary ignored him and turned the news back on. The same anchorman from earlier in the evening was speaking. "It's currently unknown how the destruction took place. The location is now a massive burning crater. Initial video indicates the destructive force came from the skies."

"Oh my God. The Pentagon has been destroyed!" President Louis quietly spoke the words as the secret service pulled him out of his chair. "We must get you to a secure location," an agent said. "I'm not going anywhere. The Pentagon was just destroyed. There isn't a secure location anywhere," he replied.

Civilization was dying. Video from around the world showed rioters and looters decimating major cities. All manner of crimes increased drastically. Law enforcement gave up and, in many instances, joined with the rioters and looters. President Louis needed to act immediately. "Call a press conference. It will start in ten minutes," he barked. He knew who Malachi was and he also knew the world was in big trouble.

"People of the United States and all citizens of Earth, I have important information to share. The individual calling himself Malachi is not a Son of God. The major nations of the world have known for over a century about the existence of alien beings. We have previously withheld this information from the public. The withholding of this information was an error in judgment. We didn't want to cause panic and were working on a way to contact the aliens in order to achieve a peaceful relationship. Malachi is not of this Earth. He has arrived to divide and conquer humanity.

Others will follow. I will now take the unprecedented step of releasing all our classified alien contact documents. Malachi is a biological extraterrestrial and a threat to humanity. He must be stopped. Almost a year ago our scientists discovered an alien armada traveling towards Earth. At the time of the discovery, we believed the arriving aliens were amicable; we were incorrect. I direct all military units across the planet to prepare for war. Do not abandon your sworn duty and prepare to fight. To align with Malachi is to align against humanity. God bless America and all of mankind," President Louis concluded.

Enzo was transfixed and couldn't stop watching the news. He longed for the time when he knew what was really happening and could control most aspects of his surroundings. He didn't like President Louis but was impressed with his frank disclosure of alien contact at long last. It was a valiant effort, but it was also too late. Malachi gave the people what they so desperately wanted and needed. Citizens of every nation were irritated with the erosion of their freedom and tired of government interference in their daily lives. The people of Earth needed something to believe in. Nearly everyone on the planet could be observed and tracked at all times. The people of Earth knew they'd lost an undeclared war with the major governments.

Enzo knew things would only get worse; humanity would be lucky to survive. His phone rang. It was Randy. "Have you been watching?" Randy asked with urgency. "I have. The situation is not looking good," Enzo replied. "I'm coming to Trundle. I learned my lesson last time. I won't make the same mistake twice. If it's alright, I'm going to bring some of my staff with me," Randy said. "We cannot defeat this enemy. Save yourself and save your people. We must be patient. Bring whoever you want to Trundle and any technology or supplies you think might help." Enzo hung up the phone and went to find Martino and Sandy.

"You've seen the danger we all face. Life on this planet is about to change drastically. The only authority on the planet will now be the invading aliens. There is no longer a need to obsess over the United States. It's likely gone forever.

Recruit every available able-bodied person in the area. We will build an underground city right here. The people you recruit will be given safety and shelter here. Let them know their families are welcome. We will take shelter and plan our strategy beneath the surface. Don't share our location with anyone who is unwilling to assist. Do you understand your instructions?" Enzo asked. "I do understand. I'm grateful for all you've done for me and will do as you wish. I'm ready to fight," Sandy said. "I understand too," Martino nodded.

Tony was warm. He'd slept too long, and the suns were high in the sky. It was time to travel. Birds chattered as he reached the summit of a small hill and scanned his surroundings. Without anyone in sight, he was free to travel safely to the rendezvous point.

He took a moment to see if he could comprehend and review the information he'd stolen. Data appeared on the screen, but he couldn't understand the bulk of the information. A report highlighted in orange appeared on his screen. The solar system was familiar; it was Sol. He activated the translation unit and accessed the data. A voice emanated from his data pad. "The advance team has arrived in the Sol System. The remainder of the armada will arrive as scheduled. The species on the third planet has advanced beyond expectations. The mission is proceeding as planned. We will overtake the humans and the planet will be ours. I will report any anomalies should any occur." Attached data revealed Annunaki bases. Tony suddenly felt dizzy and sat down. Earth was about to be attacked and there wasn't any way to quickly provide the valuable information to the Alliance. He was now in possession of the most important piece of military intelligence in the history of Earth. He stood up and sprinted as fast as possible. The data pad indicated he was now fifteen miles from the rendezvous point. He could make it in a matter of a few hours if he kept moving.

Vincent spent an hour on a hillside overlooking the rendezvous point. He didn't see anything threatening, but he also didn't see any of his friends. Just as he was about to move downhill, he saw Monique and Isabella. Monique was supporting Isabella and helping her walk. He was relieved to see the two women. After the alarm sounded, he was afraid he would never see any of his friends again.

Monique found Isabella near the rendezvous location; she was limping and not making very good progress. "Hey Bella! It's good to see you! What's wrong with your leg?" she asked. "I'm fine. I sprained my ankle when I tripped on a rock. It looks like we're the first ones here," Isabella said. "I hope we won't be the only ones," Monique replied. A few minutes later, Vincent arrived. "It's good to see you two. We need to make a shelter and stay out of sight. Our presence on Vandi has been discovered. Do either of you have anything significant to report?" he asked. Both Monique and Isabella reported safe journeys. Monique hadn't seen anyone. Isabella spotted a patrol but was able to hide. She twisted her ankle when she scrambled to a hiding spot. Vincent told the women about his encounter with Maxis at the Martian village. "The villagers were being tortured when I left. It was horrible to watch and something I'll never forget," he said solemnly. "We need to use such atrocities as motivation to free Vandi," Isabella said with conviction.

"Since none of us were found, it must be Dominic, Julia, or Tony who have been captured," Monique said. "It must be Dominic or Julia," a voice behind Monique said. "Goddamn it Tony! Stop doing that. How long have you been here?" Vincent asked. "I just arrived. My mission was successful and I discovered some terrible news. You're going to want to sit down for this," he said as he opened his data pad.

It took an hour before the team was able to understand the entire translation and comprehend the enormity of the information. "The primary Annunaki armada hasn't reached Earth yet, but an advance ship of some kind has. The information doesn't specify its purpose. The most troubling information is contained within the overall battle plan. Earth, as well as the Alliance, could fall if we are unable to act on this information in time," Vincent said somberly. "We should attempt contact with Dominic and Julia," Isabella said. "Good idea, Isabella. Go ahead and send the signal," Vincent replied. Isabella sent a simple and short transmission informing Dominic and Julia that the team on the Martian Continent were safe. "Vincent, I'm not receiving a response. It's likely one or both have been captured," she said. "We must allow them more time. Perhaps they're currently occupied or asleep. If you don't receive a response in an hour send the signal again. We've been given much to think about; it's been a long day. Everyone get some rest and we will discuss a course of action and our options in the morning. The fate of Earth hangs in the balance," Vincent said wearily.

Bazor viewed the human broadcasts with amusement. The plan was working better than she expected. One of the guards interrupted her enjoyment. "The humans have selected a leader to act as a liaison. The man is requesting to speak with you." Bazor already knew about the human from the broadcasts. The man was a priest and was advocating mankind to follow the Son of God known as Malachi. "Bring him to me," she commanded.

The priest was visibly shaking when he entered the church and dropped to both knees. "Lord Malachi, thank you for granting me the privilege of speaking with you," he said. "You are welcome. Are you prepared to serve God?" Malachi asked. "I've always done my best to serve God. How can I continue to serve Him?" the man asked. "You must teach the wisdom of God. Judgment has arrived and there is little time left for souls to be saved. Lead those who truly believe in the message from God," Bazor said. "Lord, I've humbly been selected to represent man. Those who selected me wish to have their questions answered. Is this permissible?" the priest asked. "You may ask two questions and no more," Bazor said. "Was God responsible for the destruction of the Pentagon?" he asked. "Yes, God instructed me to destroy the Pentagon and so it was done. You may now ask your final question," Bazor said. "Thousands of lives were lost when the Pentagon was destroyed. Were any of the victims with God?" the priest asked. "Those who were with God have now taken their place beside him. There were very few; the majority of those vanquished were not of God. The remainder were sinners with unholy souls and were not saved. The Pentagon is only the beginning. God will continue to take his vengeance on sinners and non-believers. Believers will receive the ultimate reward. I will answer no more questions. Go in peace and go with God," Bazor commanded.

The major cities on Earth were in chaos. President Louis didn't bother trying to restore order. At the moment, the military was mostly intact. He returned from a cabinet meeting and was extremely frustrated. The United States was trying to fight an enemy which couldn't be found. The attack on the Pentagon came from space. NASA and the Air Force were unable to locate the exact location where the destructive force originated. With reluctance, he picked up the phone and called Enzo.

Sandy did her job well. The artificial lake was drained and construction began on the small city in its place. Enzo observed and inspected the work daily. Structures began to appear on the newly poured concrete foundation. It was time to take the measures necessary to protect his small but thriving community. Randy and the small crew he brought with him from Leviathan arrived the previous day. "You're making amazing progress," Randy said. "If we're discovered it won't matter. You saw what happened to the Pentagon. We need to get this city built and buried as quickly as possible. Staying under the radar is the only option right now," Enzo said as Sandy rushed up to him with the phone. "It's President Louis!" she said.

"Mr. President, I'm with Randy Stedman. It appears you have lost control of the situation," Enzo stated. "The situation isn't what it appears to be. We are still in control of the military," President Louis replied. "The aliens consider us vastly inferior, Mr. President. The Pentagon was destroyed, and your military never even fired a shot," Enzo said blandly. "I need you to level with me; be completely honest. Do you have any method of contacting Vincent?" the President asked. "If there was a way to contact Vincent, I would have done so the moment Malachi appeared. It's my planet as well, and I don't wish to see innocent people killed. Randy has attempted to contact Vincent, but if he's not in the solar system there's no way he will receive the message.

You must try and kill Malachi. People are being converted by the millions. Dissect the body. Show mankind Malachi is not a Son of God," Enzo said. "I will consider what you've said; to be honest it's better than what my advisors have been telling me. Please contact me if you manage to establish communication with Vincent," President Louis replied.

Bazor marveled at the sheer number of people who arrived for her address. The species was grasping for change and hope. Her arrival couldn't have been timed better. She was informed almost two million humans were present. Her message would be broadcast planet wide. "Fellow believers, you have been taken advantage of by the immoral leaders on God's Earth. These supposed leaders take your money, steal your personal information and have no accountability. All current governments on Earth are immoral in the eyes of God. The leaders of this planet are prostitutes for the wealthy corporations. They take your money and live lavish, selfish lifestyles while you continue to toil your

116

days away in perpetual poverty. You provide income and entertainment for their evil. God sent me to teach and save His people. Those who hear my words are now teachers as well. We will teach the wealthy, we will teach the government and we will teach the corporate leaders. All those who perpetrate evil will be taught a lesson. Now is the time to pick up your weapon of choice. It is not the time for hesitation or engaging in negotiations. God requires you to find the non-believers and carry out his will. Go forth and destroy the evil," Bazor commanded.

Enzo realized modern civilization as he knew it was over. Warfare raged across Earth in almost every nation. There were only two notable exceptions; somehow China and North Korea managed to keep the majority of their citizens in the dark. Before Malachi began to speak, the two nations turned off all power to their citizens.

As much as he despised the governments of the world, Enzo couldn't help but wonder if mankind would survive anarchy and the impending invasion. Malachi's tactics exploited the major weakness of humanity. Societies fought religious battles for all of recorded history. The alien was simply throwing more gas on the fire and the plan was working perfectly. Time was running short and religious leaders were telling their flocks that the apocalypse had begun. Even if President Louis somehow managed to kill Malachi, another alien would likely take his place. Mankind was undergoing a psychological attack on their beliefs.

Where was Vincenzo? Enzo wondered if his nephew somehow angered the aliens and was the reason people of Earth were being punished. Over one hundred years passed without any known alien intervention. The noble and righteous goal of contacting the aliens who visited Earth in the past was a naïve attempt to gain admission to their exclusive club. The attempt was made and the aliens responded with violent vengeance. As an intelligent and cautious man, Enzo managed to survive multiple attacks on his life. He was always able to stay one step ahead of his enemy. There weren't any options he could see that would defeat this enemy. "The structures are complete. We can begin the process of moving in supplies and families. We should begin to hide the buildings immediately," Sandy said interrupting his thoughts. "Get it done quickly while we still have time. Thank you, Sandy." Hiding wasn't in his nature. There was always a solution to any problem and he would continue to search for an answer.

Rest wasn't easy under the circumstances. Vincent slept for a few precious hours. He couldn't stop thinking of all the death which occurred on Mars and the imminent danger to Earth. Mars was once vibrant and robust with a thriving civilization. Now it was a world littered with bones of the dead. He was in command of the small team on Vandi and would make the final decision on any course of action. Earth would suffer the same fate of Mars if he failed to act quickly.

"Good morning. I hope you slept better than I did. I've reached a decision. Unless someone can convince me otherwise, the data will be uploaded to the satellite and we'll activate the return sequence today. We will do everything we can to disrupt and sabotage the efforts of the Krace and Annunaki here on Vandi. If possible, we will liberate some of the enslaved members of Sol to assist us in our efforts," Vincent said. "Captain, the Alliance requested we gather intelligence for approximately ten months before we sent the satellite back through the gate. Shouldn't we try to gather additional intelligence before we send the satellite back?" Tony asked. "If the satellite leaves today it will still take over three months to return to the Rabanah System. If it leaves orbit and maneuvers too fast, the Annunaki will take notice. I spent many hours last night reviewing the Annunaki battle plan. The plan is detailed and has specifics regarding the number of ships, the location of the armada and the distribution of their forces.

The execution of their plan relies on proper timing and sequence. We must disrupt the timing to change the conditions of the battle. If we wait, it's possible we could provide some additional useful intelligence, but the risk is not worth the reward. We must act now. Isabella, I've provided a brief summary and mission update of what we've learned during our time here. Upload the data Tony recovered along with my summary immediately. When the upload is complete, send the satellite back to Rabanah. The Annunaki have been attacking the Alliance, Vandi and now Earth. It's time to take them by surprise and find their weaknesses," Vincent said.

Isabella triple checked the data to make sure the satellite received her transmission successfully. The information was received and ready to be transmitted once the satellite entered the Rabanah System. She sent the command for the satellite to depart Vandi. "Captain, the information has been successfully uploaded. The data will be received by the Alliance in approximately ninety-three days," she reported assuredly.

Vincent felt confident in his decision. The satellite would arrive in the Rabanah system quicker than the Alliance expected. The information Tony liberated might turn the tide of the impending battle. "Thank you, Isabella. We will return to the Martian village I visited. If we are to free the people of Vandi, we must find a way to deactivate their Kracian bracelets. If I can get you one of the bracelets, do you think you can find a way to deactivate the device?" Vincent asked. "It would take some time; I will need an active device that isn't attached to a person. I can't experiment on a device worn by someone. It's too dangerous," she replied. "I'll do my best, but no promises. We will leave tomorrow morning," Vincent said. "I'll research any information I can find regarding the bracelets, but I won't be able to make any real progress until I have one in my possession," Isabella said. "I'll leave a message for Dominic and Julia. I hope they're still alive," Vincent replied.

Julia was slowly learning to communicate with the village leaders. She'd been spending a great deal of time with Grice. The atrocities continually committed by the Krace were disheartening. Nearly every member of the community was disfigured in one way or another. Members of work groups frequently returned with blood streaming down their faces and backs after the whippings. Julia slept during the day and snuck into the village at night. Grice asked them to remain outside the village during the day. He didn't want his people endangered. Dominic wasn't sleeping on a regular schedule of any kind. He was fearful of being discovered and needed to study the enemy's routine.

While Julia spent her time in the village, Dominic hiked to a bluff to document the number of guards and their patrolling patterns. She watched as he carefully descended the hillside and returned to their crude shelter.

"What did you learn today?" she asked. "The amount of guards and the number of patrols is decreasing. I think guards are returning to normal operations. It's been weeks now and they haven't been able to find us; I think they've given up," Dominic replied. "It's time for us to execute the back-up plan," Julia said. "I know we're supposed to follow it, but I don't like it; it just seems too dangerous to work. Traveling across an ocean isn't easy on Earth and it's far more treacherous here. Vandi has twice as many dangerous creatures in its sea," Dominic replied.

"We should at least consider crossing. I think the best course of action is for one of us to find a port and see if it's possible to liberate a vessel. The data indicates there are slave fishing ports," Julia replied. "I have a different idea. I saw a piece of art in Grice's home. The image showed people riding in the Strithu pouch just as we did. The birds are highly intelligent and if we're lucky, one of us can travel safely and quickly across the ocean. I don't think I can make it across the ocean in the pouch, but you don't seem to mind it as much. It's probably best for you to make the journey and I'll continue to document what I can about the enemy. I'll talk to Grice tonight and find out if such a journey can be made. If I'm the one staying behind, I'll need to develop a mutual trust and a relationship with the inhabitants of the village," Dominic said. "I'll go with you; we need to make plans together," Julia replied.

Grice was surprised when Julia arrived with Dominic earlier than normal. Julia took his hand and led him to the location of the art. She drew a crude map of the planet and attempted to communicate, but it took ten minutes before Grice understood what she was asking. Dominic and Julia were motioned outside. Grice found a sleeping Strithu and climbed into its pouch. He manipulated the animal's neck and it immediately took to the sky. Julia was mesmerized as Grice and the bird flew low inside the village. He was careful and made sure the bird didn't fly beyond the perimeter. After a few minutes, Julia believed she could control the bird's flight in the same manner. The bird landed clumsily, and Grice fell out of the pouch laughing. He said a few words to the giant animal and touched it on its beak. The Strithu responded with several deep guttural sounds and lay down to rest.

President Louis was informed a ground operation would be nearly impossible. "Wherever Malachi travels, hundreds of thousands follow. A ground force attack would be met with heavy resistance. Collateral damage would be extreme. We have multiple snipers on the scene, but none of them can get close enough to his position to fire. His followers are completely faithful and devoted to his cause.

Our only option is a nighttime drone attack. We can launch a single missile causing minimal damage. With your permission, we will attack tonight," the Secretary of Defense requested. Targeting Malachi with a missile attack was a desperate and messy plan. President Louis knew such action would likely make the alien a martyr. The aliens in orbit would respond violently whether the plan succeeded or not. If Malachi were killed, he could show the world the false deity was not of Earth. Mankind would rally, and humanity might have a fighting chance against the invading force. "Proceed with the plan. Keep me updated and keep the drone as low as possible. Prepare our people on the ground to recover and secure Malachi's body as quickly as possible. The corpse is to be brought to Washington immediately," he commanded.

The President observed from the situation room as the drone approached the church. When it was approximately one mile away, a missile launched. In a blinding flash, both the drone and the missile were destroyed. "Mr. President, we have a negative impact. Both the missile and drone were blown up," a technician reported. "No shit? Where do you think I am? I just watched the same fucking thing you did!" Fifteen minutes later, military installations across the planet were destroyed one by one.

Tissa silently observed from the safety of home the night a human arrived and visited with Maxis. She waited for three days before finally questioning her husband. He rarely talked with anyone since the night of the meeting. She knew humans lived on the other side of the planet but had only seen them in images on the hidden device. It was unsettling to see such strange looking creatures. "I observed your meeting with the human. Are you ever going to speak about it?" she finally asked her husband.

Maxis led her into their chamber and quietly retold his talk with the strange visitor. Since the human arrived, Maxis was a changed person. There was a new purpose and determination within him she didn't know he possessed. His new purpose gave her hope.

She listened as Maxis spoke again with the human inside their home. Three others accompanied the man. She'd been asleep when the strange creatures arrived but awoke to the sound of Maxis greeting the aliens. "Tissa, you can come out. It's safe; there's no sense in sneaking around," Maxis said reassuringly. She ventured out and sat down quietly next to her husband.

Maxis introduced his companion to the humans. "How much have you heard?" he asked his wife. "I've heard everything. Is there truly hope for our freedom? As far as we know, you are the first members of the Alliance on this world since the war," Tissa asked.

"I can only speculate and guess at any actions the Alliance will take. We were able to obtain critical intelligence regarding the Annunaki plan. The Alliance must pursue a course of action that will alter the enemy's timing. I believe the leaders of the Alliance will decide to invade both the Earth and Vandi systems in order to disrupt the plan. The primary Annunaki invading force is planning to travel through the Vandi System and traverse through the gates of Rabanah and Earth," Vincent said.

"Is it true we originate from the same star?" Tissa asked and looked at the one called Isabella. "It's true. I've been to the fourth planet and have uncovered some of your ancient history. A friend of ours is returning to uncover as much history from your ancient home as possible. If you've been listening, you know Earth is in as much danger as Mars was in the distant past," Isabella responded. I would rather die fighting than spend another day as a slave. Do you have a plan Vincent?" Maxis asked. Before he could reply, a scream from inside the house startled everyone followed by another from outside.

Vincent went outside to find the source of the second scream as Maxis rushed over to the small Martian boy in the corner of the room who made the first one. "Zanther, we are safe. Don't be scared. These people are humans. Come sit with us. Do you remember when you asked if the Alliance would save us from the Annunaki?" Maxis asked his son. "Yes father, I remember," Zanther replied timidly. "These humans have come from the Alliance. We must not tell anyone about their arrival. We will work with them to gain our freedom," Maxis said and smiled.

Vincent discovered a young female outside the house. "Have you been listening?" he asked the woman. "Yes, but the boy's scream startled me. I saw you the night you first arrived. I just needed to know what was going on," she said. "Accompany me inside, please," Vincent said as Maxis proudly introduced his son.

"It's a pleasure to meet you, young Zanther. This female has been eavesdropping and is aware of our purpose here. Who is she?" Vincent asked. "Her name is Alixias. She is young and recently lost her partner when Kracian soldiers beat him to death. She is strong willed and lucky to be alive. The guards have tortured her many times as she remains uncooperative. I'm amazed she's recovered each time from their vicious attacks. On multiple occasions she has tried to escape from her work location. She is always trying to convince me to organize an attack on the soldiers, but none of her plans have a realistic chance of success," Maxis replied. "I think some of my plans are pretty good and worth a try. It's better to try and fight than to live your entire life as slave!" Alixias said with resentment. "You are correct if the circumstances warrant an attempt, but suicidal attempts must be dismissed," Maxis replied.

"It's a pleasure to meet you, Alixias. For now, you must keep any information you hear to yourself. Maxis, in response to your earlier question, I do have a plan. The satellite returning to the Alliance will take ninety-three days to arrive at the gate. Once it passes through the gate the information will be transmitted immediately. I believe the Alliance will take action very quickly. It can't be known for certain, however. One hundred and thirty days from now we will free as many slaves as possible. We will go into hiding and only fight the Krace and Annunaki if necessary. If my guess is correct, the Alliance will arrive in the Vandi System at approximately the same time. I believe it is probable Alliance forces will arrive within the timeframe I've outlined. In reality, it's only an educated guess and possibly an incorrect one," Vincent said. "Your logic is sound, and I would make the same decision if I were in your place," Maxis said. "I will be ready when the time arrives. I've already picked out which guards to kill first," Alixias said, her spirit suddenly rejuvenated.

"Maxis, for our plan to work, I need access to a functioning bracelet. I need to find a way to disarm the device, so you aren't all killed when it's time to fight," Isabella said. "All bracelets are attached to living Martians. I'd prefer you didn't experiment on the bracelets attached to my friends," Maxis said. "I don't wish to sound insensitive, but what happens when someone dies? Where are the bodies taken? Are the bracelets taken off?" Monique asked. "I don't know what happens to the bracelets, but the bodies are taken to the south. The guards take them to a place known as "the pit." Our people are disposed of like garbage; it's disgusting and undignified. The dead should be honored and revered," Maxis said.

"Prepare your people for battle, Maxis. You will need to fight to gain freedom. We will locate the bracelets and my friends. I will stay nearby and make contact when it's safe to do so," Vincent said as he rose to leave.

"I have more information for you, Vincent," Maxis said. Vincent sat back down ready to hear what the Martian would say. "We will need as many allies as possible. There is an indigenous species on Vandi known as Volmer. When the Alliance arrived, the

Volmer were indifferent; we left them alone and they left us alone.

However, in recent years, we've heard rumors the Annunaki have made attempts to enslave the Volmer population. The Volmer took to the sea to escape. The species is introverted and wishes to be left alone. These recent attacks might give them a reason to align and fight with us. If you have the resources, you must try to make contact and ally with them. The Annunaki keep most of their military force at the poles to repel any revolt that might occur on the major continents," Maxis said. "If possible, we will attempt to contact the Volmer. By the way, the Volmer are not indigenous. Their species also originated from Sol. The Volmer have been on Vandi much longer than your species and mine, originating from a moon of the largest planet in the Sol System," Vincent responded.

Chapter 7

The attempt on her life angered Bazor. She took immense pleasure in systematically destroying military bases across Earth. The United States was proving to be exceptionally troublesome. She sent instructions for her ship to destroy all remaining military bases and to eliminate the infrastructure of the nation.

Incessant attacks rained down on the United States. The nation was in ruins and law enforcement ceased completely. All major corporate headquarters were destroyed. Top executives were captured and hung in public executions. The death toll was in the millions with no sign of stopping. After the failed attack on Malachi, the remaining United States Military collapsed. All NASA facilities were destroyed. The technical infrastructure was failing as well. Satellites in orbit were systemically destroyed.

Air Force One was prepared and ready. President Louis and his team were likely boarding the aircraft for the last time. He assembled three hundred people to accompany him to Dulce, New Mexico. The United States maintained a top secret underground base at the location. When everyone was inside, the base would be secured, and no one would be allowed to leave. It was the safest place left on the planet.

"How long will our food supply last?" Enzo asked Randy. "Not long; more is on the way. Most people here are either farming or hunting. We're about to enter the growing season and should be alright for the next eight or nine months. We're extending the farming range and are working on greenhouses. Once it turns cold we will have a limited supply of vegetables to hold us through next winter.

Martino and Sandy have recruited and are maintaining a small group of guards. The perimeter is patrolled regularly. The guards have killed eight people attempting to steal food," Randy said. "Tell them to continue to recruit. It will only get worse. We must protect what we've built," Enzo replied.

"Do you have any new ideas to fight the aliens?" Enzo asked. "I learned quite a bit about the ship Vincent brought back from Mars. Unfortunately, we didn't have enough time to reverse engineer any of the technology. We were able to analyze the tratium and have made a similar substance, but we only have a small quantity of the material. At best we might be able to make some bullets or perhaps a missile," Randy said. "We should make bullets and keep things quiet, if possible. If any aliens show up, we can kill them and hide the bodies. If you're right, tratium bullets will pass through any protective alien armor. A missile would be a shout for attention and end our lives quickly" Enzo replied.

"We will need additional ammunition for our people. Conditions are getting worse across the plant. Famine and disease are rampant; the hospitals have been looted and are completely empty. Antibiotics aren't available for those who've become ill. The large cities are almost completely empty. The farms have been raided and crops have been pulled from the ground in most places. It's been reported that even North Korea and China have completely collapsed. There are no longer any functional governments left on Earth.

If it was Malachi's goal to get mankind to destroy itself, he has succeeded," Randy somberly stated. "If some of us can stay alive, there's hope for the future. Manufacture the bullets. We will save the tratium rounds in case we need to use them against enemy soldiers patrolling our area," Enzo commanded.

Julia was sleeping soundly in the pouch of the Strithu when the giant bird suddenly squawked. She opened her eyes as the bird descended quickly to the surface. A giant spray of water erupted when the bird crashed onto the ocean's surface. Immediately, the large raptor was back in the air. She watched as the Strithu carried a large fish over her face with its talons. Blood and bits of entrails landed on her head as the bird devoured the strange looking creature.

She was trying to clean herself as the Strithu approached a coastline. She guided the bird to the original rendezvous point. Before the bird began to descend, she saw a message spelled out in the rocks, "Nearby village. North." She steered the Strithu north and after a few minutes she could see the village in the distance and instructed the bird to land. She would sleep until nightfall and approach the village before sunrise.

Another grueling day of work was finally over. Maxis looked at his friends gathered around the nightly fire. It was time to share his amazing news. He'd been waiting his entire life for this moment and stood before his family and friends. "We were once a proud race capable of achieving anything we put our minds to. We were not meant to be slaves. We were destined to be artists, writers, musicians, scientists and so much more. Buried in each of us and our children are a people capable of greatness. The time is at hand to free ourselves. I have recently been visited by members of the Alliance on multiple occasions. When it's time to fight, our bracelets will be deactivated," Maxis said.

His words were met with complete silence. Everyone looked at him as if he lost his mind. "My husband speaks the truth. Zanther and I have met the humans as well," Tissa said. "When is this rebellion supposed to take place?" Bessax finally asked. Maxis wasn't surprised when Bessax was the one to finally respond. He was once a friend to Bessax. Their friendship ended due to a petty argument. Bessax was content to wait for the Alliance to free the planet. She didn't wish to participate in subversive activities. "I don't know for certain. In very short order," Maxis replied.

"I don't believe it. I think Maxis is so desperate for freedom he's made up this entire story. He needs a distraction so he can slither away with his family into the hills," Bessax said. Maxis was about to reply when a horrific shriek pierced the air. More shrieks followed from the village perimeter. A lone human female walked toward them. "I told you! The humans have come. I have not seen this one before." Maxis went to greet the woman. "Greetings, I am Maxis. Is Vincent with you?" he asked. Words were spoken by the human, but not translated. He gestured for her to follow him. Maxis brought her to his home and quickly returned to his friends.

This human I haven't met before. She does not carry a translation device. I will attempt to communicate with her tonight. Do not speak of this in front of the guards; we will discuss more of our future tomorrow night," he said.

After returning home, Maxis removed the device his grandfather gave him from behind the false wall and returned to the woman. She appeared nervous and scared. It took him a few moments to discover how to enable the translation function.

Julia was frustrated. Once again, she was in a strange environment and didn't have a way to communicate. She looked around the house for something to write with as a female and a small boy entered the dwelling. "Greetings, I am called Maxis. Who are you? Are you with Vincent and the Alliance?" a disembodied voice asked. She looked up and saw the Martian holding a data pad. "Thank God. I'm so happy you can communicate. My name is Julia. Yes, I'm with the Alliance. Vincent is a friend of mine. I lost my communication device and haven't been in contact with him since we landed. My friend and I landed on the continent where the humans are located, and we were almost captured. A Strithu brought me across the ocean. Can you provide something to eat and some water? Please keep me safe," she pled. "We will bring you food and water. You must hide here until Vincent returns. He is staying nearby with the rest of the Alliance members assigned to this continent. I don't know precisely where, but I will keep you safe until he returns," Maxis replied. "When do you expect him to return?" Julia asked. "He didn't specify, but I expect it won't be long," Maxis replied. "Has he learned anything since he arrived?" Julia asked.

Maxis was tired. He wanted nothing more than to put his son to bed and go to sleep himself. Tissa sensed his weariness. "Go get some rest, Maxis. I will stay up and tell Julia what Vincent has learned." Maxis put his son to sleep and took a moment to watch the two females talking. He retired to his room for the night and fell asleep listening as Tissa explained what Vincent learned.

Sunrise was a beautiful mix of red and pink. Birds flitted carelessly in the early morning sky. Vincent had never seen a sky with so many beautiful and varied creatures. In contrast, the pit was the most disgusting thing he'd ever seen. Martian bodies in various degrees of decay lay rotting. The sight was horrific, and the smell was putrid and overwhelming. "Tony do you see any active bracelets?" Vincent asked. "Nope, but we need to get this done. I can't handle much more of this," Tony gagged. "I'll remove the closest one I can find. I guess we'll have to settle for a deactivated bracelet," Vincent said. He entered the pit and found the closest corpse. A large rock was nearby. He picked it up and brought it down hard on the deceased Martian's arm. The bone snapped in half and Vincent quickly removed the bracelet and scrambled out of the pit. He continued to run until he was able to breathe fresh air. "That wasn't disrespectful at all. Don't ever discuss how we retrieved the bracelet. Let's get back and see what we can discover about this device," he said as his friends caught up with him.

It was late, and Vincent was still awake. The slaves on Vandi wouldn't be freed if the bracelets couldn't be deactivated. He rose and went to find Isabella. "Have you had any luck figuring out how to disarm those things?" he asked. "I've been able to open and analyze the device. There is a way to deactivate it, but I can't be certain until I have an active unit. There is a third display light on the unit. I don't know what purpose it serves," Julia said. "I think it's time to visit Maxis again. Bring the bracelet. We'll go late tonight," Vincent said.

Julia was going stir crazy. She'd been confined for nine days and longed to go outside where village members were once again speaking near the fire. Maxis was considerate enough to leave her the data pad so she could listen in on the discussions. She was impressed with Maxis. He was organizing and preparing his people for battle. Crude maps were provided to the villagers. Teams were organized and he explained the plan to free the other villages. He even knew where his great grandfather stored weapons when Vandi was invaded. Julia was disappointed when the nightly meeting ended. She fell asleep with the reassuring knowledge that Maxis was a great leader for his people.

Zanther was on the ground sleeping near the fire. Maxis picked up his son and brought him home. His boy was a hard worker and produced more than many twice his age. He looked at his son's fresh wounds as he laid him down for his nightly rest. The Krace would suffer for the horror they inflicted upon his child. "Rest well. Soon we will have our vengeance," he told the sleeping boy.

As leader, people looked to him for guidance. Maxis went back outside and lay down by the dying fire. He stared, fixated, at the bright orange embers and contemplated the future. Looking to the sky, he found the dim star where his species originated. It was time for his people to retake their proper place in the universe. For the first time in his life, Maxis felt he could bear the responsibility of being a leader for his people. He dozed off thinking there was now a chance for his son to live the remainder of his life free of slavery.

Vincent was still disturbed about the gory incident at the pit and almost tripped over a body lying near the fire. In his mind, Vincent thought it was another Martian corpse. "Oh my God. Maxis is dead!" he said. Maxis stirred and woke up. "Hello my friend. I have something of yours at my home," Maxis said with a smile. "Please lead the way. Tony and Isabella please go with him. Vincent and I will be with you momentarily," Monique said.

"Why aren't we going?" Vincent asked as Maxis led Tony and Isabella to his home. "We aren't going because you're still in shock. You are seeing the dead where none exist. The pit was a horrible experience and no intelligent lifeform should ever have to witness such atrocities. But we did see the horror and we know what evil the Annunaki and Krace are capable of. We must think clearly to defeat them. Get past what you saw, Vincenzo," Monique said.

He knew Monique was right. The incident at the pit was so unsettling he wasn't thinking straight. Vincent closed his eyes and took a moment to refocus his thoughts. When he opened his eyes, Monique was staring at him with a concerned expression. He put his hands around the back of her head and gently pulled her close for a kiss. "Since when do you call me Vincenzo?" he asked. "I'll call you Vincenzo when necessary. Enzo isn't here to kick you in the ass, so I guess the duty has fallen to me," Monique said as the couple went to join Maxis.

Isabella, Tony, Maxis and Tissa were waiting for them. Vincent was surprised when he saw Julia sleeping peacefully on the floor. "Thank God she's alive. Is Dominic here?" he asked Maxis. "Dominic is not here; however, Julia said he was safe when she left," Maxis said.

Julia awoke to the sound of familiar voices. "We're glad you're safe and alive," Vincent said warmly as she sat up. "I am too. It's good to see all of you again," she said as her friends surrounded and hugged her.

The quiet celebration was abruptly interrupted. A villager entered the home. "Maxis, another has died. The guards beat Suxon severely today. His daughter found him dead when she went to check on his injuries," he said. "Vincent, you and your people must leave. We are required to summon the guards," Maxis said. "Wait. I need to experiment on the bracelet. We might not have another opportunity like this," Isabella said. "Monique go with Isabella and make sure you accurately document the deactivation procedure. We all need to know how to deactivate the devices," Vincent said as Monique and Isabella left. "Maxis, we brought a deactivated bracelet with us. With your permission we will bring the body to the perimeter and place the deactivated bracelet on Suxon. It will appear as if he died trying to escape. We do not intend any dishonor; it is the only way," Vincent said. "My people haven't been honored in death for a very long time. We will do what must be done. Proceed with your plan," Maxis said.

"Julia, if Isabella successfully deactivates the bracelet, you must return to the Human Continent immediately. I will give you my data pad so we can communicate and coordinate when the time comes. Maxis, I think it would be a good idea for you to record a message. You can explain that we are here to help and that it is time to rebel. Julia can show it to any human leaders she encounters," Vincent said. "I agree we must be unified in our action. The message will hopefully unite the two continents," Maxis said as Monique and Isabella returned.

"I successfully deactivated the bracelet!" Isabella proudly stated. "Share the procedure with everyone. Deactivating the bracelets is the most important obstacle we face right now. Julia, you must return now. Maxis, I will return every few days to strategize. We will take the body to the perimeter and depart," Vincent said. "I look forward to your next visit. Travel safely brothers," Maxis said as he placed his hands on Vincent's chest.

"Mr. President we have received images from the Hawking Space Telescope from our last functioning satellite. The alien armada has arrived. The smaller vessels are in orbit. The larger ships are descending to the surface all around the planet. We estimate over two thousand will be landing. Each is approximately the size of a football stadium," the Secretary of Defense reported. "Launch the drones, and fire at will. Use whatever assets we have left to attack the enemy," President Louis said. "The attack will commence at once."

As he watched the battle unfold, President Louis knew the effort was in vain. The military hadn't been able to damage the ship Randy used to attack the White House. There was no chance against thousands of such craft.

The missile attacks had no effect on the ships as the vessels descended and entered the atmosphere. The tratium ships were impervious to mankind's weapons. One of the few remaining drones transmitted video of a ship landing. Thousands of aliens wearing body armor exited the craft. A group of nearby people opened fire on the arriving aliens. A large explosion killed the group instantly. "Send a message on every communication channel we have! Tell them I want to negotiate a truce and am willing to discuss a limited surrender," he said.

Her personal ship landed nearby. Bazor ordered her guards to fire on the mass of humanity following her. Those who weren't killed or injured quickly scattered. "Provide an update on the current situation," Bazor commanded as she entered the ship. "The humans were unable to offer any significant resistance. We are establishing hives and erecting perimeters. We will begin selecting the healthiest members of the species and distribute bracelets within the hour. We have received a message from the leader of the United States. He has requested a meeting," her second in command reported. "Send the vessels assigned to protect this system to the Rabanah gate. An invasion by the Alliance is possible and we must repel any attack. Bring the human to me; I will be in the medical chamber. It's time to get rid of this horrible disguise," Bazor commanded.

Enzo was underground and still didn't feel safe. "Is everyone inside?" he asked. "The last of the hunters just returned. The entrances have been concealed and we should be safe unless the aliens conduct an extremely thorough search. Martino and Sandy are monitoring the external video and will only engage the enemy if our sanctuary is discovered. We've been able to provide them a small amount of tratium ammunition," Randy said. "Send President Louis the instructions for manufacturing tratium. With any luck, he might still have resources available to make some weaponry. Send an update to Dalton on Mars as well. It's possible the people on Mars are the only free humans left in the solar system," Enzo said.

When the Intrepid left Earth, Patrick was hoping he would get along with the assigned government representative, Kathy. He didn't trust the government and he wouldn't trust her. She was now crying uncontrollably. For the last twelve hours they'd been watching the news broadcasts from Earth. All transmissions abruptly ceased. "I know it's horrible, but you must calm down. I'm going to get Dalton and Jose. Try to compose yourself by the time we return. There is much to discuss and we all need to be thinking clearly," he said. "I'll try my best. We don't deserve to be treated like animals," Kathy sobbed as tears ran down her face.

After unlocking the cipher, Dalton made incredible progress. This was what he was born to do. As he directed Jose to the next section of the wall, Patrick suddenly appeared. "You need to come back to the ship. It's urgent," he said. "We're making exceptional progress and making historical discoveries right now," Dalton replied. "Trust me this one time, Dalton, the reason you have to return to the ship is historical as well. Let's go right now," he commanded.

Dalton felt numb and horrible anguish when Patrick replayed the news broadcasts received from Earth. He watched the final thirty minutes of video the Intrepid received. "All transmissions have now ceased.

Earth has been completely defeated and devastated," Patrick said as Kathy continued sobbing nearby.

"Will the invading aliens come here?" Jose asked. "I don't know for sure. For all intents and purposes, we're prisoners here already. There aren't many humans on Mars and we don't constitute a threat. If we're lucky, they've forgotten about us or will ignore us," Patrick replied. "What can we do?" Dalton asked. "I've been considering our options. We can't attack in one lone ship; the attempt would be suicidal and a waste of lives. Our best course of action right now is to simply survive and exist. I recommend the three of you get back to work. Having a purpose might help keep your mind from obsessing about the situation on Earth. After you return to Cydonia I'll meet with the local leader here on Mars. Since he doesn't have a government anymore, I expect he'll be willing to coordinate and plan. Everyone left on Mars must unite and try to coexist. See if you can discover any information about advanced weaponry in the historical records," Patrick requested.

The three-dimensional printer was a godsend. Hector produced and stored weapons as quickly as possible. He printed more weaponry than there were people on Mars. When the aliens arrived, he would die honorably fighting for humanity. "The weapons won't do you any good. You need to produce habitats and

146

greenhouses," a voice said. He turned to find a stranger standing before him. "I know everyone on Mars, but I don't know you. Who are you?" he asked. "My name is Patrick Weeks. I'm sure you have a file on me somewhere.

I come from the ship parked on the edge of the dead zone," he said. "President Louis said to leave you alone this time around. Have you found any Martian technology we can use to defeat these aliens? The President said there's an ancient city buried in Cydonia," Hector asked. "We have not. We've only learned of ancient Martian history so far.

It's of paramount importance to settle our differences and work together to see if we can survive on this planet. If there's anything I can do to help your community here on Mars, I'd be happy to do so. We're also running out of food," Patrick said. "There are no longer any divisions; we are all in the same boat now. I'll find some food for you and your people. Together, we'll do what we can to fight our shared enemy," Hector replied.

The sky was dark, and it was raining hard. Monique stared at something that resembled a melon, but it was green with purple stripes. She took a picture and waited for her data pad to process the information. "Enolp, safe for consumption." Monique reviewed the attached nutritional information. The enolp would provide a good source of nutrition and energy. There were many in the area. She heard a noise just a few yards away and stood up expecting to find more birds. Instead she saw a small Krace patrol. The Krace were looking right at her and began running in her direction. She sprinted as fast as she could, crossed a small creek, and hid behind a large boulder. She sent a message to Tony, knowing Vincent gave his data pad to Julia. "Guards have found me. I've been followed. Do not try to find me. More soldiers will come." After the message transmitted, she enabled the self-destruct feature on the data pad. The device became hot in her hand and began to smoke. She threw it is far as she could toward the creek. The guards splashed through the water and were converging on her position. She began to run again. A steep hillside was nearby and climbing the hill was her only option. Monique began scrambling up the base of the hill and felt a sudden pain in the middle of her back. She tried to climb higher, but her legs wouldn't move, and she felt a new pain in her neck. Her hands stopped working and she fell. The guards immobilized her with an electrical device of some kind. She hadn't climbed far and only fell a few feet. She tried to get up and fight, but her muscles refused to respond. There was nothing she could do as a soldier raised his boot and kicked her in the back of the head rendering her unconscious.

The rain was a welcome relief. The end of the day was near, and it was hotter than normal. Maxis was growing weary. The normally bored guards suddenly gathered together and momentarily ignored their slaves. Such activity was uncommon. He tried to listen to the conversation but was too far away. Zanther was closer to the guards. Maxis hoped his son would know what was going on. When the guards refocused their attention on their prisoners, the attacks were more brutal than normal. The sound of cracking whips and screams filled the air.

When the short march to the village began, Maxis quickly found his son. "Father, one of the humans has been captured. It's the one known as Monique," Zanther said in a panic. "Did you hear any other information?" Maxis asked. "The guard said she was being taken to the north. She is to be tortured and executed," Zanther replied.

Tony and Isabella defied his order and physically restrained him. When Vincent saw the text message from Monique, he needed to save her immediately. She meant so much to him and he counted on her. Tony threw him to the ground and immobilized his limbs. "You must focus on the mission, Captain. Is one life worth sacrificing thousands, millions, or billions of others?" he asked. "We all love Monique, Captain. Do not jeopardize our mission. There are very few of us on Vandi and we can't lose both of you," Isabella said.

A few hours later, Vincent knew his instincts were wrong. He needed to set an example as a leader and he failed in this instance. It would be the last time an emotional experience would affect his judgment. "I'm sorry. It was wrong of me to order you to help me save Monique. It was an overly emotional response and it won't happen again," "If someone I loved was taken, I would have reacted the same way. We all care for Monique. She's our friend too," Isabella comforted. "I'm in command and it's my responsibility to safeguard your lives and ensure we can successfully complete our mission. My behavior wasn't acceptable," Vincent said as a data pad chirped. The message was from Maxis. "Come to my home quickly. I have information about Monique," the message read.

"Maxis has information about Monique and requests our presence in the village," Vincent shared. "Aircraft and ground forces have been in the area for hours. I'm not sure if we will be able to leave anytime soon," Tony said. "We're safe here for the moment. If we remain hidden beneath the surface I don't think the Krace will find us. We must wait until sunset and hope there won't be as many patrols," Isabella suggested.

By nightfall, the number of aircraft and ground troops began to decrease. "What are we going to do? Patrols will likely increase in the morning," Tony asked. "We'll hide where we're least expected to be found. Gather your supplies. We're moving in with Maxis, Tissa and Zanther. Let's try to make it inside the perimeter as quickly as possible," Vincent commanded with urgency.

Everyone in the village was at the nightly fire except for Maxis. His people were no longer downtrodden. The villagers were discussing how the capture of the human would influence the coming battle. Maxis was at the perimeter waiting for Vincent. He was about to return to the fire when he saw the group of humans emerge near the creek bed. His new friends ran quickly through the perimeter.

"Monique has been taken to Vath, a city located in the North. It's the Annunaki base here on Vandi," Maxis reported. "Thank you for the information, Maxis. Let's get inside and discuss our options," Vincent said. He never wanted anything as much as he wanted to rescue Monique. Vincent knew it was not the correct tactical decision and a rescue couldn't be attempted. Once inside, he sat down on the floor and began a painful speech. "I appreciate the information you provided about Monique, but we cannot jeopardize additional lives attempting to save her. She will be tortured, and she will reveal everything she knows. We would like to remain hidden in the village until the battle commences. Monique will be the first casualty in the upcoming war," Vincent said.

Maxis knew his friend was right. It would be foolish to jeopardize more lives to try and save one. "You are welcome to remain within our village. We will keep you hidden and ensure you receive proper nutrition, but you must remain indoors during daylight hours," Maxis said. Vincent was about to reply when Tony interrupted him. "I can save Monique," he said frankly.

"Earlier today you reminded me the mission was more important than one person. We will continue the mission without Monique. My decision is final," Vincent said. "Captain, I stopped you today because you were acting rash and don't have the physical attributes necessary to save Monique on your own. With my unique abilities I can save Monique and inflict damage upon our enemy's ability to conduct warfare. This isn't just about saving Monique and Vandi. The Annunaki are planning to invade both the Rabanah and Sol systems. I will stay in the north and do everything I can to weaken their ability to fight," Tony said.

Vincent thought he'd painfully made the correct decision. He was trying to protect the mission and fulfill the role the Alliance placed upon him, but Tony's request took him completely off guard. He didn't trust himself to make the correct decision. "What do you think, Maxis? Do you believe Tony's plan is a wise course of action?" he asked.

Maxis considered the plan. Defeating the Annunaki was the ultimate goal. "I believe the effort should be made. If Tony can provide a distraction in Vath, it will make our mission easier. The attempt should be made. When Monique is tortured, she will tell the enemy their battle plan has been compromised and transmitted to Rabanah. The Annunaki will quickly alter their plan. Our adversary must not know what we've discovered. The operation must commence at once and if Monique can't be saved she must be killed. Are you prepared to kill Monique if necessary?" Maxis asked Tony. "If it's absolutely necessary I'll do what must be done," Tony replied quietly.

"You will be quickly trained to maneuver a Strithu and arrive at the location," Maxis said. "I would like to have a weapon of some kind. Are there any available?" Tony asked. "I know a woman who might have access to some primitive weapons. I'll take you to her," Maxis replied.

Tony and Maxis watched as an elderly Martian woman pulled up part of her floor. A small stairway led to an underground room larger than the home above. A diverse collection of swords and other alien weaponry adorned the room. There were many different weapons to choose from. "These weapons were saved as art. Each piece has a rich history and unique story. I would like anything you take returned," the Martian woman requested. Tony found a weapon like nothing he'd ever seen. The fascinating and lethal weapon was double bladed and formed half an oval with multiple hand holds. "You've made an excellent choice. The blade is called a bullak and is very lethal. Take this small dagger as well; it can be easily concealed and will be useful," the woman said as she handed him the small weapon. "Good luck Tony and thank you. If an opportunity arises, enlist the assistance of the Volmer, but don't endanger yourself. Their species is quite tenacious and not much is known about them. Maxis is correct, if you can't save Monique you must ensure she doesn't share what she knows. If you must, kill her quickly and make sure she doesn't suffer," Vincent uttered despairingly.

Monarch Reltith was not happy. An off-world human was recently found and captured. It was very likely there were more off-worlders somewhere on Vandi. The human female was nearly killed when she was captured. Reltith planned to question the woman personally; however, due to damage inflicted by the guards, the human wouldn't be released from the medical center or available for torture for hours. She issued a command to have the guards killed. She almost lost the ability to interrogate the human due to their carelessness. A similar mistake couldn't be allowed to happen again. She needed as much information as possible before the Empress ordered the invasion of the Rabanah and Sol Systems. Many cycles passed since the last time a member of the Alliance was captured, tortured and put to death. The death of an Alliance spy was worth celebrating. Her torture and execution would be broadcast and open to the public. Reltith would take extraordinary joy in slaughtering the woman.

Tony was cold; his borrowed clothing wasn't keeping him warm. He stayed as low as possible inside the pouch but was still chilled to the bone. It was getting colder and icebergs appeared on the horizon. Much was at stake and he was tired. He closed his eyes, tried to stay warm and eventually fell asleep.

Tony woke and was surprised to be on the ground. He heard strange sounds coming from an animal of some kind. He poked his head out of the pouch and found he was surrounded by a large group of Volmer. The species was amazingly white and blended into the snow and ice perfectly. He'd seen images of the species in preparation for the mission, but to see them in person was amazing. The Volmer had six appendages which folded together and acted as a tail in the water. Finger-like tentacles were attached to the upper two appendages. Retractable fins protruded from the torso. The Volmer were content either on land or in the sea.

The voices began to make sense. The noise was being translated. "Who are you and what are you doing here?" he was asked. "My name is Tony. I'm on my way to Vath to try and free a friend of mine from the enslavers known as the Annunaki. I didn't intend to land here and apologize if I've caused a disruption. Your species is known by our people as Volmer; our species originate from the same star," he said.

"I don't care where you originate from, you are not allowed in our territory. Give me a reason not to kill you." Tony wasn't sure which of the Volmer was speaking. "Martians and humans have lived peacefully on this planet with your species for a long time. We are not your enemy. With whom am I speaking?" Tony asked. "I am known as Gly. We made a mistake by granting the request to allow your kind to live on our planet. We demand you leave Vandi," he said.

"We are not able to leave; the enslavers prevent us from doing so. There will be an upcoming battle in which we will try to remove the enslavers from this world. Your assistance would be helpful," Tony said. All Volmer within earshot suddenly began speaking.

The translation device was quickly deactivated and Tony didn't know what was being said. Gly stuck out an appendage and everyone stopped talking. Silence followed for nearly a minute.

"If we decide to assist you, we demand all off-world species leave after the battle is complete," Gly said. "When you first agreed to allow Martians and humans to live on Vandi, you negotiated with the Alliance. I am with the Alliance, but I am not allowed to agree to your request. I will ensure your request is given to those who make such decisions after we've defeated the enemy. If you allow me to depart, I will return with my friend. She is much more knowledgeable in such matters," Tony said. "I will allow you to depart. Tell your people they are no longer welcome here," Gly said. "Thank you. My friend and I will return as quickly as possible," Tony said.

Gly motioned to the Strithu and the animal quickly returned to the sky. Tony wondered what happened while he'd been asleep. The large bird was apparently very loyal to the Volmer. He was happy to be leaving alive after the unexpected and surprising visit with the introverted species.

The ice continent approached. Tony hoped to find a few small buildings, so he could get in and out as quickly as possible. Instead, he saw a massive city. There wasn't any time to waste. He guided the Strithu to the dimly lit rooftop of a small building. The building overlooked a courtyard filled with Krace who were transfixed on a massive screen. An Annunaki female was speaking. Tony turned on his data pad to learn what was being said. "Do not let down your guard. We found one Alliance spy and there are certain to be more. Our goal is to capture, torture, interrogate and kill them. Do not destroy these humans or injure them more than necessary. We must know what the Alliance is planning. I will personally torture, interrogate and slaughter the captured human at Victory Hall. I encourage everyone listening to come and enjoy the momentous event. Victory Hall can accommodate ninety-thousand of you. The celebration will start shortly. The human will be released from the medical center in the next few minutes."

This occasion was only the second time Gly viewed transmissions from the invaders. He watched once before when he led a small battle to free four of his people. It was the only time the invaders tried to enslave his species. The battle was short and quick. He freed his captured friends and killed twenty Kracian soldiers in the process. The broadcast transmissions hadn't disclosed any information about the incident at the time. Gly watched the Annunaki leader speak. Monarch Reltith controlled all within her domain. He wouldn't see Tony again because the human wouldn't leave Vath alive.

Monique was happy to be alive until she opened her eyes. Her arms and legs were bound, and she couldn't move. She could only watch as the platform she was strapped to rose onto a stage surrounded by thousands of chanting Krace. An Annunaki female began to speak as a table of knives and liquids were wheeled beside the platform. She didn't know what the Annunaki woman was saying, but her words inspired the crowd to chant louder and louder, erupting into a frenzy.

It wasn't hard to find Victory Hall. Tony simply followed the crowd and stayed in the shadows. The general population was entering the building through the main entrance. Tony went to the side of the structure. Kracian soldiers were drinking and coming in and out of a side entrance at will. He could hide himself, but he couldn't hide his weapons. The bullak stood out prominently and he knew time was growing short. He entered the building and one of the Krace soldiers shouted an alarm. Tony made it to the end of the hallway and turned to find five soldiers approaching his position. He threw the dagger into the chest of the closest one. The soldier screamed and fell to the floor. The remaining aliens were quickly upon him.

He swung the majestic weapon and with adrenaline pouring into his system, he was faster than he thought possible. With each swing of the weapon, a Krace was sliced open. The hallway was soon filled with the blood of dying soldiers.

Tony closed and latched the exterior door. He ran to the door leading to the stage and opened it. Reltith was speaking and Monique was shaking violently. A transparent wall separated Reltith from the audience. Tony was thankful. The wall could only be there to protect Reltith from the Krace on the other side. It would now prevent those in attendance from coming to her aide. Tony made his move.

Nearly every Annunaki and Krace on the planet watched in horror as a human appeared behind Reltith. The image was blurry and became translucent. It took less than a second for a metallic weapon to slice through the air severing Monarch Reltith's head from her body. Her head landed on the floor with a sickening thud. For a brief moment her mouth moved as she tried to speak.

Gly watched the scene with utter disbelief. He didn't think humans could move with such speed and agility. The Volmer leader now thought Tony might have a chance. He looked to the sky and issued a call to all Strithu within range. The message was repeated and forwarded by each of the large birds and would reach the city within seconds.

A viscous liquid splattered across Monique's face. She thought her torture had begun but couldn't feel any pain. She looked down and saw the head of the Annunaki leader on the ground. Tony suddenly appeared before her. "Get ready to run and stay behind me." he directed as he removed the restraints from her arms and legs. Monique hadn't moved in hours. She tried to get up but couldn't. Tony picked her up and carried her over his shoulder.

In a moment, it would be time to open the exterior door. If Tony was going to fail, it would be here. He opened the door prepared to fight. No soldiers were in the immediate vicinity. Krace soldiers raced toward his location from his left as he exited the building, but there were none to his right. He rebalanced Monique and began running as fast as possible. He heard the report of weapons behind him. Nearby explosions nearly knocked him off is feet. The weapons fire suddenly ceased. Tony took a moment to look behind him. A considerable number of Strithu attacked the Kracian soldiers. Some of the enemy were crushed by the giant birds while others fled. Tony knew Gly must have intervened. The distraction was enough to stop the pursuit and force the Krace to abandon their attack. The sky immediately filled with the large birds. One landed about fifty yards in front of him. "I think we're safe. You can put me down now. Let's get the hell out of here." Monique said as she and Tony climbed into the welcoming pouch of an exceptionally large specimen. The bird took flight and immediately blended in with the thousands of other Strithu in the sky. "I'm glad I didn't have to kill you," Tony said. Monique listened as he told her about his conversation with Gly.

Chapter 8

President Louis felt relatively safe in the underground shelter. All orbiting satellites were now gone. The enemy of humanity succeeded in eliminating almost all communication across the globe. There weren't any news organizations operating and he wasn't receiving any new information or intelligence. He didn't believe it likely mankind would be victorious in the near future. Intermittent drone video continued to show aliens slaughtering anyone who attempted to fight. The attempts were becoming more infrequent and those who surrendered were placed in camps. Bracelets were placed on the legs of the captured. One video showed a woman trying to escape a camp. She dropped to the ground and stopped moving when she passed beyond the perimeter of the enclosure. The aliens brought her body back and placed it in the middle of camp to rot. She was used as an example to those who contemplated escape.

Vietnam taught President Louis war was a series of battles. It was possible to lose a battle and eventually win the war. If humanity was to have a chance of winning, he needed to develop long-term strategies. He took a deep breath and prepared for what was to come. The remaining cabinet members arrived for the daily briefing. As the meeting was about to begin, the facility was rocked by an explosion. The entire structure began to shake. "Mr. President, the entrances have been breached; we are under attack," a secret service agent reported. He was suddenly surrounded by a dozen agents. "Forget about me. Go kill those sons of bitches. Give me a gun! That's an order!"

President Louis waited and listened as the sound of battle grew in intensity and neared his room. Screams echoed in his ears. He stood up, took aim, and fired when the first alien entered the room. The bullets didn't penetrate the alien armor. He was quickly thrown to the floor and bound. President Louis regretted not turning the weapon upon himself.

Gly was in awe as the Strithu descended. He was amazed the two humans survived. "Very impressive, Tony. I didn't know humans possessed such great reflexes and I didn't think you would survive," he said. "I'm an abnormal specimen. We wouldn't have survived without your help and I'm grateful for the assistance," Tony said and introduced Gly to Monique.

"Gly, there is an impending battle. The Annunaki will eventually try to kill or enslave your people. Please join us in fighting the enemy of Vandi," Monique said. "We have discussed the matter. I have met with the elders while you were gone. We will help defeat the

Annunaki provided both Martians and humans depart Vandi when the planet has been freed," Gly stated.

Monique hadn't been given the authority to conduct any negotiations or make any agreements. The assistance of Volmer forces in the upcoming battle could make an enormous difference. She didn't have a choice. Hopefully, the Alliance wouldn't be too upset with her. "I agree to your terms. We will depart Vandi after our enemy is defeated," she said.

Priex was the senior aide of Reltith. Now he was the leader of the Annunaki on Vandi. It was almost unheard of for a male to be in a leadership position. He planned to take advantage of his newly attained status. Reltith's death was shocking and unexpected. She was a demanding and effective leader. It was now his duty to finish the job she began. As her aide, he knew every detail of the upcoming invasion. The end was near for the Rabanians and the inferior and weak species in their Alliance. The capital of the Alliance would be taken and the gate to the Sol System would finally be accessible. Many of the forces on Vandi were reassigned for the invasion. With the new and ongoing threat, it was time to thin the remaining population and locate the Alliance spies.

Vincent was outside looking at the stars and worried sick. He had almost wrapped his mind around losing Monique when Tony sprung his surprise rescue plan. Now he might lose them both. Maxis interrupted his thoughts. "Vincent, your device is making noise," he said. He ran inside and found a text message from Tony. "Monique is safe. The Volmer have agreed to fight with us against the Annunaki. I recommend Monique and I stay here to coordinate and assist with their efforts. By the way, I killed the Annunaki ruler of Vandi."

"Holy shit!" Vincent exclaimed. "What did you say? I think the translation device is malfunctioning," Maxis asked. Vincent relayed Tony's message. "The Annunaki and Krace leadership will be angry. I'm glad your partner has survived." Maxis barely finished speaking as Tissa rushed through the door. "Soldiers are entering the village. We must hide the humans!" she said. Maxis went outside to greet the soldiers. He arrived as a Krace airship landed. A single soldier exited the ship and began to speak to the assembled members of the village. "Your production has been unacceptable. In three days, we will kill fifteen of you. We will closely monitor production. The fifteen least productive people will be killed. Two additional hours will be added to every workday from this time forward," the soldier said and abruptly departed.

The soldier's booming voice could be heard inside. Vincent listened to the translation. He thought it likely every village on Vandi would receive the same message. He sent a text to Julia. If the human village hadn't been visited yet, it soon would be.

Maxis and Tissa returned. Vincent knew what needed to be done. "At sundown tomorrow, we will free the villages. The battle will begin," he said hopefully. "I was going to request the same course of action; I will inform my people now," Maxis said. "The day has finally arrived to fight for your freedom. Prepare your people, it will not be easy." Vincent replied.

President Louis stood before the alien who called himself Malachi. He was surprised to learn the alien was actually a female. Five Annunaki soldiers stood behind him. He didn't have any power, no aces up his sleeve and no real options. "I offer you the surrender of humanity. We can peacefully coexist and share the planet. I will instruct my people to follow the directives you issue. I can control the people of Earth. I would like to visit the camps and ensure the prisoners are following the instructions you issue. I wish to save as many lives as possible," President Louis said.

"It's more likely you wish to visit the camps to find a way to rally your people and rebel. You offer me

167

nothing I don't already have. You were brought here for a singular purpose; therefore, it's an opportunity you should cherish. As leader of your planet, you will have the honor of being killed by the supreme leader of my species. Your skull will be polished and placed alongside the skulls of all the other races we've conquered," Bazor said. "You don't understand humans very well. I would die first," President Louis said. "So be it." Bazor said and motioned to a guard.

President Louis felt pain erupt through his back and his upper body. Blood spilled everywhere. Looking down he saw a blade sticking out the center of his chest. The end finally arrived. He smiled with satisfaction as he lost consciousness. He hadn't won the war, but he wouldn't be a slave to an alien race.

Tony and Monique were fascinated. Hundreds and then thousands of Volmer gathered. Gly issued orders and instructed his people on the best method of invading the city as the shores of the inland bay filled with Volmer soldiers. "How many of your people will be participating in the battle?" Monique asked. "We have gathered half our people for the engagement. There are approximately one hundred and fifty thousand prepared to fight," Gly responded. "In three hours, our friends will begin removing the bracelets from the Martians and humans. It will take time to organize, locate weapons and join the battle," Monique said. "The battle on the continents is of no concern to me," Gly responded.

The army was impressive. The gathered Volmer blended into the whiteness of the surroundings well. Even with his enhanced vision, Tony could barely make out the white figures. Snow began falling from the sky and Tony was no longer able to see the Volmer force. "Are they still there?" Monique asked. "I don't know. I can no longer distinguish them from the surrounding whiteness in the air and on the ground," Tony said. "The invading albino army will be virtually invisible in the snow," Monique replied with a smile.

Julia responded to Vincent's message. The human village hadn't been visited yet as they were on the opposite side of the planet. Most would be freed just before sunrise. Monique and Tony were ready in the north as the second sun descended below the horizon. "Isabella, it's time. Begin removing bracelets. Maxis will tell you which people to free first," he instructed. Isabella successfully removed the first bracelet. The freed Martian ran to the courtyard and hopped into the pouch of the closest Strithu. The bird took to the sky immediately. Maxis indicated which villager to free next and the second freed person repeated the action of the first. "This is the strangest airport I've ever been in," Vincent said wryly.

"I hope things go smoothly in the other villages," Maxis said. "Your species is highly intelligent. The people in the villages will quickly understand the message and the situation. Freedom will spread quickly and all the villages on Vandi should be free within hours. You have told me you'd rather die than live as a slave; I'm sure all your people feel the same way. It's time to exact your revenge," Vincent replied.

Monique observed from a distance as Tony spoke with Gly. She wanted to know what was going on and approached her friend. "What are you talking about?" she asked. "With my abilities, I need to take part in the attack. I'm going to Vath to cause as much damage and disruption as possible," Tony said. After witnessing Tony's capabilities, Monique couldn't disagree with his reasoning. "What can I do to help?" she asked. "Stay with Gly and coordinate with Vincent. I will inflict as much damage as possible and contact you when I can," Tony said as he found a Strithu.

After a short flight, the bird landed a quarter mile from the perimeter of Vath. Tony needed to discover the Annunaki military's vulnerability and how to inflict the most damage.

Maxis was overwhelmed. He watched as the bracelets were removed from his wife and son. The devices were attached at birth and expanded as growth occurred. His would be the last to be removed and he smiled as the device fell to the ground. "I despise this place; it's been our prison for far too long. Let's go find those weapons and retake our place in the Alliance!" Maxis led the remaining Martians out of the village. The population in the village was reduced by half after many of his friends flew with the Strithu to free other villages. Maxis hoped the store of weapons hadn't been found. He'd rather fight than hide. He found the buried cave he'd seen on his grandfathers' device and reached into a small hole in the entrance and found a lever. A few feet away, rocks tumbled down the hillside revealing a stairway that led up to a chamber. Maxis ascended the stairway and stopped when he noticed writing on the wall. "Your mind is the most dangerous weapon of all." His grandfather signed his name under the message. Maxis continued up the stairway and found a room packed with weaponry. "We must practice for a brief time and learn how to use these weapons properly," he said.

His new position granted him new privileges and Priex was taking advantage of his new-found power. The invasion of the Rabanah system was to begin the following day. He wanted to relax one last night while he had the chance. He selected three Krace females to join him for the evening. The last of the three arrived as an alarm sounded. He hadn't heard the alarm before and called the control center. "What's going on?" he asked. "We are under massive attack by the Volmer and incurring heavy casualties." Priex was surprised and angry. The Volmer were known as a reclusive species; an attack was almost unprecedented. Priex couldn't take any risks. The Rabanah invasion was the highest priority. "Launch the fleet immediately and send all remaining personnel to engage the Volmer. Recall forces from the continents to reinforce and defend the city!" he commanded.

Mox listened as Chief Minister Azira addressed the council and shared the latest developments on Vandi. "We don't have enough resources to fight the Annunaki on two fronts. The battle plan transmitted from our operatives on Vandi indicates a massive invading force will attack Rabanah. The Annunaki are planning to attack the very core of the Alliance.

Their battle plan is clever. We didn't believe their leaders would take the required time necessary to send an armada through normal space to the Sol System. The gate leading to Sol is now being patrolled heavily with automated ships in place. If the Annunaki send reinforcements from the Sol System, we will be ready. The plan called for both the Rabanah and Sol Systems to be taken simultaneously. We will attack the Annunaki before their forces enter the gate from the Vandi System. After we retake and secure Vandi, we will focus on liberating Earth. Battle simulations indicate all our military will be necessary to stop the invasion of Rabanah and to retake Vandi; it will not be an easy task. The most recent data suggests we have a sixty-four percent chance of defending our own system. The models indicate we have a fifty-three percent chance of liberating the Vandi System while defending Rabanah at the same time. We cannot divert resources to the Sol System, if we do, our possibility of victory will be significantly reduced. There is an imminent threat to the Alliance as a whole. We will continue to send probes through the gate into the Sol System but will take no offensive action at this time."

Mox stood waiting for her turn to speak. "I wasted much of my life here urging you to retake the Vandi System. I'm now the representative for Earth and will not tolerate inaction that could last another hundred years. Find a way to change the situation immediately. The Tactical Council has been too slow to respond and too slow to build a military force that can safeguard the home world and conduct offensive operations. Another slave planet is unacceptable. I will not wait for years as our military leaders debate the situation. I request assistance from any and all Alliance member worlds. I will assemble a task force and formulate my own plan. I welcome the help of any ambassadors who disagree with the constant inability of our tactical leaders to mount offensive operations," Mox declared angrily.

President Louis dreamt. He couldn't remember what the dream was about, but it had something to do with his time in Vietnam. He opened his eyes and found Bazor hovering over him. The thought of still being alive was repulsing. His injuries should have killed him within minutes. "Why did you save me?" he asked. "Because you're the leader of this planet. I've already explained you are a gift to my empress. We have wonderful medical facilities. I can kill you a thousand times and return you from the brink of death a thousand times as long as I don't wait too long. For the immediate future, you will be kept aboard my ship and accompany me when necessary. A present for the supreme leader must be watched closely," Bazor said.

Priex recalled as many soldiers from the continents as possible to fight the Volmer in the capitol. He left minimal forces to maintain security in the villages. Monarch Reltith and the rest of the council underestimated the Volmer. It was out of character for the Volmer to suddenly turn so aggressive. He assumed Alliance spies somehow enlisted the support of the species.

Video of Monarch Reltith's assassination was analyzed and processed. The human was not wearing any clothing and was able to naturally bend light. Kracian soldiers called him the shadow. Such an ability was unheard of. There were rumors of an extinct species with similar abilities, but there wasn't any information indicating humans could bend light. In the history of Vandi, there were no records of such an individual. The assassination video provided proof that the species could somehow accomplish the feat. It was a frightening new development. If all humans possessed the same ability the likelihood of defeating the enemy in a protracted war would be reduced significantly. He would take no chances; the humans must be eliminated entirely. "Send all soldiers from the Martian Continent to the Human Continent. Every human is to be killed. By tomorrow I expect them all to be dead," Priex ordered.

After searching the exterior of numerous buildings, Tony still didn't know what course of action to take. He was in the center of Vath and could hear the battle raging as Volmer attacked the outskirts of the city. Hundreds of spacecraft began appearing overhead.

The Annunaki were launching the Rabanah invasion early. He ran in the direction the ships were coming from and discovered many large hangers. The closest was only two hundred yards away. He ran through the entrance and quickly scanned the surroundings. There wasn't any obvious weaponry and he needed to find a way to deter or destroy the departing spacecraft. He glanced up and noticed the massive hanger door retracted electronically into the open position just like his old garage door on Earth. Physically, the door was held open by two massive cables anchored into the roof of the facility. Tony quickly climbed a catwalk to the roof. He didn't know how strong a weapon the bullak was, but he had to try and cut the cables. He swung the weapon as hard as he could into the alien material and the weapon made it halfway through. With one more swing, the cable snapped, and the massive door lurched.

Tony quickly made his way to the opposite side of the building. He cut the second cable and the giant door came down hard as two ships attempted to depart. The ships crashed violently into the door and caught fire.

Tony ran to the next building and repeated the process. When he reached the third building, he found the cables guarded by soldiers. The enemy quickly recognized what he was doing. He returned to the first building and found it guarded on the outside. Tony ran to the back of the building and discovered a large oval sphere the size of a small house. A dozen hoses exited the sphere and led into the building. He sliced all the hoses and liquid fuel poured over the ground, pooling behind the hanger. The smell was overwhelming. Tony ran as fast as possible before the fuel found an ignition source. When he was about two miles away he heard a large explosion followed by a series of smaller ones. With his enhanced vision, he saw burning soldiers exiting the hanger and throwing themselves to the ground. The two hangers on either side also caught fire. Tony couldn't help but smile as explosions light up the sky.

The Alliance Tactical Council selected Kapun to retake and liberate the Vandi system. He was Commander of the invading Alliance Armada and would lead his ships through the gate within the hour. The latest probe returned with the most current data. All previous probes reported no unusual activity. According to the recovered enemy battle plan, the Annunaki weren't scheduled to depart Vandi for another day. The report from the probe indicated the Annunaki fleet was leaving Vandi before their scheduled departure time, surprising Kapun. He could only guess why the fleet was leaving early. He speculated an Alliance operative on the planet was discovered, tortured and informed the Annunaki of the transmission which was sent to Rabanah.

An additional surprising fact in the report was the size of the enemy fleet. A sizeable number of ships were missing or unaccounted for. Only ninety-six percent of the expected ships were present. Four percent were either late or missing. "Set course for Vandi. Inform the rest of the armada it's time to go through the gate. There are no changes at this time in the battle plan," Kapun ordered.

Priex was screaming at his subordinates. He was receiving nothing but bad news. A hanger was destroyed, more were on fire and the Volmer were much smarter and more ferocious than the Annunaki expected. The ancient species of Sol were ignored in the past and not considered a major threat. None of his personnel could give him an accurate number of enemy Volmer. "Monarch, we are receiving scattered reports from both continents. Guards are reporting the villages are empty and all of the Martians and humans have escaped into the countryside."

The report was unfathomable. "I want my orders to be clear. All humans are to be killed. There are to be no exceptions. We will retake the Martian Continent after we kill every human on Vandi," he said. "We have analyzed the video of the destroyed hanger. The damage was caused by the same person who assassinated Monarch Reltith. It was the shadow."

Priex couldn't understand how so many operations could go wrong so quickly. "Post additional guards outside all military installations," he said. It was his responsibility to safeguard the mission and prove a male was worthy of a leadership position. He was failing on both accounts. "Send an update of all current conditions and military operations to the home planet. Request immediate reinforcements and include everything we know about the Volmer in the report," he demanded.

Maxis wanted to do everything within his power to keep his family and friends alive. Practicing with the assortment of weapons excited him. He had a means of killing the enemy and was ready for vengeance. "Let's go; it's time to take back our planet," he said. "I understand your enthusiasm. We must follow the plan. It's time to withdraw and organize. We will fight only when required and we need to try and hold out as long as possible. Alliance forces could arrive any day.

Why exactly are we travelling to the valley? It makes more sense to stay as high as possible in the mountains," Vincent asked. "There is an old city in the center of the valley. There are some underground passageways and hidden rooms; it's a great hiding spot and a safe location to mount a defense," Maxis replied. "I'm going to request an update from Monique and Tony. We need to know how the battle in Vath is proceeding," Vincent said.

Monique was uncomfortable. Gly instructed her to stay away as he consulted with his people. She didn't know how to read Volmer body language and assumed the leader was pissed off. Vincent wanted an update; she texted him to standby. Gly finally approached her. "We've lost about nine thousand of our soldiers. The storm is subsiding and with the weather change my people will be targeted and killed more easily. It's time to withdraw our forces," he said. "I'm very sorry Gly. Please know the sacrifice your species has made in this battle is greatly appreciated. It's unfortunate the battle didn't go well, and you've lost so many. Do you have an estimate of enemy casualties?" she asked. "Our best estimate is one hundred and twenty thousand enemy casualties," Gly responded. "I'm sorry I think there is an issue with the translation device. Could you repeat the number of enemy casualties?" she asked. "One hundred and twenty thousand casualties," Gly replied.

Monique still didn't believe the number she heard. She asked a third time, but Gly walked away. She wondered why the hell the Volmer forces were being recalled. They were kicking the hell out of the Krace. She wanted to ask him to reconsider but decided it would be best to speak with Vincent first.

The group was nearing the valley when Vincent received an update on the battle in Vath. "Gly reports approximately nine thousand of his species have been killed. Volmer forces have been instructed to retreat. He estimates one hundred and twenty thousand Annunaki and Krace have been killed. Do you want me to request he reengage the battle?" Monique asked.

The message was astounding. "I'll get back to you shortly Monique," Vincent texted. "Maxis, tell me everything you know about the Volmer," he said. "The species is peaceful and introverted. War is not in their nature. They aren't interested in advancing technologically and wish to be in harmony with nature and the planet. Contact with the Volmer has been very limited and it's against their nature to interact with outsiders. Before the Annunaki arrived on Vandi we had a strict no contact policy," Maxis said. "I must leave and convince the Volmer leader to continue the fight. I'll return as soon as possible. You are a great leader for your people, Maxis. Don't get overzealous. Stick with the plan and keep your people alive," Vincent said.

Priex toured the battlefield. The carnage was overwhelming. Dead Annunaki and Krace were strewn everywhere. There were very few enemy casualties. "All these lives could have been saved. Why aren't our soldiers wearing body armor?" he asked. "Body armor wasn't deemed necessary on Vandi. It hasn't been worn for generations because it hasn't been necessary. All available body armor was sent with the fleet to Rabanah," Commander Atad explained. "Begin manufacturing new body armor immediately.

Why weren't our soldiers able to mount an effective defense? There are very few Volmer bodies." Priex probed. "During the storm we couldn't see the enemy. The Volmer are suited to the snow and cold, we are not. If the enemy attacks again during a storm we may not be able to hold them back again," Commander Atad said. Priex would not tolerate excuses from the military leader. "If the Volmer attack again, I expect you and your troops to launch explosives and missiles in every possible direction. How did a storm arrive in the first place?" he asked. "Repairs were required on the weather unit; it was offline for longer than expected," Atad replied. "Utilize our technology and make sure a high-pressure system remains above Vath. If we have clear skies, we can see the Volmer. It's my job to find a way to defeat the enemy. Your task is to follow my orders exactly. If you fail, your death will not come from the Volmer. I will personally burn you alive, Atad. I hope you now have the proper motivation to do your job properly. I expect the weather unit to be fully functional immediately. See to it," Priex commanded.

It was very peaceful in the air. Vincent took a moment to enjoy the solitude and beauty of Vandi. Over the open ocean, he watched dozens of unusual species of bird diving into the salty water. The wet glistening animals returned to the air with prey in their mouths. He wondered if the invasion of Earth was underway and if Enzo was still alive. Hopefully, sending the Annunaki battle plan would pay off. With any luck, the Alliance immediately rushed to Earth and defeated the Annunaki in the same manner they did in 1947. There was a quick drop in elevation as the Strithu began descending toward a growing white landmass.

With Tony gone, Monique was going crazy. The Volmer wouldn't speak to her. The aliens only contacted her when someone threw a fish in her direction to keep her fed. Vincent suddenly appeared, and she was so happy to see him. "Thank God. It's good to see you!" she said. "I thought I'd lost you and would never see you again," he said and kissed her. She kissed him back and was grateful to be back in his arms. She held him tight and didn't want to let him go. "What's going on around here?" he asked.

"The Volmer were annihilating the Krace. Gly doesn't seem very interested in fighting again," Monique said. "That's the reason I came. The Volmer must attack again as soon as possible. The damage they've already caused is tremendous. Have you heard from Tony?" Vincent asked. "Yes, Tony damaged a couple of hangers where the Annunaki were launching their ships, but I haven't heard from him for the last eight hours. He might be resting," Monique said. "I hope he's alright. Let's go speak with Gly," Vincent said.

"Greetings, my name is Vincent Moretti. I'm the leader of the small force of Alliance operatives on the planet. We were sent here to gather intelligence and conduct operations to defeat the Annunaki." Gly nodded. "Your friend has likely told you who I am. I hope she told you we have demanded both Martians and humans leave Vandi as soon as possible. We have done our duty, now you must do yours," Gly stated firmly. "You have assisted in our effort to free all people of Sol on this planet, but the enemy is not yet defeated. We must continue to fight. Your species has been on the planet for a very long time. My friend has informed me you do not care that you are a brother species of Sol. I respect your wish for solitude, but I ask you to respect what has happened here. Three species from Sol were relocated to this world. Your species has not yet been enslaved, but the other two have been slaves to the Annunaki for far too long. Once our shared enemy kills us, your species will be next. The soldiers you sent to Vath were very effective and caused enormous damage to the infrastructure and to the Annunaki. I don't care if you don't wish to fight with your brothers, but please know that if you don't fight with us you will soon be fighting the enemy on your own," Vincent said.

"We will not attack at this time. Weather conditions have changed, and my people would be slaughtered. A large percentage of my species do not wish to engage in battle regardless of circumstances. Unless conditions change drastically in Vath, our assistance has come to an end. There are no words that will alter my position. Should the time come when we must fight the Annunaki on our own, I have no doubt we will prevail," Gly responded.

Chapter 9

After destroying the hanger, Tony couldn't find any additional high value targets to attack. All the hangers were surrounded by guards. He hadn't ever seen a storm dissipate so quickly. The sky cleared, and the sounds of battle ceased. For a brief second, he saw a strange and colorful chemical composition being released into the sky from a nearby hilltop. There were no remaining clouds in the area. He was exhausted, and his body needed rest. He climbed the hill and found a safe place to sleep. He overexerted himself and his body demanded sleep.

Something was in his mouth and it was moving. Tony opened his eyes and found a small bright red bird standing on his forehead. He watched as the creature put another live and large insect into his mouth. Normally he would have been disgusted, but he was hungry and needed energy. As a scientist he knew he needed to refuel and gain some energy. The little bird decided to feed him for unknown reasons and flew away as he sat up. His data pad indicated he received a message. Monique wanted an update immediately. "I will be taking action shortly. I'm going to investigate a device which might possibly affect the weather. A possible weather change might occur if I'm correct. I'll send an update when I learn more," he texted.

The facility on the hill was only guarded by a single soldier. Tony wanted more practice fighting the Krace. He quickly disarmed the soldier and prepared for hand to hand combat. His opponent was incredibly slow and there was nothing new to learn from combat. He plunged his dagger through the soldier's neck and noted how much pressure was necessary to slice through the skin of a Krace. The dead soldier's weapons were nearby. Tony picked up the weapons and entered the facility. He quickly killed the two occupants. He ran to the rear of the facility and found there weren't any remaining personnel. Through an open doorway he saw a soldier warming himself near a fire. Tony shot him with one the weapons he retrieved. The projectile traveled through the soldier's forehead and out the back of his skull. Satisfied he secured the building, Tony returned inside.

A screen on the wall displayed meteorological data over a map of Vath. Tony activated his data pad and translated the information. He realized it revealed the local barometric pressure. He wasn't a meteorologist, but knew lower pressure was needed to create unsettled weather. It took four hours for Tony to figure out how to change the barometric pressure and implement the required changes. He watched with satisfaction as the temperature dropped and storm clouds gathered above the city. Tony went out to the fire and returned with a burning piece of wood. He threw it into a trash bin and left. Ten minutes later, the facility burnt to the ground and it began to snow. He sent a message to Monique.

"Vincent, we have a report from Tony," Monique said. Vincent viewed the report with satisfaction and went to find the Volmer leader. "Gly, we have new information. As you can see, the weather is changing. Snow will continue to fall, and the temperature will continue to drop. Wind speed will also increase. Tony has destroyed the Annunaki weather control device and there will never be a better time to fight the enemy. The time for attack is now," Vincent said with conviction.

"The message didn't say anything about the wind or the temperature," Monique said to Vincent. "You're right, but Gly doesn't need to know. It will be snowing like hell. Wind and temperature changes will accompany a pressure change and the conditions will be perfect. The time is now or never," Vincent said.

Jose enjoyed being on Mars and working with Dalton. The man was strange, but also quite intelligent; he knew what he was doing. For the last few days, Dalton had been exceptionally quiet and focused on one particular section of the golden wall. "What has you so enthralled with this area?" he asked. "It's unusual and it appears this section was the last to be engraved. I believe it was added hastily. The translation tells us what's in the blocked chambers at either end of the passageway in this pyramid. I want you to double check my work. The translation is extraordinary, if true.

If I've translated this correctly, the most intelligent known Martian in history, Salkex, sealed himself inside the two chambers. One of the chambers was his lab, the other was his quarters. He traveled between the two through an underground tunnel. The translation also states he was paranoid and quite insane. Since the chambers are still sealed, his body is likely still inside," Dalton said. "I'll inform Kathy. She's been trying to find a way into the chambers, but she hasn't had much luck without any electrical equipment. It will likely take brute force to gain entrance. Patrick might have a few promising ideas about gaining entry as well," Jose said.

When he looked out the window, Priex became enraged. Snow was falling from the sky. He specifically instructed Atad to make certain there would be no adverse weather. He contacted the military leader immediately. "Can you please tell me why it's snowing outside? You were instructed to get the weather under control," He growled angrily. "Monarch, the facility that controls the weather, has been attacked and has burned to the ground. At this time, we cannot control the weather, but I'm working on a solution," Atad said. "Find a solution now. The weather is changing quickly. Prepare our forces for an imminent attack," he said as the alarm sounded.

Priex considered ordering all remaining soldiers from the continents to the capitol. The situation was spiraling out of control and he was getting desperate. He needed the humans killed and decided not to recall the remaining military forces. The Martians and humans must be dealt with before the two species could organize and inflict more damage.

Maxis expected to see soldiers scouring the territory for his people, but lookouts reported seeing only one small group of soldiers in the distance. "I don't understand. There should be more patrols. I expected a large battle and the need to defend our people. Where are all the soldiers?" he asked Isabella.

You and your people have been slaves to the Annunaki and Krace for generations. It only took a handful of soldiers and some technology to keep you enslaved. The Annunaki are attempting to invade the Rabanah system and Vath is under attack, so it's likely reinforcements will not be sent. I know the plan called for patience; however, if the opportunity arises to kill a patrol of soldiers it shouldn't be ignored. The conditions of battle have changed. I think you should meet with your people and discuss altering your plan as soon as possible," Isabella suggested. "We will attack the nearby patrol shortly," he replied.

Maxis didn't need to meet with his people. The patrol located earlier wouldn't be hard to find. He gathered two men and three women. Zanther insisted on coming as well. The weapons he selected were easy enough to use by all. One of the weapons he chose was a small firearm which fired an explosive the size of a small pebble. After a few minutes of practice, his team was proficient enough to strike the practice targets. "It's like a small grenade launcher," Isabella said. "Yes, it's a very effective weapon. Finally, the time has come for us to fight. We will see you shortly," Maxis said. "Good luck and stay safe. Don't take any unnecessary risks," she said with a wave of her hand.

Isabella wanted to join Maxis and fight the enemy. She desperately wanted to see the planet freed. As much as she wanted to go, she knew this battle should be led by Maxis and won solely by the Martians. Maxis confidently walked his soldiers out of the area and Isabella knew he wouldn't fail.

Maxis positioned his group on a ridge between the Kracian camp and the setting suns. The soldiers weren't actively searching and looked tired and bored. Thirteen Krace were drinking and relaxing near a fire.

He instructed his team to spread out and prepare to fire. "Let's make sure we all target different soldiers," he directed. The targets were selected, and an age-old war was about to be resurrected.

Maxis took a deep breath. He'd been waiting a long time for this opportunity and didn't want to miss. "Fire!" he said. The loud report of rifles echoed in his ears. Six soldiers were immediately blown apart. Maxis was surprised at the carnage. He fired again instantly as did the rest of his team. Only one Krace remained standing. The soldier fired blindly toward the setting suns and was immediately struck multiple times in the chest and head. Maxis watched for movement and saw none. "We will recover their weapons. Be careful, some might still be alive," he said although he knew it was unlikely any survived the attack.

As Maxis entered the camp, he didn't detect any movement. The soldiers were dead and the birds were already feeding. He glanced at one of the bodies and recognized the face of a familiar guard; he'd been brutal and whipped his son mercilessly on many occasions. Maxis was reflecting on the past when the alien's grey eyes popped open. Zanther raised a blade to finish the guard. "Wait! He has not earned the right to a quick death." Maxis said as he took the blade from his son.

"Kill me," the grey alien moaned. "Your kind is not welcome on Vandi and you have earned a horrific death. You've tortured my son and disrespected my people. Death is coming, but it won't come quickly enough for your liking. You will watch as your life is slowly taken," Maxis said. Amazingly, the soldier suffered no obvious trauma. He injured his spinal cord when he fell and lay paralyzed. Maxis took a blade and made a small incision in the creature's stomach. "Watch as the beautiful birds of this world feast on your entrails. I can't think of a more fitting end to your existence," Maxis said as the sound of fluttering wings filled the air.

Zanther helped his father collect weapons. "Father, if we can defeat the Krace so easily, how did we lose the war?" he asked. "These soldiers grew complacent and lazy. They were not expecting an attack. When we lost the war, we were overrun, and our cities were destroyed from the skies. Our next battle will not be so easy; the other soldiers will be on guard," Maxis cautioned.

Julia received a message from Isabella stating enemy forces were scarce and the battle was going well on the Martian Continent. She was surprised to learn a small team led by Maxis killed a group of soldiers. She shared the information with Grice hoping it would buoy his spirits. The human leader received unwelcome news. A quarter of the escaped humans were recaptured and returned to villages the previous day. Many who weren't captured were killed by soldiers. "I think we need to surrender; the action might save lives. The Krace are no longer attempting to capture us. The soldiers are killing my friends on sight," Grice said. "No, we must continue to fight. We should spread out into smaller groups to make their search more difficult and attack individual soldiers when the opportunity arises. Kracian soldiers have been killed on the Martian Continent. We can mount a defense and kill them as well," Julia said. Grice was about to respond when people began shouting. Air ships were arriving from every direction. Grice told his people to surrender. "I will not have any more blood on my hands. If the Alliance ever arrives, their military will have the force necessary to defeat the Krace. We've been enslaved our entire lives. A few more days won't matter," he said.

Julia dreaded the thought of becoming a slave. She knew the Krace would torture captured humans. Her role as a member of the Alliance would be uncovered. She ran as fast as she could to a nearby tree line and suddenly found herself on the ground with blood streaming down her face. Looking back, she saw explosion after explosion annihilate the area where the humans assembled. She crawled behind a large boulder and hoped she would be spared.

Tony found a small storage facility containing a great deal of military equipment; it would make a useful shelter. The storm raged outside, the sounds of war resumed, yet the noise was different this time. Missiles were fired followed by explosions in the distance. He knew the Volmer didn't have such technology. It was time to use his skills and fight alongside the introverted brothers of Sol. He ran toward the sound of the explosions to save as many Volmer as possible.

Thousands of soldiers were rushing into battle in the blinding storm. An Annunaki commander issued instructions and orders. Tony watched as soldiers ran past him into battle. The scene was chaotic and the Krace were desperate. Much like the Volmer, Tony was camouflaged well. He was cold, and he was white just like everything else within sight. He placed the bullak on the ground and stood behind a missile launcher. He observed the soldier operating the device. After the soldier fired, he knew he could operate the mechanism. He picked up his weapon and sliced it through the midsection of the soldier.

He retargeted the weapon and began firing on nearby missile launchers. Kracian soldiers rushed past his position, oblivious of the direction the weapon was pointed. Within two minutes, Tony destroyed every missile launcher within range. He fired on troops directly in front of his position and launched two missiles before nearby soldiers finally located him. A few enemy soldiers began shooting in his direction. Tony smiled as Volmer soldiers appeared nearby. The Kracian soldiers retreated as Volmer forces advanced. He dismounted the launcher as intermittent weapon fire was directed at his position. Nearby Kracian soldiers appeared confused and disoriented as the Volmer overran their position. Tony ran to the storage facility and searched for explosives.

Each report from the battlefield was worse than the one before. The only good news Priex received was from the Human Continent Commander. The elimination of the humans was underway and hundreds were dead. When the Martians were recaptured, the species would be required to work longer and harder to compensate for the loss of their counterpart. A minimum number of slaves were needed to process the necessary food for the planet. The battle on the Martian Continent would resume immediately. A group of escaped villagers managed to kill a patrol which chose to ignore the order to return to the Earth Continent. "Redeploy our forces on the Earth Continent. Send half of the remaining contingent to the Martian Continent. The Martian villagers are to be recaptured and returned at once," Priex commanded.

"Monarch, the Volmer have defeated our defenses and entered the city," Atad reported. "Instruct all senior leaders to relocate in the underground shelter. After you've issued the order, meet me outside," Priex commanded.

Atad issued the order and went outside to meet with his Monarch. The fresh air on his face was immediately replaced by searing heat. He fell to the ground and skin dripped off his face. "I told you not to fail me. You are a disgrace. Your death will not be a waste as your replacement will learn the price of failure," Priex said as he unleashed more fire from his weapon.

Maxis and his team triumphantly returned. All the Martians appeared to be in good health. "I take it the battle went well?" Isabella asked. "The soldiers weren't expecting an attack. We haven't been given the opportunity to retaliate in a long time and the Krace have grown complacent. It was a good first test for us," Maxis replied. "The situation on this continent is going well. There are very few soldiers and your people are in hiding, but the battle is not going as well on the Human Continent. I've received a report from Julia. The humans are on the run and are being killed when found. The Krace are not trying to recapture them; they want them dead," she said.

Maxis watched a Strithu descend as he considered what Isabella said. Upon landing, a battered human tumbled out of the giant bird's pouch. "Greetings, I'm Nizak; who's in charge?" the human asked. "I'm leading the Martian forces at the moment. Where did you come from?" Maxis responded. "My village was destroyed. Everyone is dead. I climbed into the well to escape. The Strithu were searching for survivors and one of them found me when I climbed out. I was brought here." Nizak said. "I'm currently organizing our forces as best I can. What can I do for you?" Maxis asked. "On my journey here, I observed many Krace abandoning our continent. I saw aircraft traveling to this continent while on my journey. It appears the Krace are returning," Nizak shared. "The information you bring is invaluable. I will have as many of our people as possible travel to the Human Continent to engage the enemy. When you return, you must tell your people to scatter and hide. With the soldiers returning, I cannot afford to send many of my people to assist. Weapons will be sent. Learn how to use them. We must organize and fight together," Maxis said. "We will thankfully accept any assistance you can provide," Nizak agreed.

Kapun was tasked with managing and fighting the Annunaki fleet in the Vandi System and the battle was not going as planned. The battle was going better than anticipated. The enemy was taken by surprise, disjointed, and unorganized. Kapun was confident the Vandi System would be retaken. He needed to ensure the Alliance could defend the system against future invasion. The most recent report indicated seventy-two percent of the enemy fleet was destroyed. Only thirty-eight percent of his fleet had been lost. The remaining enemy fighters retreated behind the last large Annunaki cruiser. It was time to proceed with the next phase of the Alliance plan. He opened communications with every craft in the armada. "Separate the fleet. Commander Evir is now in command of the liberation force. Our sensors indicate a battle is ongoing in the capital city. The expected resistance has likely been reduced. The time has come to free Vandi," Kapun ordered.

Vincent expected Gly to recall his troops at some point. Day two of the battle in Vath was underway. He received reports from Isabella and Julia. Humans and Martians were doing their best to hide and attack the enemy when possible on the continents. Vincent was anxious to return. "What is the situation in Vath?" he asked. "All troops will be retreating shortly," Gly said. "Are you sustaining heavy casualties?" Vincent asked. "No, we're running out of enemies to kill. Vath has

199

been destroyed and the land will soon return to its natural state. The battle was disorganized in the beginning. We defeated the Krace on the outskirts of the city and encountered heavy resistance when we attempted to enter the city proper. Tony intervened and saved the lives of many of my people. He destroyed the missile launchers. If he hadn't, I would have likely recalled my forces a day ago. The Krace retreated to the buildings. Tony destroyed many buildings with explosives. Some survived the blasts. My soldiers waited to ensure the Krace wouldn't regroup and wage war," Gly responded.

"On behalf of the Alliance, I thank you for what you've done. Your species is honorable and noble. I will be returning to the continent now," Vincent said. "Remember our agreement. Goodbye human. You're not as primitive as I originally believed," Gly responded. Vincent considered asking the Volmer leader to relocate his forces and help with the battle on the continents. He knew Gly wouldn't agree to an additional battle. He decided to leave on amicable terms. He definitely didn't want to become an enemy of the Volmer. "Goodbye, I hope to see you again," he said. "I hope not; we wish to be left alone," Gly responded.

Tony had been running on adrenaline for far too long. His body was crashing, and he felt dizzy. He couldn't remember the last time he had anything to eat or drink. He knew what his prognosis was if he kept going. Volmer soldiers were gone and there weren't any Krace soldiers within sight. He found a recently killed Kracian soldier. The bullak was an excellent cutting instrument. He used it to slice the grey animal open. The beast's heart was located just above the stomach. He removed the organ and roasted it over the remains of a burning building. He consumed the entirety of the organ and lapped water from a puddle on the ground before passing out next to the smoldering ruins.

"Maxis, Vincent reports Vath has been destroyed. There will be few, if any, reinforcements coming from the north to assist Krace on the continents. It's time to go on the offensive. We need more weapons. Vincent is on his way back and will arrive shortly," Isabella said. "I will make preparations for battle and wish to speak with him as soon as he arrives," Maxis replied. He sent instructions for all Martians to relocate to the Human Continent as quickly as possible. After issuing the directive, he found the closest Strithu and explained what was needed.

With the assistance from the Volmer, victory was now within reach. Vincent wondered why the Alliance hadn't arrived. He received a new message from Isabella. "We are relocating to the Human Continent. Please rendezvous at the indicated coordinates." Vincent instructed the Strithu to change course.

He'd never seen anything like it; there were thousands of Strithu in the sky and all were travelling in the direction of the Human Continent. All the birds were carrying passengers. "Thank you for your help. We couldn't have done this without you," Vincent said to his bird.

"My research and development people have successfully weaponized an additional two hundred and fifty tratium rounds," Randy said. "I hope we don't have to use them. Our tiny community won't stand a chance if we are forced to fight," Enzo replied. "We can't live underground forever. A few people want to leave, but so far, I've been able to talk them out of the idea. Morale is getting pretty low," Randy said. "Let's go pay a visit to everyone. Perhaps we can lift their spirits a bit," Enzo suggested.

The people of Trundle were hard workers and Enzo enjoyed their company. He led Randy into a room filled with children. A woman was on the ground laughing with a small girl. "Welcome to school, gentleman. Thank you for keeping our children safe and alive. My name is Gail Marie. I don't consider myself a teacher. Around here the children teach themselves," she said. "It doesn't look like any school I've ever attended. How do you teach them?" Randy said. "I find if you give children the tools to learn and give them fun problems to solve, they learn on their own. Teaching down to them doesn't work. Each child takes joy from discovering something new. The students I've taught have tested higher than those who have received a traditional education. I much prefer to teach outdoors; however, under present circumstances it looks like I won't have the opportunity for quite some time," she said.

"The students appear to be enjoying themselves. You're doing a wonderful job. I wish you and your students could go outside as well. These children need to learn outdoor survival skills. When we're finally able to leave this place, the world will be completely different," Enzo said. "I agree and have always felt it's important to connect with nature and be in harmony with the environment. It's something we need to get back to," Gail said. "If you ever need anything, come and see me. I'd be happy to help in any way I can," Enzo replied.

"I wish I had a teacher like her when I was in school," Randy mused as the two men continued their underground visits. "We will need educated people when we regain our freedom. It's something we need to take into consideration as we move forward. We need more educators like Gail. The children of today will be called upon to run this world if we can defeat the enemy," Enzo replied.

He was about to say more when Sandy came running down the hallway. "We've spotted a patrol. There are five aliens coming our way. Martino and his men are on the roof preparing to fire," she urgently reported. "Let's go join him. Randy will you go the security room and see if there's anything you can do to assist?" Enzo asked. "Sure, I'll contact you immediately if necessary," Randy said.

Aliens approached the underground community. The soldiers were almost on top of one of the entrances. There were nine other women and men on the roof with Martino. He assigned two shooters for each alien target. "Prepare to fire. Remember, keep firing until the aliens are down and immobile. We have no idea how effective these bullets are, or if they even work." One of the aliens moved the shrubbery which camouflaged one of the entrances. "Fire!" Martino commanded.

Enzo and Sandy joined Martino on the roof as he and his men began firing on the aliens. Two of the targets fell immediately, followed quickly by two others. The only alien left standing fled. Enzo fired a shot into his back and the soldier went down. "Martino and Sandy, come with me. The rest of you stay up here and be on the lookout for more patrols," Enzo commanded as he ran toward the exit. "We have no idea what time this patrol is due back at their base and we'll need to move the bodies far from here," he said. "We should cut one of the bodies open so we can learn where their vital organs are located. A couple of my shots didn't seem very effective; on a human they would have been immediately fatal." Martino said as the trio exited the building.

"Wow, these grey bastards really stink," Sandy said covering her nose with her sleeve. "Each has an electrical device of some kind wrapped around their upper arm. It's likely a communication device and a tracking system," Enzo said.

"We need to get those devices as far away from here as possible," Enzo said. "We cannot keep one of the communication devices to study and replicate. The alien gadget would be stationary for too long and our location would be compromised. Let's bring the closest body inside," Enzo said. A grey alien was brought into a storage room and placed on a large table after the communication device was removed. "Who wants to slice this thing open?" Enzo asked. "I'll do it; I'm very interested in the anatomy of these creatures," Martino volunteered. After removing the alien's armor, he took out his knife. He made an incision just below the elongated neck to the top of the strange looking genitals. Orange blood oozed from the body. Martino counted fourteen large ribs that were much thicker than human ribs. Just below the neck was an air sack. Martino hunted many animals and hadn't seen anything like it. "If I were to guess, I'd say it's an air reserve of some kind. The lungs and heart are much lower than I expected. We need to aim about a foot lower when we fire," Martino said.

Sandy inspected the body armor. "The modified bullets seem to work well. Their armor proved ineffective against the tratium rounds," she said. "I'll ask the local doctor to perform a more thorough autopsy. In the meantime, we need to dispose of the rest of the bodies and relocate the communication devices," Enzo said. Randy entered the room. "Ugh! What a disgusting smell. We located the vehicle they were using for travel. It's a Jeep about a half mile away," Randy said.

"Apparently, they find our vehicles useful. Send someone to bring it here. We will leave the communication devices on the bodies and place the aliens inside. The device we took from this alien will be placed inside as well. Martino and I will visit the petrol station in Trundle. Let's get moving; we don't know how much time we have," Enzo said.

The four bodies and all five communication devices were quickly placed in the Jeep. Martino followed Enzo in a separate vehicle. Enzo sped as fast as possible to the petrol station and parked the vehicle next to one of the pumps. He doused the Jeep with gas. "Would you please do me the honor? I think I splashed a little on my sleeves," Enzo asked. Martino threw his cigar toward the vehicle and a fireball rose into the sky. "They'll be well done in a couple of minutes. What do you think they taste like?" Martino asked. "If they taste anything like they smell, I doubt they'd be any good. Someday we might run out of food, but I hope it never comes to that. Let's get the hell out of here," Enzo replied.

Chapter 10

Vincent landed and found Julia waiting for him. "What's going on? I saw thousands of people traveling here," he asked. "From what we can tell, the Kracian military forces have abandoned the Martian Continent and have been reassigned to the Human Continent. Soldiers are still killing humans on sight. We will engage the enemy and fight together here. Has there been any sign of Alliance forces?" Julia asked. "No, there hasn't been any communication. I hoped reinforcements would be here by now," Vincent replied.

"I've assembled all the village leaders. We've been waiting for you to arrive before debating a course of action," Julia said. "We still face extreme danger and there is no sign of the Alliance. Let's go discuss our options. Feel free to speak up if you think I've missed anything," he replied.

Julia brought Vincent to a courtyard. He found humans and Martians sitting on the ground waiting patiently. "Greetings, my name is Vincent. I'm the Alliance leader for the small task force that was sent here. I understand your desire for retribution. You have been tortured and mistreated for generations. I urge you to spread your people far and wide across the land. An attack in Vath decimated the capitol city. Annunaki and Kracian reinforcements will not be sent in the short term. It would be foolish to gather in a singular location. The enemy still has advanced weaponry and the ability to strike from the air, so we must make their task as hard as possible and kill them one by one," Vincent said.

A debate began among the assembled village leaders. "We have waited for generations for this day of uprising to arrive. We wish to fight, free our children and liberate all future generations," one of the leaders said. "If we were on equal terms with the enemy, I would urge you to fight. However, the Annunaki and Krace will attack with advanced weaponry. The handful of antiquated weapons we possess is no match. You are intelligent beings and know this to be true; follow your mind not your heart. Remain alive and share your wisdom with your children. Grow old with your families," he said. A new but familiar voice spoke. "We will be victorious if we remain patient. I agree with Vincent. I have known him for quite some time now and I trust him to guide us on the correct course of action. We should follow his advice," Maxis stated.

Evir expected a long and protracted battle to recapture Vandi. As commander of the planetary invading force, it was his responsibility to defeat the Annunaki on the planet. His fleet was about to enter the atmosphere and the latest report indicated the

Annunaki capital was on fire and the villages were now liberated. The remaining forces on the planet were disorganized and attacking humans and Martians when possible. "Commander, we've detected an underground structure in the capitol. The only remaining Annunaki life signs in the area are inside," he was told. "Target the structure and destroy it completely," Evir ordered.

Priex attempted to recall all remaining Krace from the continents, but the communication equipment was no longer functioning due to battle damage. He left the safety of the underground shelter and boarded an airship to the Human Continent with a dozen guards. He would personally redirect troops to the capitol. "Monarch, the capitol reports the remaining subterranean structures are under attack from the air," his pilot said. Priex knew it could only be newly arriving Alliance ships. The remaining Annunaki and Kracian leaders in the shelter were doomed; there was no longer a way to wage war. "Find the closest village and land immediately. We will take refuge in the local guard barracks," he commanded.

President Louis would have rather stayed in his cell; he deserved nothing less for his failures. Bazor summoned him to dinner again. The Annunaki leader apparently enjoyed tormenting those she controlled. "Earth is the latest conquest of my species. Soon we will be in control of all Alliance worlds. In the end, you will be a minor footnote in our history," Bazor sneered. The meal was interrupted by an aide. "Five members of a patrol are dead on the Australian Continent in a small town called Trundle. The patrol was refueling their vehicle, and something went wrong. The fuel caught fire killing all five." "Send out a safety memo as to how to fuel vehicles properly; this is the second time it's happened. What's the status of the most recent patrols?" she asked. "We are still encountering sporadic resistance from those in hiding. There are very few natives left on the planet who remain hidden. The current estimate is approximately two thousand," the aide reported. "Find the remaining holdouts and kill them all. We don't need any strong-willed people in the camps. It's easier to guard the weak minded," she ordered.

For the first time in months, President Louis smiled. He knew who was responsible for the deaths in Trundle. Enzo Moretti had always been a pain in the ass and an enemy. The mafia boss knew how to cover his tracks. Somehow the man was the first person on Earth who managed to kill any members of the invading force. Enzo managed to provide a small glimmer of hope for mankind.

Vincent was pleased and believed the citizens of Vandi were making it as difficult as possible to be captured or killed. The members of Sol heeded his advice and traveled in small groups. The Strithu were put to use once again to relocate the travelers as close as possible to water sources. He traveled with Monique and they were dropped off on a hillside overlooking a small lake. "What do we do now?" Monique asked. "We find shelter, look for food and survive," he said as his data pad chirped at him. "Kracian aircraft are arriving at my location. Soldiers are being deployed and there are more ground troops than we expected. The aircraft are firing on anyone within sight," Isabella texted. "Goddamn it! Every time I think we're making progress, more lives are lost," he said. "We're following the best course of action under the circumstances. Let's get down to the lake and find somewhere to hide. We knew this mission wouldn't be easy," Monique said as she heard the sound of an approaching aircraft.

Shortly after arriving at the pristine lake, his data pad demanded his attention again. Vincent was sure it was another member of his team reporting more death. He activated the device and received a live audio transmission. "Captain Moretti, this is Commander Evir of the Alliance. We have arrived and are preparing to assist. I have analyzed the tactical situation. Forces have been deployed. Your work here has made my task quite easy. I will arrive at your location in five minutes. The planet will be liberated within the hour."

Vincent dropped the data pad as Monique fiercely hugged him. They both began to cry. "We did it!" they said in unison. Vincent called the rest of his team and shared the good news.

The sight was surreal. Birds lolling on the lake scattered as a sleek ship with the bright emblem of the Alliance landed on the shoreline. A hatch opened and a Rabanian male appeared. "I'm Evir. Well done, Captain. I don't know how you did it but taking out the capitol made the mission very easy for me. The remaining enemy forces will either be captured or killed quickly. Climb aboard; we still have work to do." The Alliance ship quickly returned to the sky. Vincent watched as bird poop landed on the front viewport. "There sure are a lot of birds on this planet," Evir said. "You have no idea," Vincent replied.

Maxis kept Tissa and Zanther within his field of vision at all times. He observed with his wife and son as two airships fired on a position across the valley killing more of his friends. Suddenly he heard a new noise as eight aircraft flew low, directly overhead. A few seconds later, all eight of the aircraft unleashed their weapons on the slow moving Kracian ships. The ships were quickly obliterated. Maxis hoped none of the people on the ground would be harmed by the falling wreckage. He took hold of Zanther and placed his hands on the chest of his only child. "We are free now, my son."

Across the Human Continent, Kracian ships were outnumbered, outgunned and offered little resistance against the invading forces. The remaining ground troops surrendered. Large Alliance ships descended from orbit and landed. Injured people were escorted inside for medical assistance and those who hadn't been injured were given communication devices.

People ran toward the ship as it landed in the center of one of the abandoned villages. "Commander Evir, it will take time for everyone to return. We decided to spread out across the entire continent. I felt it was the best plan under the circumstances to save as many lives as possible," Vincent said. "It was a good plan and saved lives. We will find everyone; there are many rescue vessels retrieving the citizens of this world. It won't take as long as you think. The major cities have been destroyed and many Krace have surrendered. Those attempting escape in spacecraft to the Annunaki system are either killed or captured," Evir said as a Strithu landed a few yards away. He watched as a human female exited the bird's pouch. "It looks like we'll have help retrieving everyone. This is a strange planet; I like it," Evir remarked.

Mox regretted accepting the position as Earth Ambassador. Unbelievably, she was once again representing an enslaved planet. She was beyond frustrated and summoned her aide. "Have any of the member worlds contacted us offering assistance?" she asked Sarah. "We have only received a few offers of tactical and supply assistance. There have been no offers of direct military support," Sarah responded. "I didn't expect anything more. I let my anger and frustration push me too far. Asking for assistance from other member worlds was foolhardy. We have two choices: we can wait for the Alliance to act or we can request assistance from a non-member world," Mox said.

"Are there any non-member worlds that can help?" Sarah asked. "There might be one. The species is known as Cardonian, but I really can't think of a reason why they would help. We have nothing to offer," Mox said. "Who are the Cardonians?" Sarah asked. "They were once a member of the Alliance. Civil war constantly rages on their planet. The Cardonians are tremendous warriors. Unfortunately, the only enemy the species ever fight is themselves. When they were members of the Alliance, their ambassador changed every time their government changed hands. The Cardonian Civil War has raged for centuries. The species was placed on probation and eventually their membership was revoked. The Cardonians are still being observed and will be offered membership again if they can become internally harmonious. I'll find out who the current leader is and initiate contact. It's been forty-seven years since their membership was revoked. Perhaps the species has progressed into a more peaceful existence," Mox said.

"Vandi has been secured sir. We now control the planet, but there is an unusual anomaly. A shack near a village on the Human Continent is currently guarded by twelve Kracian soldiers. Sensors indicate an Annunaki is inside," Reported the intelligence expert. "We must capture and interrogate this person. We will kill or capture the guards as necessary, but do not kill the leader under any circumstances," Evir said.

"Any unnecessary forces on Vandi are to return to the fleet at once," Commander Kapun ordered. The Annunaki on the planet were finished; it was now time to defeat them in space. For a day, there was little progress. The enemy fighters took refuge with the mother ship and the military escorts. "Sir, the Annunaki are breaking formation and their fleet is spreading out." Kapun knew what was likely to happen and dreaded the moment. The Annunaki leader understood no help would come from the planet and was preparing to sacrifice the remainder of his ships to reduce the Alliance fleet as much as possible. "Redeploy our ships as planned. Prepare for an immediate attack," Kapun ordered. He defeated the enemy and the remaining Annunaki leadership knew it as well.

Kapun issued orders as the battle unfolded. Many of the Annunaki fighters were disabled and utilized their last remaining power reserves to collide with and destroy Alliance ships. The attacks by the Annunaki were ruthless and suicidal. After another half day of fighting, the mother ship was destroyed and the Annunaki space fleet defeated. "What percentage of our fleet remains?" he asked. "Twenty-nine percent," he was informed. Set course for the Annunaki gate. We will defend the system should reinforcements from the Annunaki home planet be sent," Kapun said.

Priex hadn't heard from the capitol or from any of his soldiers for hours. He was defeated and knew all was lost. "Alliance airships are approaching. What are your orders?" one of the lowly Kracian soldiers asked. "You are to protect me. Blow them out of the sky," he said as multiple explosions erupted outside. "I will stay inside and personally guard you," the soldier replied. "No, I'm no longer in need of your services," Priex said as he withdrew a blade and sliced open the soldier's grey skull. He heard the aircraft approaching and decided one last act of defiance and sacrifice would be made for his Empress.

Evir expected a violent last stand and was surprised. A single Annunaki exited the structure, shed his clothing and waited for capture. The alien was unarmed and made no act of defiance as the restraints were placed on his limbs. He was quickly ushered aboard the ship. Evir always wanted to meet a member of the Annunaki species in person. He greeted his prisoner as the ship rose into the sky. "I am Evir. You will be required to cooperate with us. We will use any means necessary to extract the information in your brain," he said as three guards led the alien into a holding cell. "Greetings, my name is Priex. I will be happy to cooperate. It's time for peace between our races and I would like to propose a truce. Hostilities must cease for negotiations to commence," the naked alien said. Evir hadn't heard of the Annunaki ever proposing peace and the species overtly rejected the Alliance's proposals in the past.

Something was wrong. Priex was male and didn't have the authority to make such an offer unless something drastically changed in the Annunaki hierarchy. He was hiding something. Evir turned on the security console and scanned Priex. An explosive mechanical device of some kind was inside the alien's stomach. Priex began laughing. Evir didn't know how much time he had and suspected it was very little. He immediately called the command center. "Pilot, descend immediately," he said as he unlocked the door to the holding cell. "Let's get him to the hatch," he told the three security guards. "Pilot, are we low enough to open a hatch?" he asked. "We will be low enough in fifteen seconds. The depressurization will be severe. Hold on to something and close the hatch as quickly as possible. The extremely low temperature can kill us in seconds and there will be very little oxygen. You can now open the hatch."

Evir and the guards tossed Priex on the ground in front of the hatch. After waiting to make sure the guards were prepared for depressurization, Evir opened the door. Priex was quickly sucked out of the craft. Evir couldn't breathe and closed the hatch as fast as possible. As he tried to catch his breath, he glanced out the window in time to see the Annunaki leader blown into hundreds of bloody pieces. A variety of colorful birds converged for an unexpected meal.

Maxis and his family boarded an Alliance shuttle. The craft was beautiful and a wonder to behold. The time in the air was short and the craft landed quickly. Vincent was waiting when he exited the ship. Maxis was about to place his hands on the human's chest when Vincent wrapped his arms around his shoulders and clutched him tightly. "I apologize my friend. It is a human gesture," Vincent said. "No apologies necessary. The name Vincent Moretti will be remembered on Vandi forever," Maxis replied. "I have endured very little compared to the people of Vandi. Your rich culture and history must be brought back to life and revered. It is the people of Vandi who should be celebrated," Vincent said. "Have no doubt. We will renew and celebrate our culture. We will also have a special place in our hearts for you and your friends. Have you heard from Tony?" Maxis asked. "No, I haven't heard from him in quite some time. I'm worried he didn't survive the battle, but for now, let's gather the people of Sol and celebrate this victory," Vincent replied.

Tony wasn't sure how long he slept and was incredibly thirsty and hungry again. He sat up and found he was surrounded by containers of water and a large variety of fruit. Three Strithu were nearby. He spent thirty minutes refueling his deprived body. The Strithu were certainly taking good care of him and a large one licked his face. "Thank you, sweetheart. Let's go see what's going on," he said as he climbed into the enormous bird's pouch.

Tony didn't know how long he slept but knew it was much longer than normal. He was at peace and knew once the capitol fell, everything else should have fallen into place. He hadn't meditated for days and instructed the bird to land near a small creek. He found a solitary rock barely breaching the surface and sat down. His mind reached a point of serenity. Physically, he knew his body would not live a long second life. The battle in Vath took a greater toll on him than it should have for a man of his apparent age. A new undertaking awaited him. He would discover his forthcoming purpose and fulfill the destiny which had been thrust upon him. After two hours of meditation, he resumed the journey.

The giant bird descended toward a large gathering of people. Martians and humans surrounded a centralized stage as hundreds of Strithu circled over the crowd. Just as Tony landed, a Rabanian male began to speak. "Citizens of Vandi, I'm Commander Evir of the Alliance. This planet was intended to be a refuge for the people of Sol. For many generations, Vandi served its purpose, but we failed your ancestors when we lost the planet to the Annunaki. On behalf of the Alliance, I apologize for your enslavement. We were unable to defend your people against the invasion.

We must now look to the future. Vandi has been liberated. The Alliance will place a transitional government on the planet until the populace elects new leaders. Any citizens of Vandi who wish to leave are welcome to do so. The Alliance will transport you to

221

any accepting member worlds. Governance of this planet will be transferred to local leadership as quickly as possible," Evir said.

"I guess nobody told him about the agreement with Gly," Monique said. "I guess not," said a voice that wasn't Vincent's. "Damnit Tony, you need to stop sneaking up on us! Where have you been anyway? We thought we might have lost you," Vincent asked as he hugged his friend. "It took me a little while to recover from the battle in Vath, but it's good to learn the effort wasn't made in vain. I'm fine now." Tony said. "I'm glad you're alive. If you hadn't aided the mission in Vath, we would likely still be fighting. Excellent work, old man," Vincent replied with a grin.

Vincent needed information and was anxious to meet with Evir. He found the Commander in his quarters eating a meal. "I apologize for interrupting Evir, but can you please update me with any information you have regarding the Sol System and Earth?" he asked. "You will not like what I'm going to tell you. The Sol System has been taken by the Annunaki and we do not have the necessary military force to retake the system at this time," Evir morosely relayed. "That's all the information you have? How many have been killed? What is the situation on Mars?" Vincent asked. "Probes indicate the destruction on

Earth is extreme. It is the opinion of the Tactical Council that approximately three billion lives have been lost on Earth. Your species has been unable to successfully repel the enemy and has been enslaved. I don't have any information about Mars. You have my condolences and sympathies, Vincent," Evir said.

All his friends were finally together. Vincent looked at the members of his team and felt lucky to know each of them. Together, the crew accomplished a great deal and he took pride in how the mission concluded. Telling everyone about the situation on Earth had been painful. "It's time for us to return to Rabanah. We must assist the people on Earth and Mars in any way possible," he said. Everyone agreed with the decision.

Commander Evir was laughing with a local human leader as Vincent approached. "The captured Kracian soldiers will be kept prisoner in the villages they used to guard. The situation is quite ironic," Evir said. "What is to become of them? Are the Krace going to be killed?" Vincent asked. "The prisoners will be transported to a planet called Qoopax. The Kracian species thrives on the planet. We've been placing captured solders there for generations. The species can run the planet as they see fit. We only restrict them from producing weaponry and spacecraft. In time, we hope the Krace will decide to align with us, but a mutual trust must first be established. The Alliance is planning on negotiating with the leaders soon," Evir said.

"Commander, my team is ready to leave. We must get back to Rabanah as quickly as possible to see what we can do to help Earth," Vincent said. "I anticipated your request and there is a ship waiting for you in the small valley to the east."

"Come on, let's get moving. We need to walk a couple of miles," he said. As Vincent and his team approached the valley, the ship came into view. A name was stenciled on the vessel. It was the Santa Maria. "I'll have to thank the Chief Monarch when we get back. It was very considerate of him to send us our ship," Vincent said. "A Martian female is waiting for us," Tony said. Vincent could see it was Alixias, the woman who was eavesdropping outside Maxis' home. "What are you doing here?" he asked. "I'm going with you. You helped save my world; I will help save yours. I've spoken with Maxis and he agrees. In the near future, Vandi will deploy volunteers to help free Earth. Maxis has made it one of his first priorities," she said. "Thank you for joining us. We gladly welcome anyone willing to assist," Vincent said warmly.

Tony entered the Santa Maria and knew his destiny would not be found on Rabanah. "I'm going to remain on Vandi," he informed Vincent. "What are you talking about? You already agreed to return to

Rabanah," Vincent said. "I cannot return to Rabanah. My unique abilities will best serve the Alliance if I remain on Vandi," he said.

Tony successfully accomplished missions Vincent thought were impossible. He didn't understand what forces were driving the man, but knew Tony would likely succeed in whatever he put his mind to. "You are my friend and helped in more ways than I could have ever imagined. I hope to see you again. You mean more to us than you'll ever know. Good luck," Vincent said and hugged his friend. He watched as Tony ran at an amazing speed up the hillside.

Chapter 11

Empress Zovad rarely grew angry. By some astounding act of insanity, a male ascended to power on Vandi. As Empress of the entire Annunaki realm, she would ensure such a travesty would never happen again. She finished reviewing the data from the last automated probe which returned through the gate. After reviewing the information, she couldn't believe the system was completely and totally lost.

The unqualified male failed in spectacular fashion. She reviewed the extenuating circumstances of his failure. The plan she'd authorized failed from the beginning. Her plan depended on surprise and guile, yet somehow the Alliance learned of the attack and acted quicker than she anticipated. She needed to have both the Vandi and Sol systems. Resources were becoming scarce, planets within the realm were overpopulated and some were becoming uninhabitable. It was time for her to take the initiative and take the Alliance by surprise. She recalled forces from other solar systems and ordered an increase in production of all military vessels and weaponry.

The joy of liberating Vandi was replaced by feelings of loss, frustration and anger due to the invasion of the Sol System. The crew of the Santa Maria arrived on Rabanah and learned conditions were unchanged on Earth and Mars. There would be no immediate attempt to retake the Sol System. "What do we do now?" Isabella asked. "We meet with Mox. We all heard her speech; she appears as frustrated as we are. Hopefully she's made some progress recruiting forces to free Earth. We should get some sleep, refocus and regroup. I'll request a meeting with the Ambassador in the morning," Vincent said as the door chime sounded.

Julia answered the door and a diplomatic aide entered the room. "Chief Administrator Azira requests your presence for a grand celebration of our victory and the liberation of Vandi tomorrow evening," the aide requested. "Please inform Azira we will not be attending. We are in the process of analyzing the situation on Sol and are unable to attend a celebration of recently gained freedom in the shadow of torture and death on Earth," Vincent replied.

"An appropriate response," Mox said from the doorway as she arrived with Sarah. "You are dismissed. I shall consult with my people. Return to the Chief Administrator and relay the message you have been given," she said to the aide. Sarah hugged each of her friends and was overjoyed to see them all alive. "Is there any hope?" Vincent asked. "Earth will not be freed tomorrow, next week and it will likely not be freed next year. We require a significant increase in military capability and I'm working on it," Mox said.

"I've been thinking about possible courses of action. Vandi has been liberated. We can send humans to Earth by the thousands. Our presence went undetected on Vandi, so we can conduct the same operation on Earth," Vincent said. "Your logic is sound, but you lack experience. The enemy force on Earth will be actively searching for pockets of resistance for years to come. Vandi was occupied for generations and all resistance was eliminated for decades. The situation is not the same on Earth," Mox said.

"What about Mars?" Vincent asked. "The Annunaki have ignored Mars so far. The aliens are in search of resources and Mars offers none. It is unlikely Annunaki forces will take an interest in the planet for the moment," Mox replied. I have a friend on Mars in the ancient Martian city. There are hundreds of humans on Mars. You are the ambassador for Earth. Make a request to have my team sent to Mars and we will plan a rebellion from there," Vincent said.

Mox was growing frustrated. She wanted nothing more than to see the Annunaki defeated as well. She knew hundreds of humans on Mars would die if they brought attention to themselves. "The Annunaki Armada in the Sol System is massive. A few hundred humans on Mars cannot free Earth under any circumstances. You cannot mount a rebellion from the planet and you can't defeat the Annunaki," she said. "Submit a request to have two of us sent to Mars. We can plan and strategize if the request is granted. There are only a few humans in the ancient city. The remainder of the people on Mars cannot enter the city due to an electrical force field of some kind. We need to at least give the humans on the surface the ability to go underground and hide. I understand your position, but please understand mine. Make the request for us to go to Mars with a thousand ETS units," Vincent pled.

"Against my better judgment I will make the request. The primary reason I will make the request is for those on the surface of Mars. Everyone on the planet should be afforded as much protection as possible under the circumstances," Mox replied.

Vincent was present the next morning when Mox made the request. The debate was short. Council members shared the same arguments Mox made the previous evening. In the end, it was agreed only one person would travel to Mars. The mission plan had many restrictions and only passive action was authorized. The humans outside the dead zone would be provided ETS units to enter the ancient city, but any attempt to send reinforcements to Earth, negotiate with the Annunaki, or engage the enemy in battle was unauthorized and forbidden.

From their shared quarters, Monique watched the short debate on the screen with the rest of the crew. The situation was disheartening, and Vincent wouldn't be satisfied with the result. The door opened, and Vincent entered with Sarah in tow. "Goddamn it! How many people are dying on Earth while we wait for the Alliance to act?" he fumed. "Stay focused, Vincenzo. We will send someone to Mars who can help the people stranded there. The situation is not ideal, but we can still make use of this opportunity," Monique said.

"We must continue searching for options. Is there anyone who would like to volunteer for this mission?" Vincent asked. Alixias raised her hand. "I would like the opportunity. Perhaps I can uncover ancient knowledge from my ancestors that could prove helpful. I would like to see the planet from where my people originated." "Unless there are any objections, the mission is yours. You will follow the parameters the Alliance has set, but I have one additional duty for you to perform. You will send a message to an Earth leader. Prepare for immediate departure," Vincent said.

Bazor read the troubling update from Empress Zovad. Reinforcements would not arrive from the Vandi system anytime soon. It was up to her to secure the Sol System and repel any intrusions from the Alliance. It came as a great surprise to learn Rabanah and the heart of the Alliance hadn't been taken. News that the Vandi system had been lost was shocking. She redeployed the entire fleet to the gate. If Alliance forces tried to enter, the ships wouldn't get far.

Earth's population was approaching a more manageable number of approximately three billion people. Pockets of resistance were becoming more and more infrequent. Bazor decided to reduce the number of patrols and focus on the productivity levels of the slaves. Before she arrived humans severely overpopulated the planet and nearly poisoned the atmosphere beyond repair. She would ensure the planet would be hospitable for all future Annunaki visitors. Her Empress was preparing for a new battle and Bazor was to construct military craft on Earth as quickly as possible. When the time for battle arrived, Bazor would lead an armada through the Sol gate for a combined direct attack on Rabanah.

Patrick awoke to a Leviathan communications alert. The channel hadn't been active in over a year. With Earth decimated, he wondered how anyone could possibly communicate. He activated the message and was stunned by the image on the screen. Vincent spoke and was flanked by a Martian female. "Hello Mars ground crew. I hope you are managing despite the tragic circumstances. This is Alixias. She is a Martian and will arrive at your location in approximately one hour. I apologize for the short notice, but under the circumstances it was best to transmit the message as close to Mars as possible. She will land within a half mile of your location and emerge from stasis. Please assist her as necessary and she will update you on the current state of affairs inside and outside the solar system. Circumstances have prevented the rest of us from returning with her. I hope to see you again in this lifetime. Take care my friends."

The message kept repeating and was beyond belief. Patrick let out a yell which woke Jose. "Keep it down man. I need my rest," he grumbled. "Help might be on the way! Go to Cydonia and retrieve Dalton and Kathy," he said. "What is it?" Jose asked. "Just go get them; I'll tell you all at the same time," he said.

The video transmitted by Vincent and the Martian was mesmerizing. Patrick couldn't stop watching; he played it in slow motion and froze the image of Alixias on the screen. "What's going on Patrick?" Dalton asked as the trio entered the command center. Patrick turned the screen toward his three friends and played the video. "She's a fine specimen. I can't wait to get her into the lab," Dalton said after watching the video. "Jesus, Dalton there's the minor matter of the enslavement of humanity. Let's worry about the future of mankind first. Later, we can debate

232

the differences between ancient and modern-day Martians," Kathy said. "It's almost been an hour; let's go look for her," Patrick said.

Dalton opened the exterior door in time to see two large parachutes descending directly in front of him. "What are attached to those parachutes? Why attach a parachute to a large rock?" he asked. "I don't know. Let's go find out," Jose replied. Patrick watched as the asteroids gently touched down. In an instant, the exterior of the asteroids morphed, and he made out two containers. One was square and the other was cylindrical. As he approached the cylindrical container, the top slid back and he saw the glow of an ETS unit. He looked into the stasis tube as Alixias woke up. "Welcome to your ancestral homeland," Patrick said. "Thank you, do you have anything to eat? I'm starving," Alixias replied.

Safely aboard the Intrepid, Patrick waited patiently for the Martian to fully awaken. "Forgive me, I know you have many questions. I have a recording that will summarize the current situation," Alixias said as she handed Dalton a virtual drive. Dalton quickly plugged in the device and watched as an alien appeared on the screen. He was addressing a large group of aliens, explaining why Earth couldn't be rescued and celebrating the liberation of a planet called Vandi.

A message from Vincent followed. "Hello, my friends. I apologize for not coming. Alixias volunteered for this mission and may prove useful in rediscovering ancient secrets and technology. We made a choice to help free a planet of refuges from the Sol System. At the time, we didn't know Earth was in danger. Tony recovered the Annunaki's battle plans and only then did we discover the threat to Earth.

We sent one thousand ETS units with Alixias. Get everyone on Mars into the ancient city in Cydonia. Do not engage in any offensive operations or draw attention to yourselves. A portion of the craft that delivered Alixias to Mars will continue to Earth. I have prepared a message for Enzo and Randy. Do not try to contact Earth under any circumstances. Stay alive until we can defeat the Annunaki. Alixias will give you additional information regarding any questions you might have. I'm sorry I don't have better news. Please survive. I want very much to see you all again."

"Goddamn it. What chance do we have if an advanced alien race can't save us?" Jose asked. "Vincent and his friends undertook a grave risk. I would not be free, and the Alliance might have been defeated if not for his efforts. He risked his life and those under his command to save an entire enslaved planet. We were killed, beaten, tortured and humiliated by the Annunaki. His quest was noble. You will heed his instructions and stay alive. We will learn as much as possible and do what must be done.

Would someone please take me on a tour? If I'm not mistaken, I'm the first breathing Martian on this planet in thousands of years," Alixias asked. "My apologies. At times our frustration overshadows what is best for us. It is a great honor to meet you and to welcome you home. I believe Dalton would be best served to escort you. He has uncovered a great deal of information about your ancestors. I will begin the process of issuing the ETS units and relocating people on the surface into the ancient city. First, however, I would like you to tell me more about the Alliance," Patrick said.

Hector was updating the food inventory when Patrick entered. "How are things at Cydonia? Have you guys figured out a way to save mankind yet?" he asked. "Not yet. We have a new arrival, however," Patrick replied. "I thought all Earth spacecraft were destroyed. How did someone make it here?" Hector asked. "Our new arrival is from outside our solar system. She is Martian, and her name is Alixias. The advanced alien race we've been studying relocated a group of Martians in the distant past. A war decimated Mars and the aliens rescued survivors. Our new arrival has brought advanced environmental suits for everyone. All those on the surface can now come to Cydonia and live in the underground city. There is enough room for everyone. I will hold a meeting tonight with Alixias and we will share her information. Tell your people to pick up their ETS suits at my ship. I'm going to go find Alixias and prepare for the meeting," Patrick said. "I'll send a message to everyone and will be there shortly. I've been dying to see the dead zone ever since I arrived," Hector said.

Alixias marveled at the strange, yet familiar architecture and history of the ancient past. Dalton led her up a stairway to a chamber with inscribed gold walls. "This is the written history of your people. We've begun to slowly translate the information. So far, we've translated most of it. There are some sections which are confusing and don't make sense to us. Do you understand what is written?" Dalton asked. "Yes, I understand it. We still use the same language, essentially. There are some deviations and words which are no longer in use, but I comprehend the majority of what I'm reading."

Alixias was amazed at the history she was learning. She was reading about the first attempt at space travel when Patrick interrupted. "Your species accomplished so much. I hope we can all live freely, learn from each other and live in harmony someday," he said. "We were doing so on Vandi before the Annunaki invaded. It's time we defeat them once and for all. I will spend most of my time here learning the history of my people," Alixias said. "You will have plenty of time to do so, but right now we need to prepare to address those on the surface who will soon arrive," Patrick replied.

Enzo was winning and enjoying a rare glass of wine. He was in the small meeting room playing pinochle with Randy, Gail and Martino. "A run and one hundred aces. I believe it's another game for Gail and me," he said as an alarm sounded on a nearby console. "What in the hell? It's the Leviathan deep space frequency. With the satellites gone, the transmission source must be very close," Randy said as he activated the message. Vincent Moretti's image appeared on the screen. "It is my hope this information reaches Enzo Moretti, Randy Stedman, or anyone who can relay the information I'm about to provide."

The video was long and interesting. Enzo hoped the information would help somehow. He watched as humanity was granted membership into the Alliance. Vincenzo stood proudly and nominated a Martian female as Earth's Ambassador. The Assembly celebrated the liberation of the planet Vandi, but Vincenzo and the rest of the crew were notably absent from the celebration. Enzo got angry when he learned the tactical situation left the people of Earth to fend for themselves. Vincenzo appeared on the screen again. "We are exploring other options that don't exactly fall within official Alliance channels. It's highly unlikely an invasion and rescue will be attempted in the immediate future. A file has been attached with this message. All information the Alliance has gathered about the Annunaki and Krace is contained within. I don't know if it will be of any help, but we were able to liberate Vandi by weakening and confusing the enemy before the invading fleet arrived. Perhaps you can do the same. I wish I was there to help and I'm determined to see you as soon as possible," Vincenzo said.

"He did what was asked and he did it well. If the planet Vandi could be freed, Earth can as well. Randy, get as many people as needed to review the information about our enemy. At least we have names for them now. We must begin to consider proactive operations that will inflict damage upon their infrastructure. We must find a way to make the Alliance reconsider their position. Analyze the hell out of the information; there must be an answer in there somewhere," Enzo said.

"I'll distribute the information to my older students. I have some talented problem solvers who have demonstrated great intelligence. My students are not experts and don't have college degrees, but they're passionate and willing to tackle any problem given to them," Gail said. "We need as many people working on this as possible. I'll provide the information to everyone in the community. A week from now we will meet and share what we have discovered," Enzo said.

A crowd of the most disgusting looking humans he'd ever seen was waiting for Alixias to speak. The people on Mars removed their normal space suits once safely ensconced inside the Alliance ETS design. Patrick couldn't remember ever seeing a group of people in such desperate need of a shower.

"Greetings, my name is Alixias. My species originated and evolved on this planet. We advanced into intelligent animals and a society in much the same way as mankind. I will summarize the recent events that have put Earth and this solar system in jeopardy."

Patrick listened as Alixias spent considerable time explaining the recent events on Vandi and how the battle left Earth and Mars vulnerable and inaccessible. "You have been ignored here on Mars. It is a mistake by the Annunaki. Power still flows from an ancient source and you have learned to grow food and we have water. There is no reason we can't survive underground, but we need to do more than just survive. We must thrive, learn, and plan. My ancestors made this city their home. We will make it ours and learn the secrets they left us to find. This city has enormous potential; therefore, we must repair as much of the damage as possible and bring it back to life. On Vandi we were enslaved for over one hundred years. Enslavement is torturous and horrible; we must find a way to fight back. We are citizens of Sol and we will overcome," Alixias said.

Patrick listened as the newly arrived Martian woman spoke and waited with the crew of the Intrepid. Nobody said a word, and no one stirred in the courtyard as Alixias finished speaking. A solitary woman rose from the floor at the back of the chamber. She slowly approached Alixias and hugged her. "Welcome home. We shall accomplish much working side by side." Silence reigned until Hector clapped his hands together. The courtyard quickly erupted in applause and celebration. Patrick was impressed. The dirty assemblage was given a purpose and hope for the future. "She's smart. I think we can have the city up and running in a couple of months," Dalton said. "Yes, and she is determined. If we can remain hidden, we might have a chance," Patrick replied.

The mist of the rushing water felt good on his naked body. It was a pleasant distraction from the frustration of not knowing a course of action. Tony sat on top of a waterfall, meditating. He knew he had a purpose but was having difficulty discovering what it was. He spent days trying to figure out what he needed to do. He needed to satisfy the strange hunger in his soul and figure out his destiny. At last he understood part of his need. Answers would not be found on Vandi, Rabanah, or Earth. He understood it was time to explore as he heard a worried friend approaching.

Maxis was growing concerned. Tony isolated himself from everyone in the community. The human was currently residing on top of a nearby cliff overlooking a waterfall. Maxis knew the man was unique and found it unusual he hadn't accompanied his friends back to Rabanah. He really didn't like interrupting whatever the human was doing. "Excuse me, Tony, I wanted to see if all was well with you," he asked gently. "I appreciate your concern. You are a credit to your species and a good father. Are there any available Alliance ships? I require one," Tony replied. "For what purpose and where are you going?" Maxis asked. "I do not know the answer to either question," Tony replied. "Commander Evir will have an answer for you, but he will likely ask you the same question I did. I recommend you give him a different answer if you truly want a ship," Maxis advised. "I will consider your words. Let's go find Evir. I'd like to get underway as soon as possible." "He is planning on entering the pyramid in my village tonight. A large meeting and celebration is planned," Maxis said. "I will celebrate with you. It will be good to spend one last night with friends before I leave," Tony responded.

In the center of the village, the pyramid's entrance was reopened. Commander Evir inspected the structure. It was an empty shell. Anything inside was removed by the Annunaki. He welcomed Vandi citizens as they arrived to view the interior of the structure. From the center of the crowd, Tony and Maxis approached. "It's good to see you. I hope this pyramid will once again be useful to the people of Vandi," he said diplomatically. "I need to leave this planet and require a ship," Tony requested.

"You were offered transport to Rabanah with the rest of your friends. Why do you need a ship now?" Evir asked. "I'm not going to Rabanah. I require a ship to travel to an alternate location," Tony replied. "What is your destination?" Evir asked. "I do not have an exact destination, but my purpose is to help the Alliance. I need a ship to do so," Tony said. "Your request is denied. We need all available vessels to guard the gate. Our enemy could attack at any time and I am not willing to give you any of our ships. You do not have a thorough mission planned. I cannot approve any mission that doesn't inherently increase our chance of success," Evir said. "I respect your position and your decision. I had to ask," Tony replied as he and Maxis walked away. "What will you do now?" Maxis asked. "I will improvise as necessary to accomplish what must be done," Tony replied. "What is it you need to do?" Maxis asked. "I don't know, but I will not fail," Tony replied cryptically.

Evir returned to his quarters and reviewed the available Alliance data regarding Tony. For a recent arrival, there was a great deal of history about the human. The man's metamorphosis was astounding. He faced nearly impossible odds in Vath and succeeded. Evir would have granted the human's request if it didn't violate standard operating procedures and if he knew what Tony's plan entailed.

Evir was hungry and began preparing a meal. Just as he was about to eat, he received an alert. "Commander Evir, a small attack fighter has been stolen and is leaving Vandi. What are your orders?" his second in command inquired. "Let it go. Do not waste additional resources on the craft. Track the course of the vessel if possible and leave all functions available for the pilot. Do not lock out any systems; I know who the pilot is. The mission is classified and is not to be discussed," Evir commanded.

Stealing the ship proved surprisingly easy. Tony was glad he didn't have to injure anyone to take the craft. He was in open space and needed to choose a course. "Computer, how many gates are there in this solar system and where is each located?" he asked. "There are four. The systems of Rabanah, Annunaki,

Cliv and Alliance System 28 are accessible through the gates," the computer reported. "Provide all information available about the Cliv System," Tony asked. "The Cliv System is young. There are currently fifty-five planetesimals. In approximately eight hundred million years it is estimated the system will have seven to ten large planets. It is estimated two planets will be in the habitable zone of the star," the computer responded. "Provide all information about Alliance System 28." Tony asked. "Alliance System 28 is a dead system. One planet circles a dying brown dwarf star. Evidence of a long dead advanced race has been discovered. The planet has been proclaimed a historical site and is protected from mining." Tony set a course for Alliance System 28.

Kathy earned advanced degrees in her fields of study and always worked hard. She could solve almost any problem she encountered. Entering the chamber of the insane Martian was proving more difficult than she thought possible. Small explosives damaged the door but didn't inflict enough damage to open an entrance. She didn't want to damage what was inside and resorted to manual tools. With help from new arrivals, she finally gained entrance to the chamber. Upon entering, she found three sets of Martian remains. Two were in sleeping chambers and the third was near a stone table. Golden tablets were stacked throughout the room. Kathy went to find Alixias and Dalton.

Alixias was spending her time assisting Dalton. With her help, they translated the more complicated sections of the walls quickly. They were learning additional details of Martian history when Kathy approached. "With all the new help, we've finally been able to break into Salkex's chamber. He died sitting in front of a stack of golden tablets," Kathy said. "Let's go see what he accomplished; however, from what I've read about his mental condition, the information is likely to be useless," Alixias said.

Tony navigated the ship past the brown dwarf star and landed on the lone planet of the system. He activated his ETS suit and exited the stolen vessel. The landing location he chose was in the center of what was likely a small town in ages past. He knew this had to be where he'd find his answer. "You have arrived, strange creature. We've been expecting you," a voice next to him said. "You are like me. I didn't know you were there. What is your name?" Tony asked. "My name is Maakla, but I am not like you. You are similar to us in a primitive way," the alien said. "Are there others here?" Tony asked. "Our entire species is here. We haven't been on the surface of this world for thousands of years. I came to the surface only because I knew you would not stop looking for an answer and would eventually find us," Maakla replied. "How many individuals are here?" Tony asked. "There are ninety-two members of our species remaining. Our race will be extinct very soon. We are chemically bound to a rare element that exists here and nowhere else. Just as you seem to be," Maakla said. "What is my purpose? What am I meant to accomplish?" Tony pled for his long-sought answers.

"You have accomplished what you were designed for. Sanity is simply a matter of perception. The chemicals that infected you have served their purpose. You were brought here, but there is no grand design. I don't know what you were meant to accomplish other than arriving here. We have no answers and you must find your own purpose. You will not be allowed to stay here," Maakla said. "Can you help me find enlightenment and guide me to inner peace?" Tony asked. "A species such as yours is repulsive and beneath us. As an individual, you cannot understand what a unified mind like ours has to offer. We choose not to assist an inferior life form. I was gracious enough to return to the surface to meet you, but my hospitality ends now, and I will not answer any additional questions. Leave at once and do not return under any circumstances."

The words from Maakla were confusing and disrespectful. He came for answers and was told there was nothing left to accomplish. Tony wanted to speak, but words would not come. His quest came to a horrible end without resolution and he was angry. "Do not dare speak again and return to your craft," Maakla said. Tony slowly walked away and reentered the ship. He gracefully piloted the fighter off the surface and activated the weapons systems. Nothing in his previous life compared to the absolute rage he felt. The infrared targeting system displayed seventy life forms near the surface. He fired four missiles and killed all of them in an instant. He opened every communication channel available. "There are twenty-two of you left beneath the surface. I have found my purpose and will return. Prepare better answers for my primitive questions," he demanded.

Tony knew the toll of addiction. He was an addict and wasn't getting his fix. What he'd done was very wrong. Maakla insulted him and turned him away. The murderous response was insane. He would follow Maakla's advice and find his own way. It was time to meditate and make a decision on what to do next. He returned to Vandi and landed on the nearest mountaintop.

Alixias entered the lab of the long dead scientist and began translating the tablets. Most of the information was either gibberish or mathematical.

Occasionally, the insane Martian interspersed concerns about being hunted by fourth dimensional beings. She understood the Martian language but did not understand higher mathematics and advanced science. She was unable to make any sense out of most of the information. She translated all the data word for word. With any luck, the humans would understand the advanced mathematics and make use of it.

Patrick was thrust into a leadership position for the inhabitants of Mars. Alixias translated instructions explaining how to divert power and repair the power grid. Slowly but surely power was rerouted and the ancient systems were coming back online. "The transportation tunnel now has power. We can load a pod and see where it goes," Jose said. "Yes, we can, but we don't know if the tunnels are clear and we don't know where we're going," Patrick said. "We will likely be down here for a very long time. Alixias has looked at the controls and says the tracks are free of debris between here and the next stop. If there are additional resources available, we must find them. I am willing to make the journey alone," Jose said. Patrick didn't like the unknown. It was dangerous, but he also knew Jose made a good point. "Use extreme caution and report your findings immediately," he said. "I will. We are surviving, Patrick. We must find new resources and see what else this city has to offer. Who knows what we might find?" Jose said. "Don't kill yourself and take all necessary precautions at the next stop. You will be alone should you injure yourself. If we weren't isolated and in desperate need, I wouldn't let you take such a risk, but go see what you can find," Patrick said.

Enzo paced back and forth with growing frustration. He wasn't used to being isolated and lacking control for so long. "We must do something. Vincent's information indicates the Annunaki have authority over the Krace. We need to target them if possible," he said. "As far as we know, there are only a few Annunaki on the planet," Randy said. "We need to find a way to assassinate the leaders. The last broadcasts showed ships landing in Las Vegas. I think they made sin city their base," Enzo said. "What about producing missiles with the remaining tratium and firing them at selected targets? Or we could try to detonate a nuclear weapon in Las Vegas?" Randy suggested. "No. We will do this the old fashioned way. The Annunaki have technology to detect and destroy missiles immediately. We must get someone close enough to assassinate the leaders," Enzo said. "How in the hell do we get someone from here to Las Vegas?" Randy asked. "I'm working on it; just give me a little time," Enzo responded.

His solitude was short lived. Tony heard the unmistakable sound of Evir approaching. "Did you find what you were looking for?" the Commander asked. "Not yet, but I will return to finish the mission," Tony said. "Why should I let you return? You stole a ship. I should take you into custody. Will this mission of yours help the Alliance defeat the Annunaki?" Evir asked. "Our enemy is evil, and I will do whatever I can to defeat them," Tony replied. "What are you waiting for? It's time for you to quit feeling sorry for yourself. Get off your ass and help the Alliance," Evir said and walked away. It had been quite some time since someone called him out and it was time to act. "You're right. I need to finish what I started," Tony said to himself as he entered the fighter. He intended to complete the mission he started, no matter the cost.

A short time later, Tony returned to Alliance System 28. It was time to communicate with the arrogant species and he opened all communication channels. "Everyone is to remain below the surface of your world except for one. Send one of your kind to the surface. If you fail to follow my instructions, the rest of you will die," Tony said and activated infrared scanning. Shortly after sending his message, he found one heat signature above ground. "Tell the one on the surface to travel north. When your representative is sufficiently far enough from the entrance, I will bring him aboard my vessel. Tony waited for two hours as the heat source moved to the north. There were no other heat signatures present and when he brought the ship down he felt energized. The planet's rare element was affecting him. He exited the fighter with the bullak in hand and approached the alien.

The alien was invisible until Tony activated his infrared display. He proceeded to place restraints on the arms and legs of the alien. "Your species previously did not wish to answer my questions. Are you prepared to give me answers?" Tony asked as he activated a recording device. "I will answer your questions," the alien said. "What is your name?" Tony asked. "My name is Jharaad," the alien responded. "Tell me everything you know about the element that brought me here," Tony said gruffly. The alien proceeded to give him all the acquired knowledge about the element. "It has gone extinct on this planet and isn't found anywhere else. There are still trace amounts scattered in the soil. We have searched for the element in every solar system we could access without success. It can't be reproduced," Jharaad said. "What does your species expect to accomplish in your remaining time?" Tony asked. "We expect to die. Our life span lasts for two thousand of your years, but we are the last and have chosen not to reproduce. Misery and certain death would await any offspring. None of us can leave and those who have tried did not survive long. Without the element, we perish within hours after leaving this planet. Two hundred thousand years ago, we sent autonomous technology into deep space. If the element is found, we will eventually receive a signal. We have hope our species will flourish in the distant future. Embryos have been stored in the event the element is found. Those who remain listen and wait for success," Jharaad explained.

Tony didn't wish to live for two thousand years craving a drug he didn't have access to. "What is my expected lifetime?" he asked. "It's impossible to say. You are not indigenous. You are still young, however. Without the element you might live for another two hundred years, but this estimate is likely inaccurate. We don't know anything about you." Tony couldn't think of any more questions. "I will release you to your people now. Thank you for answering my questions. I offer my apologies for killing many of your remaining species. It's unfortunate I needed to kill your people to receive answers to my questions," he said. "Suicide is not allowed. You did them a favor," Jharaad replied. Tony removed the restraints, deposited the alien near the entrance and set a return course for Vandi.

The news was immensely satisfying. In a nearly unanimous vote, Maxis was elected Ambassador for the citizens of Vandi. He would travel to Rabanah with his wife and son. "Ambassador, your ship has been prepared and is ready for departure," Commander Evir said. Maxis was having difficulty transitioning from slave to leader. "My family and I will be ready shortly," he said.

Maxis joined Tissa and Zanther as their friends gathered nearby. "We suffered together. Now we will enter a new age and will prosper together. Never again will our people be slaves to another species. I will make the Alliance strong and keep Vandi safe. Farewell my friends. If you come to Rabanah please visit," Maxis said as he led his family onto the ship. "We're really going into space?" Zanther asked. "We are, my son. Our lives have been changed forever and you will see wonders you never thought possible," he replied. "Your father and grandfather would be proud of you, Maxis. I know I am," Tissa said.

"Ambassador, we are receiving a message from Commander Evir. He asks we delay departure for a short time. Another passenger will be traveling to Rabanah with us," the navigator relayed. Maxis had been waiting his entire life to see a new world, so a few more minutes didn't matter. "Who is the passenger?" he asked. "The Commander didn't provide the individual's identity," the navigator replied as the hatch opened.

Maxis was surprised when Tony rushed into the ship. "I request permission to accompany you to Rabanah. There is an issue I need to discuss with the council," Tony said. "Permission is granted. I'm a little worried about you, human. We'll have time to talk during the journey, but if you wish to address the council you must first speak with me. Your abilities need to be reassessed as well. It is time for you to visit the physicians on Rabanah. At some point you must explain how you intend to help our cause. We've endured many dangers together, my friend. My family and I will enjoy your company during the journey," Maxis said. "First I need a few days of solitude and rest; I promise we will speak afterwards. I intend to be an asset to the Alliance for all of my remaining days," Tony replied.

Chief Administrator Azira rarely received unplanned visitors. He opened the door and found Ambassador Mox standing in his entryway. "Ambassador, I wasn't expecting any guests tonight," he said. "I didn't wish for you to know of my arrival. You prepare for debate too well," Mox replied. "Why don't you use proper protocol for discussing Alliance matters? What topic do you wish to debate?" Azira asked. "What we discuss must remain between us for now. All citizens of Sol must know the entire truth,"

Mox said. "For what purpose? There is no benefit in revealing the entire history of their solar system," Azira said.

"I've learned a great deal during my lifetime. The majority of intelligent life becomes distrustful when their representatives keep secrets," Mox said. "You have a valid argument but releasing the information does not serve any tangible purpose," Azira replied. "I would argue that disclosing the information does no irreparable damage," Mox said. "Given enough time, I would agree with you, but in the short term, the people of Sol may become distracted which would have a negative impact on operations and decrease the odds of eventual victory," Azira said. As the representative of Earth, Mox wasn't satisfied with political excuses.

"If you don't tell the Martians and humans, I will," she said. "You are still bound by the oath you took while on the Tactical Council. The information has been deemed classified and is not to be shared outside the council. If you release this information, you will be removed from your position and banished from Rabanah." "Such action is of little consequence. My days are numbered. I will do what I must to help the people of Sol. I grow weary and frustrated with your excuses. Good evening, Chief Administrator," Mox replied and left.

Too much time passed since Jose traveled out the transit tube. Patrick found Alixias and asked her to translate the data on the control panel. "He's returning now," she said. "How can you tell? Please explain the information on the console," Patrick said. "Lift your head up. The tube is approaching. You humans make everything so complicated," she walked away laughing.

Jose looked no worse for wear. "What did you discover?" Patrick asked. "The pod stopped at a location very similar to this one. There are many chambers and vast areas to be explored. There's no telling what we might find," Jose said. "I'll meet with Alixias and Dalton. We'll select a group of people to accompany you to the new location. We will expand operations and explore the area. Make sure you stay in contact and share any information that proves useful. Take as many people as necessary," Patrick said.

Chapter 12

Tony did not try to attain inner peace and realized the attempts were an exercise in futility. Instead, he tried to find balance. If he could continue to perform to the best of his ability, he would still be an asset to the Alliance and could help free Earth. He needed to find a way to placate his sudden addictive cravings. The new goal of meditation was to figure out how to keep his sanity and control his anger. A chime indicated someone was at his door and he had no doubt who it was. "Enter," he said.

"Good day to you, Tony. Have the last few days been beneficial for you?" Maxis asked. "The days have not produced a satisfactory answer to my questions, but I'm dedicated to assisting you and Vincent in any way I can," he responded. "You have kept yourself in isolation and meditation is a valuable tool for mental health. It is a practice many advanced species make use of, but there are times when a person needs to share their pain and inner turmoil to learn from it. You need to share what you have been hiding," Maxis said. "Each of our emotions defines us, including pain. My pain, if properly channeled, will help me succeed. Inner turmoil is part of who I am for better or worse. Pain happens in life and helps to define who we are," Tony said.

He'd been living inside a shell and keeping to himself for far too long. Tony wasn't afraid of speaking about what he'd done. Judgment would come from others, but none would be harsher than his own. The friend in front of him truly seemed to care about his well-being, so he told his tale.

Maxis listened to the unusual human's extraordinary story. The Alliance believed the race to be extinct, but Tony found them alive and living under the surface. "The action you took was not appropriate considering the circumstances. You were under no immediate danger or direct threat," Maxis said. "I disagree. Maakla's unwillingness to assist me with this addiction threatens my very existence and my sanity. His obstinacy was not the act of a moral species and was also disrespectful," Tony said. "You should have come back to Vandi and asked for help. As Ambassador of Vandi, I would have made a request for Commander Evir to assist you in obtaining information. You are my friend, Tony, and always will be, but I must report this incident to the Alliance as part of my new responsibilities. It's time for you to heed the advice and opinions of others. You have reached a crossroads and require help," Maxis said. "You're probably right. Once we get to Rabanah I will surrender myself and seek help from my friends," Tony said.

Enzo gathered the entire community in the dining area. "We must strike back at our enemy. I received a message from Vincenzo and for the immediate future we are on our own. There will be no assistance from the aliens Vincenzo has aligned with. We must begin taking small steps and small risks. I must get one person to the United States and conventional travel is out of the question. We need a different way to transport a person a great distance without the enemy detecting the movement. I want you to think about alternative modes of travel and provide any possibilities directly to me. This will not be an easy task and will likely take some time. Be patient and have faith in the process. We must bide our time and gather information. That is all for now," Enzo said. The crowd began filing out when someone spoke up.

"I know how we can get someone across the ocean," a small voice said. Enzo loved children. They always had an answer for anything. He watched as everyone paused and looked at the teenage girl who spoke. "I welcome any suggestion that can help our cause. What is your name young lady?" he asked. "My name is Apollonia. One of our challenges in class was to find a way to cross an ocean under present conditions. After much debate, we arrived at a singular conclusion," Apollonia said. Enzo was amused and interested. "What was your conclusion? How do we solve the problem?" he asked.

Adults rarely took her seriously. Apollonia was annoyed with the big bully; he wasn't taking her seriously. "Modern technology and traditional transportation methods cannot be used. The use of such technology would be immediately detected by the aliens. Patience and a long ocean voyage is the only solution. Unfortunately, Earth's oceans are filled with garbage. Massive amounts litter the Pacific. A vessel camouflaged with the waste that litters our oceans can successfully reach the west coast of the United States. I urge you to discuss this matter with Randy and the experts he brought with him from Leviathan. It's unlikely any of them have come up with a better solution," Apollonia said and abruptly exited.

"You and your staff have been challenged by a fourteen-year-old girl. Do you have a better solution than the one she offered?" Enzo asked Randy. "We've analyzed every option, every variable and the kid is right. There aren't any modern options that could work successfully with any reliability. Our best course of action using modern technology is to fly an aircraft at an extremely low altitude across the ocean at night. My analysts believe there's only a ten percent chance of success and have recommended not trying it. A life would likely be lost," Randy said. "I will give Gail my compliments. Her students are wise beyond their years. Find Gail and retrieve all the research her students conducted on the ocean voyage. I'll meet with Martino and Sandy. An assassin is required. Has there been any progress on the file Vincenzo sent about the Annunaki? Are there any weaknesses we can exploit?" Enzo asked. "The file is still under review, but so far we haven't found anything useful," Randy replied.

Martino listened as Enzo described the upcoming mission. He led a full life and knew his skill set would likely ensure a successful mission. This task would be his last. He would assassinate the leader and find more aliens to kill before he was cut down. "I'll do it," Sandy volunteered. "Wait a minute. This is the perfect assignment for me. I have the experience to ensure it's completed," Martino said. "You've trained me well; I can do this. Do you even know how to sail? As a teenager I used to sail the Pacific Ocean with my parents. You're perfect for the mission, but not for the travel. The community here doesn't need me. The people here need you and your experience, Martino. I'm not needed here, and you are. I don't plan on dying and will make it back here somehow. I'm determined to return to the community and finish what we've started," Sandy said.

Martino wanted to go to Las Vegas and knew he could complete the mission successfully. Sandy was right about the travel. He didn't have any idea how to navigate a sailing vessel. His duty and obligation was to protect Enzo and his interests. The mission to kill alien leaders was a unique opportunity he didn't want to miss. There was no choice but to relent. "You will go to Las Vegas Sandy, but remember what you've learned and be careful," Martino said. "We are in agreement. Sandy will leave as soon as the camouflaged vessel has been prepared," Enzo said.

The primitive boat was absolutely disgusting; oceanic winds would power a small sail and a simple propeller would be used when necessary. "Once you reach the west coast, you must remain hidden and travel to Las Vegas. Use any means of travel necessary, but don't be discovered. Travel only at night. The students promised it wouldn't smell too bad, as most of the garbage surrounding the ship is plastic commonly found in the ocean," Enzo said. "You worry too much. I'll be back before you know it. I don't mind the smell of the sea. I won't disappoint you," Sandy replied.

The tablets were extremely interesting. Alixias was amazed at the brilliance and insanity of the scientist; the Martian was paranoid to the end. "Did Salkex make any discoveries that will help us?" Patrick asked as he walked into the recently unsealed chamber. "It appears he might have; there are two major accomplishments he references. One is summarized and the other is not. The discovery not summarized is highly mathematical. It's not something I can translate and understand. Mathematical experts are required," Alixias said.

"What is the summarized discovery?" Patrick asked. "Salkex found a method of transmitting data through a gate. His research focused on dark matter and how it affected the gates spread throughout the galaxy. He modified the transmitter at the top of this pyramid to send messages to the Alliance, but he never tested it due to his paranoia. According to the information, the signal would be weak but would reach anyone listening on the other side of the gate," Alixias reported.

"What about the second discovery? Do we know anything at all about it?" Patrick asked. "We do not. It's advanced and theoretical. I've asked others to review the data and nobody has figured out what it means so far; it's beyond the current knowledge base here," Alixias replied. "Can we send a message to the Alliance with the modified transmitter?" Patrick asked. "Theoretically speaking we can, but it's untested and unknown technology," Alixias said. "We must attempt to send the Alliance as much information as possible. I want you to summarize what we are doing on Mars and send every piece of information Salkex documented.

We must look at the larger picture. In the grand scheme of things, we are nothing here on Mars. The ability to communicate through a gate could very well change the tide of battle for the Alliance. Communication is essential in any war and we might be able to make a difference. It's a great discovery and the ability to gather intelligence behind enemy lines will be extremely advantageous.

The Alliance must attempt to solve the problem of the second discovery. How long before you can send a message?" Patrick asked. "It won't take too long; all the information has been translated. It's simply a matter of documenting what we want to send. I will also send the information the stasis tube instruments recorded. I reviewed the data and Annunaki ships were traveling in the direction of the Rabanah gate. It's likely the ships are guarding the entrance to this solar system," Alixias said. "Send the information as quickly as possible," Patrick directed.

With help from Dalton and Jose, Alixias prepared a message and was ready to transmit. "The inscriptions Salkex made have been translated word for word and are ready to be sent through the gate on your command. I've encrypted the transmission according to Alliance standard operating procedures," Alixias said. "Activate the modified transmitter and send the information," Patrick ordered. The top ten feet of the pyramid opened, and the fifty-foot transmission device rose into the sky. Salkex's discoveries were sent through the gate to Rabanah.

Chief Administrator Azira prepared to meet with the Tactical Council. The victory at Vandi came with a high price and the Annunaki response was unknown. "Chief Administrator, we have received a weak transmission from the Sol system," his aide reported. "Transmissions cannot traverse the gate. You are in error," Azira responded. "The message comes from Mars and indicates a scientific breakthrough including data transmission through a gate," the aide reported. "Send me the information immediately. Azira read the translated information. A summary of the conditions on Mars indicated the planet was ignored by the Annunaki. A long dead and mentally unstable Martian scientist made two discoveries. The first documented how to communicate through a gate, but the second hadn't been understood by those on Mars. Azira forwarded the message to the science council. "Research everything you can about the Mars transmission. As far as I know, it's been impossible, until now, to send any data through a gate. If the discovery is confirmed, it is tremendous and affords us new options. Work as quickly as possible to decipher the second discovery and confirm the first."

The meeting with the Tactical Council was due to start very shortly. The information sent from Mars would ensure the meeting would be long and smattered with considerable debate. Research on the gates had been ongoing for millennia and the new discovery was astounding. Azira hoped the second discovery would be as groundbreaking as the first.

Sandy arrived too far south. She was near San Diego and sailed north along the coastline and landed near Long Beach. The students' travel plan was quite accurate. She drank the last of her water as the sun appeared above the horizon and fell asleep knowing the next few days would be difficult.

She awoke to a beautiful sunset and prepared herself for the task at hand. She found a beat up old motorcycle and began the journey to Las Vegas. Traveling under a full moon provided enough illumination to travel at a reasonable speed with her lights off.

The glow coming from Las Vegas was bright. Sin City appeared as normal as ever from a distance. Two miles outside the city she hid the bike and walked the rest of the way. The streets and businesses south of the airport were abandoned. She entered the post office across from the airport and began her observations.

President Louis was sick to his stomach. He was forced to watch as his people were put through hellish torture. He wanted to see no more. The Krace were massacring people in atrocious ways to stave off a rebellion. Medieval devices were resurrected to accomplish the required result. He watched in horror as a teenage girl was put on a rack and stretched to death. Bazor forced him to go on a tour of slave encampments. The brutal tactics used by the Krace were varied, efficient and sent a powerful message to those who considered rebelling.

In one camp, slaves slaughtered dogs and cats in preparation for consumption. The guards considered the animals a delicacy. "I'm familiar with your history. At least the mailman won't need to worry anymore," Bazor smirked. President Louis was disgusted. The slaughtered animals were devoted and treasured companions. Many of the slaves recognized him and gave him dirty looks or extended their middle finger toward him. He was angry at his failure and the people of Earth were justified in their hatred. "You underestimate mankind. You will die at our hands in the end," he told Bazor. "Empty threats from a small mind. We were always meant to return and claim this planet as our own. I think I've been entertained sufficiently for the moment. We will return now."

President Louis was given all the time he needed to think. Rarely was he given a chance to interact with anyone since he became enslaved. He regretted the role he played as president. The founding fathers of the United States tried their best to create a system for the people. Through the years politicians lost their morality and focused solely on wealth and power. The Constitution of the United States was perverted and distorted for personal and financial gain. Politicians stopped caring for the people a long time ago. He knew he deserved the dirty looks from his enslaved people; the government should have been working for the people. Instead, the people were working for the government. The shame he felt was overwhelming and he desperately wanted one chance to atone for his selfishness and strike back at the enemy.

McCarran airport was devoid of activity. Sandy located a slave encampment to the west of what used to be a golf course. After three nights of observation, she hadn't seen anyone guarding the people inside. On the fourth night she decided to make contact. She found a young, male teenager lying in the grass. "Hello, my name is Sandy. I'm here to kill the Annunaki leader. Can you tell me where he's staying?" she asked. The boy laughed. "You're funny; I haven't laughed like that for a long time. He's staying at the Bellagio with the President. You might as well kill them both at the same time," the boy said as he continued to laugh. "If you'd open your eyes you'd see I'm not wearing a bracelet and can travel freely. Is he really at the Bellagio?" she asked. Suddenly, the young man sat up and noticed she was armed. "Yeah, he's really there and bullets don't work against alien body armor. They wear it all the time and never take it off," the boy said. "Don't worry, I've got magic bullets. Thanks for the help," Sandy said over her shoulder as she left.

Getting into the Bellagio wouldn't be easy. After two weeks of scouting with high powered binoculars, Sandy observed very few humans entering. Those who were allowed entry wore white robes, but no one ever came out. She didn't understand the significance but knew when an opportunity presented itself.

A woman in a white robe travelled toward the Bellagio. Sandy ran quickly and intercepted the woman before she could enter the foyer. "Why do you wear the robe? What happens inside?" she asked. "How could you not know? Bazor has spread his message throughout all the camps. If we choose to die, we are allowed to save a loved one. I'm dying for my daughter today. She will be spared by the Annunaki," the terrified woman explained. "Tell me your name. I will replace you. I'm not known here by the Annunaki, give me your robe, go home, and take care of your daughter," Sandy said confidently.

The woman hugged Sandy and took off the robe. "My name is Linda Ferrer. I don't know what your purpose is, but thank you," she said and ran down the street as quickly as possible. Sandy removed her clothing except her holster and gun and put on the robe.

"Look, more of your people arrive to save family members," Bazor said triumphantly. President Louis was becoming numb. He'd seen so many atrocities and such evil he didn't care about anything anymore; his failure was absolute. He glanced at the monitor as the latest victims were brought to Bazor and he recognized one of the women. He remembered her vividly. She was violent and responsible for murdering a soldier in Trundle.

Sandy was placed on a strange alien gurney. "Your sacrifice has saved a life. Very few have the honor of being killed by our leader. You have chosen an honorable death and Bazor appreciates your sacrifice," a soldier said. Sandy studied the male Krace. He would die after she killed Bazor. She was placed in a room with six soldiers. The door opened and she tried to reach for her weapon. Automatic restraints suddenly pinned her arms and legs. She couldn't reach her gun. The Annunaki leader's face appeared above her. He ripped open her robe and discovered the weapon. "Another who believes I can be harmed by primitive devices. You have disqualified yourself. Your daughter will be killed, and you will precede her into the afterlife," Bazor said as he plunged a knife deep into her abdomen.

President Louis observed the horror many times before. The woman before him was associated with Enzo. He needed to speak to her before she died. It was possible she knew information which might help in the fight against the invaders. Bazor was surprised when he entered the chamber. "I'd like to comfort this person as she dies. She is someone I once knew and cared for," he lied. "Do as you wish. Her time is very short," Bazor replied.

Sandy was coughing up blood and beginning to lose consciousness. President Louis appeared before her. She hated the man and all he represented. His government was responsible for the death of her entire family. "You've betrayed mankind," she said. "I haven't. Why did Enzo send you here? I must know!" he asked. Sandy knew she was dying and was given no choice but to trust the man. "The gun. Tratium bullets. Will kill Bazor," she said weakly.

President Louis held Sandy's body in his arms. "I apologize for my interruption, but she was a friend to me in the past. May I keep her weapon as a remembrance of our shared history?" he asked. "Keep the weapon. Your primitive devices are amusing and useless," Bazor responded blandly.

Vincent's crew was bored; they needed something to do. He asked Monique to accompany him on a visit to see Mox. Sarah answered the door when the couple arrived. "She is resting right now and is too old to continue much longer. The schedule is wearing her out. I've spent more time assisting her as much as possible and she has taught me a great deal," Sarah said. "Please summon her; I promise to keep the conversation as brief as possible," Vincent said.

Sarah returned carrying Mox and gently placed the aged woman in a chair. "I apologize for entering in such a manner. I didn't wish to expend unnecessary energy attaching all the required apparatus to my body," she said. "No apologies are necessary, Ambassador. We completely understand," Monique said. "We need to take action. The situation on Earth is intolerable. Have you been in contact with Cardonia and is there still civil war on the planet?" Vincent asked. "I received two separate responses from the Cardonians, one from each faction. Both responses are similar in nature and are not very encouraging. Peace has eluded the species and war continues. Each side is willing to help, provided we help them defeat the other faction. It is an offer we cannot accept. The Alliance will not take sides in a civil war," Mox said.

"Recruiting the Cardonians would not be an Alliance operation. The governing rules do not apply. I'm sure I can convince Maxis to send assistance from Vandi and the combined strength might be enough to sway the Tactical Council and convince them to invade. The combined strength of the Cardonia and Vandi militaries will fight side by side. We must try to enlist the assistance of the Cardonians," Vincent replied.

"It may not be an official Alliance operation, but I will not interfere with an internal war. It simply isn't an option. Without Alliance resources, the battle will be lost. Vandi has no military or space-faring craft and the Cardonians have a formidable force. Half of their military is not enough against the Annunaki. We must have the entire military of Cardonia and it's impossible to unite the two factions," Mox said. "Allow my crew and I travel to Cardonia. Let us attempt to negotiate a truce between the two sides. If we are successful I will work with both factions and have twice the force," Vincent said. "There is much danger on the planet. You may get caught in the crossfire and it's easy to be deceived. It will appear tranquil during quiet periods, but the tranquility is interrupted by immediate death from the skies. The planet is violent, and the risk of death is always present. I would advise against the attempt," Mox said. "Goddamn it, we have to do something! I won't stand by doing nothing while the

Annunaki decimate my world. Give us the chance to try!" Vincent exclaimed.

"I believe a successful outcome is unlikely. If I'm wrong, we will gain a valuable ally. I will send a message to dock operations authorizing your departure. Once the council learns of the operation, I will likely be removed from my position. You better start thinking of a replacement for me. Take Sarah with you; I'm sure she's tired of looking after me and she could prove useful during negotiations," Mox said. "You need someone to assist you," Sarah said to Mox. "You are not irreplaceable and it's time for you to learn on your own. Do what you can to help mediate a truce. It will likely prove to be impossible. I will recruit one of my previous aides for assistance. Don't worry about me," Mox replied.

"Thank you. I'm in your debt and promise I won't assist one faction in defeating the other. We will either return with the promise of both governments or we will return with none," Vincent said. "You are not in my debt and the odds are not in your favor. Your mission is likely doomed to fail," Mox replied.

"You are a member of the Alliance and have the unique distinction of becoming the first human to violate our laws," Chief Administrator Azira said. Tony wasn't overly concerned with the Alliance justice system at the moment. "You've spoken with Maxis. He is concerned for my well being. Your new Ambassador is a good Martian. I only broke one law. I conducted my own research and discovered the only law I broke was stealing a ship," Tony said. "This isn't Earth. We don't judge only by what is written. Any crime deemed immoral is reviewed and justice is served. You committed genocide and don't show any apparent remorse," Azira said. "You have no idea how much remorse I have, Chief Administrator. On Earth I saved lives as a doctor and scientist. Taking lives needlessly has made me question my sanity. The only reason I haven't taken my own life is the possibility of helping Earth. If you take away my freedom, I will have no reason to continue this existence," Tony responded.

"If not for your courageous acts on Vandi, the sentence would be swift and immediate. You played a key role in liberating the oppressed. It is a mitigating factor. You will report to your captain and follow his orders. If you deviate from my decision and act out on your own, you will be imprisoned indefinitely," Azira said. "You are a wise leader. I would have handled this situation in precisely the same manner. I regret what I've done. You won't be disappointed in your decision. I will be able to help the Alliance in ways neither you nor I can fathom right now," Tony replied.

The Santa Maria passed swiftly and silently through the gate and into the Cardonia system. Vincent was happy to have his crew together again and Tony was a welcome addition. He missed his unique friend. "Azira has placed you in my custody. We have been through tough times together, but don't overestimate our relationship. You are to adhere to the restrictions that have been placed on you. If you test me, I will report you to the Chief Administrator. Your recent decision making has been flawed. We will arrive in orbit around Cardonia shortly and I expect you to follow my orders," Vincent said. "I'm glad to be back with you, Captain. I've made one bad decision and I don't intend to make it a trend. I promise to help ensure the success of this mission," Tony replied.

"Enough with the legalities already. The planet is approaching," Dominic said. "Isabella, contact the leaders of each faction. Let them know we have arrived and are ready to commence negotiations. Only Sarah and I will leave the ship. I don't know the extent of the danger. The Cardonians have guaranteed a cease fire until we depart. Monique will assume command and return to Rabanah should Sarah and I fail to return. Do not attempt further negotiations if we are killed. Descend to the designated landing location," Vincent commanded. Isabella deftly piloted the Santa Maria through the atmosphere and landed gently on an isolated island. There were only four Cardonians on the island: two leaders, each accompanied by a single guard waiting in the landing zone. One leader was dressed in ornamental orange clothing, the other in yellow. "An interesting race, their pictures don't due them justice," Sarah said.

Vincent was nervous. The Cardonians outside the ship looked ferocious. The species had four legs on their lower body used mainly for locomotion. Their abdomen boasted four arms and the guards wielded multiple weapons. To top it off, the small necks and heads looked highly disproportionate on the strange creatures. "Let's go Sarah. Remain vigilant and prepare for emergency departure if necessary," Vincent directed as he and Sarah exited the safety of the Santa Maria. The guards led them to a small building made of stone.

"Welcome to Cardonia, Captain. My name is Ussi. I am the current leader of my people. The name of my colleague is Yelt," the strange creature in the doorway said. Sarah nodded at Vincent. The two humans dropped to one knee and spread their arms in the air. "We are honored to be here," Vincent said. "You have reviewed our customs and researched our history and we appreciate the gesture," Yelt said.

"We arrive with full diplomatic respect for your species. It is our hope you can rejoin the Alliance in the future," Sarah said. "Your words are satisfactory. The

Alliance has not condoned this meeting. Mox informed us this is not an official negotiation," Ussi replied. "Technically you are correct; if the mission succeeds, we are prepared to vote for Cardonia's admittance back into the Alliance. Our primary purpose is to help your species resolve the continuous war that rages between your two factions," Sarah replied.

Vincent listened to hours of negotiations. Ussi represented the faction known as the Kreti and Yelt was the leader of the Ruti. War raged for centuries over two sacred books called the Nalis. Each side possessed a book. Fighting never stopped as each side tried to recover the book the other possessed. The religious leaders of each faction told their followers the combined knowledge of both books would save their souls. "Why can't the two of you meet together with the books and share the knowledge with all?" Sarah asked. "An ancient edict forbids such an arrangement. A singular leader must unite our people. We don't agree on many issues, but the edict is not one of them. It states there is evil that must be expunged before enlightenment can be attained. The faction that gains possession of both books will have the power to eliminate the evil. The war has been waged to determine which faction deserves possession of the texts."

Vincent hadn't spoken since the introduction and allowed Sarah to proceed with the negotiations. "This has been an historic day that I hope will be a new beginning for the citizens of Cardonia and the Alliance. We should take a break and consider today's conversation. I suggest we rest and resume at sunrise," Vincent said. Sarah, Ussi and Kreti agreed.

The safety of the Santa Maria was welcome. "How were the negotiations?" Monique asked. "Please provide a summary Sarah," Vincent said. The crew listened as Sarah explained the religious war over the sacred texts known as the Nalis. "I don't see how we can unite this species and convince them to help Earth. We should find out which side is most likely to eventually win and assist them," Dominic said. "I told Mox I wouldn't aide one side against the other. It's a course of action we can't consider. Perhaps she was right, enlisting the help of the Cardonians might prove impossible," Vincent said.

"I have an idea. Let me steal the ancient texts so the Cardonians won't have anything to fight over," Tony suggested. "We're here on a diplomatic mission trying to earn the trust of these people. This idea is ludicrous, Tony. If you are caught, the relationship between the Alliance and Cardonia will become hostile. The Cardonians would likely declare war on the Alliance and we don't need new enemies. We can't even defeat the ones we have!" Sarah said. "It's not time for radical plans. We'll meet with the leaders as long as necessary and I have faith we'll eventually find a solution. We must exercise some patience; negotiations usually take a while," Vincent said.

Chief Administrator Azira stared at the report on his screen. Mox was proving just as troublesome in her current capacity as she had previously when she represented Vandi. She approved passage of the Santa Maria without authorization. Somehow, she managed to acquire a security clearance for the ship. Azira wasn't surprised. Mox recruited many allies during her time on Rabanah, but this subversive act would be her last.

The council was meeting and Mox knew it would be her last day as a politician. She was informed by her sources that Azira knew the Santa Maria entered the Cardonia System solely on her authority. The Chief Administrator would put on a show and declare her an outcast. She hadn't decided if she would debate her old nemesis one last time or simply walk away. Any debate would be a repeat of old arguments. She would not give Azira the satisfaction of a lengthy reply. She told her aide to stay home; she would stand alone to face judgment.

"A new situation has occurred which must be addressed before all other issues," Azira said as he addressed the council. Mox dozed off as the Chief Administrator launched into a tirade.

Azira thought he could catch Mox off guard. He should have known her sources would tip her off. As he continued to speak, she continued to sleep. It was time to call for a vote to have Mox removed as Earth's Ambassador. The vote ended quickly and was thirty-seven to eleven in favor of removal. "Former Ambassador Mox, do you have any final words before you leave?" Azira asked as Mox continued to sleep. "Mox, wake up!" Azira shouted.

The sleep was welcome. She heard the Chief Administrator the first time and enjoyed listening as he became more frustrated. "I do have a response for you Azira. I request a more comfortable chair and a pillow for the next Earth Ambassador," she said as she stood up and strode with a strength she no longer knew existed. She heard scattered laughter as she exited the Great Chamber.

The second day of negotiations proved to be worse than the first. Ussi and Yelt fought their old battles and gave up trying to make peace. Sarah attempted to get the discussion back on track but was failing. Vincent was fed up and frustrated. He slammed his fists down on the table. "Your species has been fighting over the Nalis for centuries; it's asinine! Do you wish to eventually join the Alliance? Your war is juvenile, and your species doesn't deserve to be a member. Sarah and I will now return to our ship. Negotiations for today are over but consider what I've said; we will return in the morning," Vincent said as he led Sarah out of the building.

"Damn it. I was slowly making progress," Sarah said. "I didn't see any progress. The leaders were sitting there arguing with each other," Vincent responded. "Yes, but at least they were communicating. Now you've completely screwed up all the progress I made," Sarah said. "Those two needed a kick in the ass and a dose of reality," Vincent argued. "We'll see how your plan works in the morning. Next time, consult with me before you take any unilateral action," Sarah said.

Vincent began to regret his outburst during the negotiations. He didn't see a way the two leaders would ever come to an agreement over the Nalis. Perhaps Tony was right, a more radical plan might be necessary. He summoned Tony to his quarters. "Tell me more of this plan to steal the books. I might consider acting on your suggestion if negotiations fail," he said. "It was an idea I came up with, but I honestly didn't think you'd take it seriously. Stealing the books would prove very difficult. I could probably get one without a problem, but stealing both would not be easy," Tony said. "Perhaps we only need one of the books. Each faction wants both books. If we have one of them, we can negotiate from a position of power," Vincent said. "If we are to gain the assistance of the Cardonians, we must change the status quo. I will need to steal both of the books if you command it," Tony said. "Negotiations will resume in the morning. If there isn't any progress in the next few days, I will implement your plan. Make any preparations you deem necessary in the meantime," Vincent said.

Vincent found Tony waiting for him when he left his quarters in the morning. "I need to hear what's going on during negotiations. Try to ask as many questions as possible about the Nalis. Find out how many guards are protecting the books and their exact location. I will listen and transmit questions as necessary," Tony said as he placed a small transmitter on Vincent's belt and a translucent earpiece in his ear.

Sarah was pacing nervously when he arrived. "Take a deep breath; I'm sure it won't be as bad you expect. Let's resume negotiations," Vincent said. The guards were not waiting when he and Sarah departed the Santa Maria. "Very odd, the guards have accompanied us the previous two days," he said. "Their absence likely has something to do with your outburst yesterday," Sarah said as the duo traveled the short distance to the stone building. "Let's try to make some real progress today," Vincent said.

"Monique, Cardonian ships are converging above our location," Isabella reported. "How many do you detect?" Monique asked. There are thirty and more are arriving every few seconds," Isabella replied. "It appears Vincenzo has pissed off our hosts. Prepare for departure and be ready to activate all stealth capabilities on a moment's notice. Dominic, inform Vincent about the arriving ships and tell him he is in danger," Monique ordered.

"I must apologize for my words yesterday. It was not my intent to offend you and your people, but I felt the negotiations were stalled," Vincent said. "Our species was a member of your Alliance for a brief time. The political niceties required of Alliance representatives don't suit us. The words you spoke yesterday were honest and suited to the occasion and you made your position perfectly clear. I believe you called our sacred religious texts 'asinine.' All people of Cardonia are united in our opinion of you, Captain. You have no respect for our beliefs and customs. The only goal you care about is saving your pathetically weak planet," Ussi said and nodded to the guards.

Sarah was about to respond when blood spurted out her chest. Vincent watched in horror as the guards fired multiple shots into her. "Do you want to be invaded by the Alliance? Stop now!" he said. "You don't represent the Alliance. You are here to beg for your weak and dying species. Take your ship and leave. You will live with the dishonor of knowing she's dead because of your actions. This punishment will haunt you every day for the rest of your life. We will keep the body of your female and add her to our collection of off-world species," Ussi said.

It felt like it took an eternity for the Santa Maria's exterior door to open. Tony moved quickly and was inside the alien building in seconds. The guards were confused, but quickly noticed his arrival. He didn't have any weapons and the two massive guards converged on his position. Vincent tried to tackle the closest guard, but only managed to distract him for a moment. Tony believed the alien's small cranium was a vulnerable target. He choked the approaching guard and twisted his small head until he heard bones snap. When he glanced at Vincent, the second guard slammed two burly legs down on his left arm.

Tony watched as his ulna bone erupted out of his lower left arm. The guard pinned both of his legs and he couldn't get up and fight. The guard bent down and whispered in his ear. "Your species is inferior and juvenile. You're a disgusting race. Perhaps we'll join the Annunaki and exterminate your race. You will be the next casualty," the guard said vehemently. The massive alien raised his hefty appendages over his head. With his right arm, Tony quickly removed the protruding bone from his useless left arm. He was fast and took pleasure as he punctured the neck of the cocky guard with his own bone.

"Don't move or you will die," Vincent said. He recovered a firearm and was pointing it at Ussi and Yelt. "Captain, Cardonian ships are surrounding our position, putting us in a precarious situation," Dominic said. "Quick, get Sarah to the Santa Maria's medical center," Vincent instructed Tony. "I can't. I only have one good arm. Give me the weapon and I'll cover you. You must bring her back to the ship," Tony replied. There wasn't time to debate a course of action or have a discussion. Vincent considered his options and decided to kill the two leaders. Removing the leaders might disorient and confuse the remaining military. "How many millions of lives have been lost over the interpretation of your ancient Nalis? Where are the books?" Vincent asked. "The Nalis are heavily guarded. There is no point in requesting the location. We will die before giving them up," Ussi said. Vincent fired the strange weapon and blew the tiny head off the Cardonian leader.

"Where are the books?" he asked Yelt. "The location of the books is common knowledge. The information is in our historical records," Vincent regretted not conducting enough research on Cardonian history. "I don't have access to a database right now. Tell me where the books are," he demanded. "One of the books is five stories beneath this structure. The other is on the exact opposite side of the planet," Yelt said. "Thank you. I appreciate the information," Vincent said as he activated the weapon. Yelt's lifeless body fell to the ground. Vincent handed the weapon to Tony, picked up Sarah and ran to his ship.

"What the hell happened? Dominic asked as the three crewmembers entered the ship. "Not now. We have to try and save Sarah," Vincent said as he rushed the dying woman to the medical center and placed her in the chamber. "The patient has a sixty-five percent chance of recovery," the computer stated.

Tony observed as Isabella tended to his arm. "I don't know why the Alliance built this ship with only one medical chamber," Isabella said. "Clean the wound and stop the bleeding. I might get light headed but will survive. Place me in the chamber when Sarah has recovered. Until then, we will both do everything we can to help," Tony said as Isabella scanned the wound with a medical scanner. "Oh my God!" she exclaimed. "What's wrong? What is it?" Tony asked. "Your body is healing the wound at an extremely rapid rate. The changes you are undergoing apparently include accelerated healing. Your ulna is in the process of being regenerated. You can now add this discovery to your list of abilities. I expect you will be fully healed within the next few hours," Isabella said.

"Jesus Tony, you can do just about anything. Thank God Sarah will recover. Let's get to the command center; we're not out of danger yet," Vincent said. Isabella was worried about Sarah. She knew the computer would do everything possible to save her friend and decided to join the others in the command center. She needed to know what was going on if she was going to help. Tony was in pain and was very dizzy. No further damage would occur if she moved him. "We need to help Vincent if we can. You can rest in the command center," she said as Tony leaned on her for balance.

"What's our present status?" Vincent asked as he entered the command center. As Monique opened her mouth to respond, the Santa Maria was rocked by a blast. "I've engaged all stealth functions and am piloting the ship out of the atmosphere. Luckily, we are faster and difficult to locate. There are over fifty enemy ships. It's likely the ships are firing on our projected course," Monique replied as the computer interrupted. "Emergency bulkheads engaged due to a hull breach," the computer reported. "Where is the location of the hull breach?" Vincent asked. "The hull breach occurred in the medical center. Medical assistance is no longer available. The patient receiving treatment is no longer onboard the ship. All remaining capabilities are functional. Bulkheads are in place," the computer reported. "Isabella, take over piloting duties and bring us back to the surface. Return to the original landing location and prepare to fire missiles," Vincent ordered.

"I've done what you're about to do. Don't kill these people." Tony said. The pain in his arm was agonizing. He knew what the consequences would be if Vincent sought vengeance. "I'm only going to kill a few Cardonians. I'm going to give the species something to think about. The civil war has been ongoing for too long and it's time to give these people a reason to fight for peace. If I destroy the Nalis, the Cardonians won't have anything left to fight over," Vincent rationalized.

"We have returned to the landing location," Isabella reported. "Remain directly above the structure. Fire missiles and ensure all subterranean facilities have been completely destroyed," Vincent said. "Belay that order!" Monique interjected. "I'm the Captain! What authority do you have to countermand my order?" Vincent asked. "Your order might very well start a war between the Alliance and the Cardonians. The order has not been approved by the Alliance and is short sighted due to your anger. A war with the Cardonians will stretch the already thin Alliance military. I'm sorry Vincenzo, but you don't have the authority to conduct a military operation against the Cardonians. If the Nalis are destroyed, the Cardonians will unite against the entire Alliance in all out war," Monique said.

289

Vincent was pissed. He loved Monique and she embarrassed him in front of the entire crew, but deep down he knew she was right. "Let's get the hell out of here. Set a return course for Rabanah. Isabella, do what you can to help Tony," Vincent commanded. "We are leaving the Cardonia System. Enemy ships are numerous and scattered. It appears the Cardonian fleet is unable to locate our position. A small number of enemy ships are traveling toward the gate, but we are not in danger. The Cardonian spacecraft do not have sufficient speed to catch up or overtake us, assuming they manage to locate our ship," Monique reported. "Take command Monique; I'll be in my quarters. Notify me if we come under attack," Vincent said as he stormed out of the command center.

Sarah was correct when she scolded him about interfering in negotiations. He didn't have the required training and she was dead because he'd been impatient. Vincent looked at himself in the mirror and was repulsed. He thought he knew all the answers and could win any battle. This mission was an absolute failure. He picked up a glass and shattered his image in the mirror. The door to his quarters opened. "I'm sorry, Vincenzo. Sarah was a close friend to all of us," Monique said softly. "Aren't you supposed to be in command right now?" Vincent asked. "There is no danger. We are safe and will pass through the gate shortly," Monique replied.

Isabella suddenly rushed through the doorway. "We've passed through the gate. An Alliance escort was waiting for us. We no longer have control of the Santa Maria and appear to be on course for Rabanah," she said. "This just keeps getting better and better. Advise the escort we have suffered one casualty. It's unlikely they'll respond, but I'm sure someone will be listening," Vincent replied.

Chapter 13

One more adventure awaited Mox if she could live long enough. She made all the necessary preparations and would meet with Vincent one last time. After the meeting, she would never be seen on Rabanah again. "Captain Moretti has arrived and is waiting for you," her aide said. "Prepare for departure and inform Vincent I will be with him momentarily," she said.

The crew of the Santa Maria was allowed to disembark; Vincent was instructed to report to the Great Chamber the following day. Mox sent word for him to report to her immediately. He was anxious and waited for half an hour for her to appear. "Life offers many painful lessons, Captain. I hope you learn from this one," Mox said from behind him. "I should have listened to you. My impatience cost Sarah her life," he replied. "You have a good heart and want what is best for your people. Wisdom comes when we learn from our mistakes. You can choose whether pain destroys you or makes you stronger. This is a pivotal moment in your existence; the choices you make now will define you forever," Mox said.

Vincent always liked Mox. In the past, he failed to put the proper value on her words and he would not do so again. "What happens next?" he asked. "Tomorrow you will report to the Great Chamber. You and your crew will be grounded for the immediate future. Show Monique your gratitude. She saved you from a much worse fate. If you destroyed the Nalis, you would have been banished forever. The position of Earth Ambassador is vacant, and you will once again choose someone for the position. Try to get one of your crew to accept the position, as you cannot be the next ambassador. Your order to destroy the Nalis has been viewed by all member worlds. Your decision making is in doubt and the other ambassadors do not respect you right now," Mox said.

"Your bluntness is refreshing. I will request a volunteer. If I don't get one, I'll assign someone to the position. What about you? You don't have a future here anymore, so what are your plans?" Vincent asked. "I've always wanted to see my ancient home. Until now, my duties and Alliance regulations have prevented me from doing so. This is my last and only opportunity. Perhaps I can assist the small contingent on Mars and do some good with my remaining days. Do not share my plans with anyone else. The next ambassador must be able to plausibly deny any knowledge of my plans. I believe our business is concluded. Do you have any further questions?" Mox asked. "I do not. Thank you for your time Ambassador. I will do the best job I can." He waited for a reply, but there was none. Mox departed surprisingly quickly.

Monique and the crew waited impatiently for Vincent to return to their quarters. "Do we have any booze left?" Vincent asked as he entered. Monique opened the last bottle of champagne and poured a drink for her lover. "What happened with Mox?" she asked. "We need to choose a new ambassador and I've been told my poor decision making eliminates me as a candidate. Does anyone wish to volunteer for the position?" Vincent asked. Among the remaining crew, he didn't expect anyone to volunteer. The task was too daunting, and the position would be overwhelming. He was prepared to assign Isabella the task as she was young, smart and enthusiastic. If she was able to retain the position, she would gain experience and eventual wisdom. "I would like the opportunity to be the next ambassador for Earth. My father is wise. He knew I needed more experience and I've learned much during my time in space. My father knew how to recruit allies; I will do the same," Dominic replied.

"Your father would be proud of you Dominic. I'm proud of you also. You've been an invaluable friend. Serve the interests of Earth to the best of your ability because war is coming. Do what you can for your father and everyone on Earth. The position you are accepting comes with great responsibility," Vincent said. "I welcome the opportunity. I've been waiting to prove my worth to my father for my entire life," Dominic said. "I appreciate the fact you wish to prove yourself to your father. Keep in mind you are representing all of humanity, so proving yourself to your father is not of primary concern. Please remember my words when I select you for the position of ambassador tomorrow," Vincent said.

Council was in session and Vincent felt like he was back in school being scolded by the teacher. Azira was angry and rightfully placed most of the blame on Vincent. "You and your crew are restricted to Rabanah until further notice. Who have you selected for the position of ambassador?" Azira asked. "I have been selected for the position of Ambassador," Dominic stated boldly. "You have much to learn, Ambassador Moretti. I suggest you don't follow the example of your predecessor or your Captain," the Chief Administrator stated.

The plan was audacious and dangerous. Mox called in every ally and favor she had remaining. She didn't enjoy traveling in space and didn't have the experience to command one ship. She was now in command of seven ships recovered from the salvage yard. Only two possessed weaponry and all were unmanned. All tracking devices were removed from each of the ships. She would command her small fleet remotely and the assortment of vessels was fast approaching the Sol outpost.

The boredom of the past was gone. Samya was now responsible for coordinating all Alliance military vessels and ensuring the gate was protected should the Annunaki attack from the other side. "Sir, we have visually detected seven Alliance ships traveling toward the gate at high speed. We've attempted to communicate and haven't received a response. At present speed, the small fleet will reach the gate in two minutes," the intelligence officer reported. "Override their computer and bring the ships in," Samya ordered confidently. "The override command has been sent and I attempted to reroute the ships but failed. The override command is ineffective. Estimated time to gate arrival is now seventy seconds," the officer conveyed. "Send all available fighters to intercept the vessels," Samya ordered. The communications officer sent the order. "Sir, our transmission is being jammed. We are unable to communicate with any of our ships. Fifty-two seconds until gate arrival," stated the officer. "Use the emergency channel. We are out of time! Intercept those ships now!" Samya ordered. "I've contacted the fighters on the emergency channel. The order has been received and acknowledged. The lead pilot reports the fleet will not be intercepted before it reaches the gate. He wants to know if you want him to pursue the ships through the gate." Samya sighed heavily. "Instruct all fighters to return to their previous positions. Under no circumstances are any of the pilots authorized to traverse the gate. Send an update to Chief Administer Azira and include all data retrieved when we scanned the vessels," Samya ordered.

Mox watched her display. It was very close. The fighters almost had enough time to catch up. She refocused on her upcoming task and entered her stasis tube with the data pad. Her ship would be the last to travel through the gate. The two ships with weaponry would go through the gate first and fire on the closest Annunaki vessels. She closed the lid on the stasis tube hoping it wouldn't become her coffin.

"Commander, Alliance ships have traversed the gate and are approaching!" Commander Caltez was given the high honor of guarding the gate and in command of Kracian forces. "Fire at will. Alert Bazor of the enemy incursion," Caltez barked. The Commander observed the first two Alliance ships as they came through the gate and focused their fire on the closet Kracian ship. The lightly armed Alliance transport was destroyed quickly. Five additional ships quickly appeared, but none offered any resistance. "Continue to fire at will. A large invading force is imminent!" she ordered. The ships were successively destroyed in short order. The last vessel exploded magnificently. Shrapnel from the ship traveled quickly in all directions. Caltez opened a channel to the entire fleet. "I expect a large invading force. Prepare for the battle of your lifetime and remember what you're fighting for."

The satisfaction of killing the enemy was overwhelming. Caltez cherished the battle ahead. Time continued to pass without any additional enemy craft entering the Sol System. "What's going on? Where is the invading force?" she asked. "No additional ships have traversed the gate, but we are prepared for battle," a male Krace replied. Caltez was anxious and looked at the display. Debris from the destroyed Alliance ships was everywhere. No intact vessels remained and there were no ships coming through the gate. In all the destruction, she failed to notice a large piece of debris traveling toward the inner solar system and another smaller piece floating back toward the gate. "Stand by. The bulk of the Alliance force will be arriving shortly," she ordered.

Dominic woke to an urgent alarm on his data pad from Chief Administrator Azira. "Guards will arrive in five minutes to escort you to my location." He couldn't help but wonder what was so urgent. Sending guards meant Azira was either worried about his safety, or he was considered an immediate threat to the Alliance.

Azira was pissed; he should have known Mox wouldn't go away quietly. At least she'd sent a probe back through the gate with data on her suicide mission. She also sent a message. The image of his old adversary appeared on the screen. "I apologize for the disruption in your routine, Azira. I'm attempting to reach Mars and offer my assistance. I hope the battle data from the probe will provide some useful information to our military leaders. I have respected your wishes and have not revealed our shared knowledge with the humans. You must find a solution and save the people in the Sol System quickly. Goodbye, my old friend."

"What shared knowledge are you withholding from us?" Dominic asked from the entryway. "It's none of your concern. Do you make a habit of eavesdropping on people?" Azira asked. "I wasn't eavesdropping; I just walked in the room. Perhaps you should shut your door if you wish to keep secrets," Dominic replied. "You are the Ambassador of Earth. Did you have knowledge of Mox's plan?" Azira asked. "I haven't spoken with Mox since we returned. She didn't share any information with me. What did she do?" Dominic asked. He listened as Azira told him the story.

The small stasis craft entered Martian orbit and awoke Mox as programmed. She was confused and unsure of her location, but after a few moments her memory returned. She touched a display activating the landing procedure and the small craft descended toward the surface.

Dalton was happy to be outside again. He'd spent too long under the surface. The dim light from the sun was welcome as he conducted his research in the lost city. As he glanced toward the horizon, he detected movement. Looking more closely, he couldn't believe what he was seeing. An elderly, frail Martian female was slowly walking toward him. She looked as if she would collapse with each step. He ran to her. "Who are you and where did you come from?" he asked. "People help old ladies where I come from," the woman responded. "Of course, my apologies. Let's get you underground," Dalton said as he helped support the weight of the Martian.

Alixias assisted Patrick as they attempted to reroute power to a portion of the living quarters. Dalton ran up out of breath. "What's wrong?" Patrick asked. "Nothing is wrong. We have a new visitor; she is a very old Martian female. I found her walking toward Cydonia. As soon as I found a place for her to lie down, she fell asleep. She hasn't told me anything and I don't know where she came from," Dalton replied. "Are you serious? A Martian? Bring me to her," Alixias said.

Patrick was worried. Change made him nervous. It meant the status quo was no longer constant. Any change had the distinct possibility of danger. As they approached the new arrival, Alixias shrieked.

"It's Ambassador Mox from the Alliance! She used to be the Vandi Ambassador and was the Ambassador for Earth when I left. I don't understand what happened," Alixias said. "Should we wake her?" Patrick asked. "No, let her sleep. The walk must have been exhausting for her. I wonder why she is here," Alixias replied. "Dalton, take Alixias and find out where she landed. See if you can find any supplies, messages, or anything that might be useful," Patrick said.

Mox was surprised she survived the journey to Mars. Like many sessions in council chambers, she rested and still remained fully aware of what was transpiring around her. "There is no need to locate my landing craft. You won't find any supplies or messages," she said and sat up. "Ambassador Mox, welcome to Mars. If there is anything you need, please let me know immediately and I will see to your needs," Patrick said. "Thank you, I look forward to helping in any way I can," Mox said. "What happened Ambassador? Why aren't you on Rabanah?" Alixias asked.

The trio listened as Mox relayed Vincent's failure on Cardonia and how she arrived on Mars. "Is there any possibility you have been followed?" Patrick asked.

"An explosive charge ejected my craft in the general direction of Mars. Propulsion and navigation were not engaged until my craft was well clear of the area. It's highly unlikely I was detected," Mox replied. "Is there any chance the Alliance will invade in the near future?" Dalton asked. "Under present circumstances, the Alliance does not have the military resources available to successfully retake the Sol System. The current priority of the Alliance is to protect the Vandi System and to safeguard Rabanah. Vincent had the best of intentions and was desperate to save Earth. The Cardonia mission was unlikely to succeed, but he chose to attempt it anyway. He felt there was no choice but to try.

"I slept for a very long time on my way here. I've recovered from my walk and I would like to see my ancestral world," Mox said. "If you are prepared, I would enjoy showing you, Ambassador," Alixias said. "I'm no longer an ambassador. Call me Mox."

He was grounded and couldn't take any action. Vincent didn't know what to do next. He was playing Donkey Kong when Tony interrupted him. "Monique was wrong. She never should have belayed your order." he said. Vincent laughed. "I love you like a brother Tony. I appreciate your support. My decision was wrong. Mox told me it was wrong, I lost the opportunity to represent Earth on the council, and Azira has grounded me. Monique was right." Vincent said.

"What options do we have to save Earth now? There are none. Are we supposed to wait for hundreds or thousands of years for the Alliance to finally come up with a plan that might allow us to reclaim our home? Azira is sending a diplomatic ship to Cardonia to reestablish diplomatic negotiations and apologize for what happened. I have researched the Nalis and produced facsimiles that will serve our purpose. I can slip onto the diplomatic ship and steal the texts when we arrive on Cardonia. It's surprising how easily a species can be manipulated with religious dogma. Your decision to destroy the texts was incorrect. Holding the books ransom until Earth is freed is the answer. The Cardonians have been fighting their civil war forever and we must use their experience and tenacity to our advantage. I promise to give myself up if I'm caught and I won't kill anyone unless absolutely necessary, but this will only work if I can trade the false texts for the real ones. If I can't do it successfully, this won't work. I'm supposed to be under your supervision. You will need to report me AWOL when I leave," Tony said.

Vincent wondered why Tony continued to throw surprises at him. First the rescue with Monique and now this. His head was spinning, and he didn't know what to do. "I need time to think, Tony. You've once again taken me completely by surprise. I'll have an answer for you tomorrow night," Vincent said. "I'll see you tomorrow and remember, the ship leaves in two days," Tony replied as he left.

Self doubt and frustration reigned inside his head. Vincent no longer wanted to be in a leadership position. He was unable to determine right from wrong anymore. Tony's proposal made sense and he desperately wanted to authorize the plan. He would request advice and then resign as captain. Monique could lead the small group of humans on Rabanah from this point forward. He called his friend, the Ambassador of Vandi, to request an immediate meeting. He didn't want to share the plan with any of his shipmates.

Maxis arrived within fifteen minutes. "What can I do for you my friend?" he asked. Vincent told him the plan Tony suggested. "He has put you in a difficult position. As a member of the council, I've seen all the information and data on your unauthorized trip to Cardonia. You are not in their good graces at the moment," Maxis said. "This will be my last decision while I'm in command. I'm filled with self doubt and am unable to make a simple decision on my own. Monique will be promoted to captain and I will do what I can to assist her," Vincent replied. "You are too hard on yourself, human. If it weren't for you, Vandi would not be free. Your decision making is not in question as far as I'm concerned. The choice you made on Cardonia was wrong and was made in anger, but It was the only poor decision I've seen you make. You must have reached your own conclusion regarding Tony's proposal. I will not offer you my opinion until I hear yours," Maxis said.

"The plan is too risky. I'd pursue less dangerous options, but there aren't any that will free Earth soon. There are no alternatives other than to wait indefinitely for the Alliance to act. Without any advice, my decision is to let Tony undertake the mission, so I would appreciate your input now," Vincent said.

"A leader who doesn't seek the council of others is a dictator and dictatorships rarely last. He who seeks opinions from others is wise. One individual is unlikely to be more intelligent than many. I am in a unique position to offer you guidance. I was a slave with no possibility of hope or rescue on Vandi. I watched as my family and friends were tortured on a daily basis. Those on Earth are in the same position. I watched time slip by as many of my friends died. It is not a fate anyone should endure. You sought out my advice. I would approve the operation if I were in your position. From what I know about Monique, she would not, so I suggest you retain your command, Captain. You were right to seek assistance. Such questions must be asked by any sentient being. If Tony fails, the Assembly will banish you. A great leader must take risks. Follow your instincts and do anything you can to save your people," Maxis replied.

"Thank you, Ambassador. You are one of my most valued friends and I will continue to seek your council when necessary. I will remain in command and take responsibility for Tony's upcoming mission on Cardonia should the need arise," Vincent said. "Time is running short, Captain. You must go over the mission details and plan for any contingency with Tony immediately. Your fate is in the balance," Maxis said. "I will meet with him immediately."

Mox expected to find a downtrodden and beaten group of humans living in squalor. Instead, she found a determined and cohesive team of individuals restoring life to a long dead city. "What have you learned so far?" she asked. "When we activated the transmitter and sent our message using the formula Salkex supplied, the problems with the power grid disappeared. We don't understand why, but the dead zone surrounding Cydonia is no longer active. Some of the ancient technology such as the internal power sources were working despite the dead zone. We just don't know how. Salkex was brilliant. Just today we found a new cache of hidden gold tablets," Patrick said. "Bring me to his work location. I will attempt to uncover the secrets he was hiding. I plan to live where he worked. I require a decent bed and someone to bring me food and water, please."

The living quarters Salkex subjected himself to were sparse. Mox was used to the comforts her position afforded her on Rabanah, but she would make do with the few comforts the humans could provide. Salkex definitely was insane. Mox was familiar with the old Martian language and understood every word Salkex documented. The clear majority of the latest information was useless; Salkex rarely recorded a coherent thought, but when he did the information was astounding. She reread the latest tablet once more to make sure she hadn't missed anything. "What does it say?" Patrick asked. "Salkex truly was a genius. Technology, biology, astronomy and so much more. He knew it all. The tablet states a civilization prior to the Alliance and the Annunaki seeded the Sol System. The DNA of both Martians and humans were manipulated," Mox said. "Why?" Patrick asked. "For the purpose of reproduction. According to Salkex, the DNA of Martians and humans were manipulated for the specific purpose of eventual interbreeding," Mox replied.

"So, there was an intelligent species in this galaxy before the Alliance?" Patrick asked. "Yes, in the distant past, an unknown and likely extinct species ruled our galaxy. The Alliance discovered evidence of their past existence and has been attempting to discover their accomplishments and cause of their eventual extinction. These questions have occupied the council for millennia, but there have not been any satisfactory answers," Mox said. "Why did the ancient species manipulate the DNA of Martians and humans for mating purposes?" Patrick asked.

"I don't know. On Vandi very few Martians and humans interacted. There were scattered records of successful interbreeding on Vandi. When humans arrived, Martians were distrustful, and it took time to forge a relationship between the species. Martians and humans only began socializing thirty years before the Annunaki invasion. There were a very small number of recorded offspring. If my memory is correct, I believe there were three in total. In one of the last reports received from Vandi before the invasion, it was reported three young hybrid children were killed by the Annunaki due to their uniqueness. There was a rumored fourth child, but no records were found to confirm the existence of a fourth. Sexually, both Martians and humans found their counterpart repulsive for the most part. All research conducted on the hybrid children was destroyed in the invasion," Mox said.

"Why would an ancient species want Martians and humans to live separately and eventually find each other to reproduce? It doesn't make any sense," Patrick asked. "You ask a very good question. Perhaps it's time to find an answer. Unfortunately, I'm past child bearing years. Salkex offers a hypothesis which must be tested, and the results will likely be interesting. We must find Alixias." Mox said.

"Let me make sure I understand your proposal. You wish for me to mate with a human?" Alixias asked. "You understand precisely. You must find a suitable human male and attempt reproduction," Mox replied. "I love science and history, but this request goes beyond both. What you ask is very personal. Reproducing with a human is unnatural; I will not do such a thing," Alixias said.

"Our species and humans were specifically designed to interbreed by an extinct and very ancient civilization. We must discover why, but you are correct; this decision is a personal one. Bringing a child into this world and on this planet is unfair. Death is a real and likely result for such a child. Mating for the purpose of science is unnatural. Reproduction is normally left to nature, but nature's course was disrupted by the Annunaki and the Krace. You are the only female Martian available and capable of reproduction. Are you willing to mate with a human?" Mox asked.

"I will consider your request. I am willing to be a mother to any child I'm able to produce, but do not count on my loyalty for any other purpose. If I can produce offspring with a human, my loyalty will lie with the child. Should such an attempt be successful, the child must be protected at all costs. I will not allow my offspring to become a specimen in a lab.

If I choose to mate with a human, the choice will be mine alone. The human will be required to be a father to our child. If you do not agree to my conditions, I will refuse to participate," Alixias said. "Your conditions are not unreasonable. A mother must protect her child and I know this request goes beyond nature and pushes the boundary of socially acceptable behavior. Your participation is appreciated. Please keep me updated as the situation progresses," Mox said. "I haven't decided to participate for certain. I will consider the information you've shared," Alixias responded.

Vincent watched out the window as cargo was loaded onto the diplomatic ship for departure. Tony was trying to find a way to stash the reproduced versions of the Nalis safely. He watched as the lid to a munitions locker was quickly lifted and lowered. It was extremely unlikely munitions would be used. There wasn't a safer place for the false books. The loading process continued for the next hour. By now, Tony was on the ship and there wasn't anything left for Vincent to do. It was time to raise the remaining crew's morale, so he returned to their quarters and found Monique waiting for him.

"We need to do something. Everyone is going crazy without something constructive to do. What can we do to help Earth?" she asked. "I've taken action and if I fail, you will be in command. There is nothing left to do at the moment," Vincent replied. "What action have you taken?" Monique asked. "I cannot tell you. You would disagree with my decision. If you have knowledge of what I've done, you will be just as guilty if I fail. A new leader with a new vision will be necessary if I'm unsuccessful. I'm still captain and will be held accountable for my success or failure," Vincent replied. "I hope you haven't done anything foolish," Monique said. "We shall see. I will take ownership of the results good or bad. Perhaps it's time for my luck to change," Vincent replied as Monique rolled her eyes.

Tony wasn't having trouble staying hidden on the diplomatic ship but he was having trouble getting food and water. He found many places to hide and sleep which were out of the way and hidden. He took no chances and moved very slowly and deliberate when travelling was necessary. It was easier to eat discarded food than risk entering the dining area. The practice was useful for what would be required on Cardonia. From the disjointed conversations he heard, the ship would be landing within the hour. The craft was scheduled to stay on Cardonia for approximately nine days depending on negotiations. The timeline would prove problematic if he didn't act quickly.

The first of the ancient books was nearby, but the other was on the opposite side of the planet. To get both and return to the ship in time for departure would be a challenge. He waited in the hatch as the lead diplomat from the Alliance approached. The replicated sacred texts were in wrapping that matched the ship's surface. He hoped the man wouldn't detect the anomaly. The Cardonians were only allowing one diplomat from the Alliance to attend negotiations. Tony only had thirty-six seconds to exit as the hatch opened automatically. The diplomat departed and Tony waited. He jumped from the ship right before the hatch sealed.

It took him twenty minutes to travel one hundred yards from the ship. He moved faster when dusk arrived and increased his distance from the ship. After another ten minutes, he was running full speed toward the first location. It took twelve hours and the theft of two ground vehicles to arrive at his first destination. The small temple was guarded by a dozen soldiers. Tony knew he didn't have the luxury of slowly sneaking past the soldiers, so he parked the ground vehicle as close to the structure as possible. He parked it within inches of another vehicle. Many Cardonian citizens visited and paid pilgrimage to the book inside the temple. He set fire to the vehicle and ran to the opposite side of the structure. The guards were distracted, and he entered. Four guards inside the building were given the distinguished honor of protecting the book and all four ran to the window when the vehicle exploded. Tony seized the opportunity and made the exchange, exiting the temple before the guards returned to their posts.

Chapter 14

"Dominic, as Ambassador for Earth can you please find out how I can learn more about the transmission from Mars? I'd like to help if possible. If nothing else, I need something to do," Isabella said. She couldn't handle the boredom any longer and needed to do something. She heard about the transmission that made it through the gate from Mars and wanted to know more about it. "I will speak to Azira. It's time for all of us to contribute more and I think the Chief Administrator has been frustrated with Mox's final actions. I believe he has an ongoing issue with those of us from Sol, but I will speak with him. It is time for me to use the skills I learned from my father," Dominic replied. "I will come with you; an ambassador needs an aide," Monique volunteered. "Good luck and don't do anything reckless," Julia said.

Monique followed Dominic as the two representatives from Earth walked down the ridiculously long hallway leading to the Chief Administrator's office. An alien he didn't recognize was leaving the office and traveling in their direction. From what he could remember, the alien didn't belong to a member world. Dominic took out his data pad and while pretending to study the device he surreptitiously recorded the advancing alien.

Azira was worried. A probe recently returned from the Annunaki System. The enemy was amassing ships at an unexpected rate and was preparing to retaliate immediately. The Annunaki fleet possessed the strength necessary to overwhelm the remaining ships protecting the Vandi System. The Alliance was in serious danger of complete collapse. The battle to free Vandi reduced their military capacity and a new invasion would endanger both Vandi and Rabanah itself.

His thoughts were interrupted as the Earth Ambassador entered his office. "Welcome Ambassador. How may I help you today?" Azira asked. "Those I represent here on Rabanah are growing restless and wish to contribute to the effort to free Earth. I have received a specific request from Isabella who would like to assist in deciphering the message from Mars," Dominic said. "I know you are new to this position. Such trivial matters should be addressed with my senior aide. She can find duties for those who make such requests. I will grant Isabella's request, but please coordinate with my aide for the remainder of your personnel," Azira said.

"Thank you, Chief Administrator. I appreciate you taking a personal interest in this matter. I look forward to working with your office. If there is anything I can do to assist you with any matter in the future, please let me know. I can be very discrete should the need arise," Dominic said. "I require no assistance. On Rabanah we are open and honest with each other. Discretion is not needed here. You must learn the ways of the Alliance," Azira said. "Of course, Chief Administrator. Like you said, I'm new to the position and still learning. I offer my apologies; I meant no disrespect. Good day to you, sir," Dominic said as he left.

"Nice try, but I don't think Azira requires any assistance with problems from the rookie Earth Ambassador," Monique said and laughed. "You might be right, but I think he's hiding something. Did you see the alien we passed on our way in? I haven't seen that species before. I took a video of the individual. I couldn't really tell the sex to be honest. Since you've taken the position of my aide, I want you to find out everything you can about the unknown alien," Dominic said. "For what purpose? I'm sure Azira meets with many different species," Monique said. "My instincts tell me he isn't being completely honest, so we need as much information as possible. Besides what else do you have to do?" Dominic replied.

The simplest part of the mission was behind him. Tony now needed to travel across the planet to secure the second of the sacred books. He liberated another ground vehicle and drove to the flight center he and Vincent reviewed on the maps. Once inside the center, he found flight schedules, but there were no flights directly to the continent. He expected as much. Enemies normally don't visit each other. He found a flight that would land on an island within sixty miles of the continent. The area was constantly changing hands and battles raged sporadically.

Tony didn't face any difficulties boarding the craft. He was able to enter the airship unseen and was riding in a dirigible of some kind. The trip was very unsettling. The dirigibles on Earth didn't fare well and he was on a planet at war. Perhaps civilians were off limits. It was the only reasonable answer. The strange craft landed, and it was time to follow the plan he discussed with Vincent. He traveled to a nearby seaport and located a small marina. There were many vessels to choose from and Tony chose one that was small and sleek. He hoped the vessel would perform like similar watercraft on Earth. He waited until nightfall to begin his journey to capture the second of the sacred books.

Arguments filled the room as she entered. Isabella hadn't seen anything like it during her time on Rabanah. The walls of the room were littered with displays showing complex mathematical computations. She observed as the scientists and mathematicians

317

argued with each other. It was her purpose to try and help, but she realized she was in way over her head. "It's good to see you again, Isabella," a Rabanian male said as he approached. She recognized him instantly. He was the first Rabanian she ever met. "Azmune, it's good to see you again! We didn't know what happened to you after you left so abruptly. How are you recovering?" she asked. "I apologize for my hasty departure, but after my experience on Earth I was anxious to return to my home world and desperate to be with my own people. My recovery is going well. Physically, I've recovered completely and I'm here to assist and strengthen my mental recovery. The people in this room have the most advanced minds available within the Alliance. I studied theoretical science and mathematics; unfortunately, I'm unable to add much to the debate. The calculations are extremely complex and are beyond my present ability. My purpose here is to try and regain my mental focus and become productive again," Azmune said.

"I'm glad you're recovering. We all wondered what happened to you. I apologize on behalf of Earth. We simply didn't have the necessary knowledge or technology to help you. Can you tell me what the problem is here? I thought math was relatively straightforward," Isabella asked.

"Most mathematical computations can be easily solved. The problem everyone is attempting to solve relates to dark matter. It's an equation involving multivariable quantum interdimensional computations. Clearly, it is proving difficult. Dark matter is still not totally understood and exists in multiple dimensions. Variables change and at the present time no one here can quantify the changes. Salkex apparently found a solution, but the research transmitted from Mars was incomplete. The last tablet is missing, and everyone is attempting to complete the computations. To be honest, it's a complete mess," Azmune said.

"Salkex found a way to communicate through the gate, didn't he?" Isabella asked. "Yes, it's how we received the information," Azmune said. "Has a transmission been sent to Mars requesting a search for the missing tablet?" Isabella asked. "I haven't heard a confirmed report, but I'm sure they must have," Azmune said. "Why don't you ask to make certain?"

The chatter in the room ceased when Azmune issued a high pitched shriek interrupting and drowning out all conversations. "Has a request been sent to Mars to try and locate the missing tablet?" Azmune asked. Everyone in the room looked confused. Finally, the information officer responded. "I have no information regarding such a request. If the request was made, I was not informed. Quite often the information is compartmentalized," he said. "Send an immediate request to Mars. We don't have time to find out if a request has previously been sent," Isabella said matter-of-factly. "A message will be transmitted to Mars immediately," the information officer responded. "I knew there was a reason why I was here," Isabella said.

An emergency meeting of the Tactical Council was called. "Report the current military status of Rabanah, Vandi and the remainder of the Alliance," Chief Administrator Azira ordered. "The Annunaki possess more reserve ships than we anticipated. They likely recalled forces we were unaware of from other solar systems. An armada is gathering behind the Annunaki gate. Our most recent probe suggests we will lose both the Vandi and Rabanah Systems. Currently, the Tactical Council recommends evacuating both Vandi and Rabanah. We must retreat to other Alliance worlds to mount a proper defense," the commander replied. Azira was overcome with regret. The decisions he made in the past were now coming back to haunt him. "Initiate emergency evacuation procedures and call an emergency session of the full Assembly," he ordered.

The assignment was a fool's errand. Monique was given a task to keep her busy and nothing more. As an official aide, she could access all unclassified records in the Alliance database. She uploaded the video of the unknown alien. The species was not a member of the Alliance and was known as Osarian. Only a handful of the aliens had ever been observed on Alliance worlds. There was very little information, but she discovered the species didn't apply for membership and their world was visited only once for negotiations. The report indicated planet Osaria was not offered membership into the Alliance due to extreme decadence. According to the report, the Osarians were obsessed with mind altering drugs, sex and corruption. All deviant behaviors and addictions were acceptable, and all desires were satisfied on the planet.

With limited information about the Osarians, Monique decided to study Azira's habits. The alien identified in the picture visited with Azira often. After each visit, the Chief Administrator went on leave for approximately fifteen days and never reported his location. She suspected his absence had something to do with the Osarian and called Dominic. "I've found something, and I'd like to get your opinion."

Dominic arrived, and Monique provided him a summary. "Azira has called an emergency meeting beginning in less than four hours. It's possible he's been supplying the Osarians with money or resources. We have very little time," she said. "Azira told me the Alliance was based on honesty and trust. Perhaps the trust has gone too far, and the ambassadors don't seek out dishonesty any longer. See if you can connect Azira to the Osarians. I will attend the meeting on my own. Continue to work and send me any relevant updates. I think it's possible Azira has been redistributing resources, finances, or both. If that is what's happened, we will need proof. If I were to make a guess, I'd say the Osarians are blackmailing him somehow," Dominic said.

Chief Administrator Azira called the Assembly into session as he'd done thousands of times before. He knew this would be the last time he would do so on Rabanah. "An emergency military declaration has been issued. The Tactical Council calls for retreat. All relevant information has been forwarded to each of you. As per the rules which govern this body, debate on the subject will begin within five minutes. If no member worlds challenge the ruling, it will be effective immediately," Azira said. Dominic awaited word from Monique and with only ten seconds remaining in the debate he addressed the full council for the first time.

Dominic slowly stood. "I have reason to believe Chief Administrator Azira has engaged in illegal activities with the Osarians which has weakened our military. The action he's taken endangers all Alliance worlds." The assembled members were shocked and began talking at once. Dominic was attempting to implicate the leader of the Alliance without any evidence. Azira called for order. "Do you have any evidence for your accusation? If you don't, you'll be removed from this Assembly immediately," Azira warned. "Yes, I do. You've met with an Osarian representative on multiple occasions. The species is not a member of the Alliance, yet you've developed a personal relationship with one of their representatives. Can you explain why you take time away from your duties after your meetings with their representative?" Dominic probed. "I meet with many species to recruit new members and strengthen the Alliance. My personal time has no bearing on any negotiations. We are under threat of imminent attack. I will not bother to respond to a personal attack by the newest member of this council. Unless you have data to back-up your claim, this debate is concluded," Azira said.

Dominic was about to counter when he received a message on his data pad. He couldn't decipher it, but he knew he was out of time. "I have data to back up my claim. Please review transaction CDV2193. I request a fifteen-minute recess in order for all member worlds to review the transaction," Dominic said. "I will not grant the recess. We are short on time and this is an exercise in futility," Azira said. "I invoke council rule sixty-nine. The full council will vote on the request," Ambassador Maxis said. "The request made by Ambassador Maxis of Vandi will be granted according to the rules governing this body. When the recess ends, we will vote," Azira said with finality.

"What the hell is transaction CDV2193?" Dominic asked as Monique arrived in the Great Chamber. "We were all looking for answers and Vincent found an unusual transaction. Azira was diverting tratium and other supplies from the Alliance's military. There are no records indicating where the shipments ended up, but Azira authorized the order. Vandi, and now Earth, have suffered due to the diversion of resources and military equipment. We suspect there are many other transactions that benefitted Azira and weakened the Alliance's ability to wage war," Monique said. "Find as much evidence as possible. The council is about to resume, and I must return," Dominic said. "I'm coming with you," Monique replied.

Time expired, and council was back in session. Dominic and Monique waited as an information officer addressed the Assembly. "Chief Administrator Azira has been found guilty of treason and has been arrested. We are in need of a new leader. Nominations for the position of Chief Administrator will be accepted for the next five minutes. The vote to elect a new leader will commence in fifteen minutes," the information officer stated.

"Holy shit! Justice is swift here," Monique exclaimed. "You did well. The upcoming evacuation might have been avoided if his crimes were discovered earlier," Dominic replied. "Are you going to nominate yourself for the position of Chief Administrator?" Monique asked. "Are you insane? I don't have any experience and I know virtually nothing about the Alliance. I won't nominate myself and I don't know any of these ambassadors well enough to vote for one of them," he replied. "I was just checking. I wanted to see if your new responsibilities and power had gone to your head. What about Maxis? If he's nominated will you vote for him?" Monique asked. "Maxis has more experience than I do, but not much. I doubt if he will be nominated and I wouldn't vote for him if he were. He has good morals, is highly intelligent and if he had more experience I would vote for him," Dominic replied.

The nominations for Chief Administrator appeared on all chamber displays. Eighteen individuals in total were nominated. Dominic was shocked to see his name among those listed. "What the hell? Who could possibly believe I'm capable of leading the Alliance?" he asked. "You uncovered Azira's deception and apparently you've impressed someone," Monique replied. Dominic indicated he was abstaining and waited for the results to be announced. It was the longest ten minutes of his life. Finally, the information officer approached. "The results have been tabulated. The new Chief Administrator is Kizak of the Pokara System. Voting results have been posted on your screens," the information officer reported.

Dominic took a deep breath. He didn't want to be Chief Administrator. He was barely able to function as an ambassador. He looked at the results. Kizak was elected with fifty-eight percent of the vote. Dominic received only four percent of the vote. "It looks like a couple of people voted for me. I'll need to find out who and talk some sense into them," he said. "I think you're right. I wouldn't have voted for you," Monique replied. "I'm glad I have such great support from my aide," Dominic laughed. "Quiet, Kizak is about to speak," Monique said.

"We begin anew today. The Alliance is facing the gravest of dangers. I would like to thank the Earth Ambassador for uncovering the immoral and traitorous acts of Azira. The Alliance is based on trust and honesty. Those in a position of power must be more closely scrutinized than the populace they represent. From this day forward, all activities of the Chief Administrator will be monitored and recorded starting with myself. The resources Azira gifted to the Osarians will be recovered. I will assemble a task force to recover our property and negotiate with the Osarians.

Ambassador Moretti, I've chosen you to lead the task force. Do you accept the assignment?" Kizak asked.

Dominic could only handle so many surprises in one day. "I will do what I must to protect the Alliance. I will require a briefing and intelligence regarding the Osarian mission. If I'm sufficiently prepared with the required information, I accept the task. I would like my shipmates from Earth to accompany me on the mission to Osaria," he replied. "I would like to accompany the task force and assist as necessary," Maxis interjected. "The requests from the Earth and Vandi Ambassadors are both granted. Azira is being questioned now. We will obtain as many details as possible about his time on Osaria. The information will be forwarded to you as soon as possible, but time is short. Begin conducting research and prepare for departure tomorrow. Additional information will be sent regarding their society once you are en route.

Immediate evacuation orders have been issued for Vandi and Rabanah. We must regroup and fight the Annunaki on all possible fronts. It is likely Vandi will be retaken and Rabanah will be lost for the first time in history. Council members will not evacuate at this time as the Annunaki threat is not yet imminent. We will continue to meet until ordered to evacuate by the Tactical Council. Evacuation of the general populace commences now," Kizak ordered.

A transmission arrived from the Alliance. Patrick summoned Mox and they reviewed the information, "A missing tablet? We sent the Alliance every piece of information from all the tablets we could find," Patrick said. "The message is urgent. We must search for the missing tablet; any of Salkex's travelled areas must be searched," Mox replied. "I'll gather as many people as possible and the search will begin at once," Patrick said.

Just shy of a day later, the search hadn't yielded any results and Mox slept most of the time. Nature called and she painfully bent down and removed the doorstop leading to Salkex's personal bathroom. It was heavy and wrapped to keep it from sliding across the floor. Mox unpeeled the wrapping and discovered the missing tablet. She called for Patrick and directed him to have Alixias translate the information and send it to the Alliance at once.

Vincent watched as events unfolded in the council chamber. He was happy to have something productive to do but was worried about Tony. "Dominic, you've performed a miracle. Good job, it will be nice to have something to do," he said. "It wasn't me. Your girlfriend did all the hard work and research; thank her. Time is short before we are scheduled to depart and we must review every piece of information

Kizak provides us about the Osarians. We don't want to screw this up," Dominic replied.

The water was calm, and Tony was travelling as fast as possible in his stolen boat. The coast was quickly approaching, and he didn't plan on committing suicide. Military forces on the shore wouldn't let any unidentified boat approach too closely. He was able to see the shoreline through the light fog about three miles away. Not knowing how well the coastline was protected, he jumped off the vessel and prepared himself for a long swim. The boat continued unpiloted and came within a mile of the shore before it was destroyed. Luckily, the swim was not difficult. He even managed to catch a fish and eat it along the way. It took him a few hours to reach land and after a twenty-minute rest, he clambered up the hillside into a small town. All the businesses in town were closed for the night. Every building was elevated and stairways were required for entrance. The land was strange and despite traveling inland he was in a swamp. Most of the elevated dwellings displayed a singular orange light. Tony found an empty dwelling without a light and entered. He fell asleep immediately.

Morning came much too quickly. The residents of the town were screaming for an unknown reason. Tony peered out through a crack in the structure and observed as a large mammal was hunted and killed. A sole villager approached the beast and signaled its death. The townsfolk attacked the huge beast and took as much meat and flesh as possible.

The savagery was surprising. If first appearances were any indication, this continent was vastly different than the one he just came from. The populace was more brutal and primitive. Analyzing different aspects of their unusual society could wait. He refocused on his singular task; to stay on schedule he would have to travel quickly. After an hour of running north, he found an elevated track and followed it until he reached a supply depot. A heavy cargo carrier designed to transport tons of material approached. For the next hour the supplies from the depot were loaded, but only a quarter of the capacity was used. When he entered what he thought was an empty container, he noticed a lone individual in the opposite corner sleeping. Tony was sure he wasn't seen. It was time to sleep and prepare himself for the danger ahead.

When the carrier stopped, the Cardonian in the container walked right past him and disembarked. Tony couldn't believe his luck. When he looked around, he knew the underground temple was only a few hundred yards away. Within fifteen minutes he stole the book, left the replica and was back in the carrier. He was ahead of schedule and finally possessed both sacred books. The exertion and stress left him sweaty and worn out. He suddenly felt light headed and needed to lie down. As he was falling asleep, he noticed the stranger was back in the corner of the container.

The crew of the Santa Maria finally had something productive to do. The command center was filled with activity as departure approached. "Maxis, I'm pleased you are here. Why did you make the request to accompany us?" Vincent asked. "The citizens of Vandi will be evacuated successfully and my people will be safe very soon. I wanted to help, but also gain experience negotiating with a non-member world. Kizak was impressed with Dominic. He is new to the position of Chief Administrator and let his emotions overwhelm his sense of duty. He should have sent a more experienced task force to Osaria. He could also be testing you. Either way, you and your crew lack experience. I have very little myself. On Vandi I spent my youth and much of my adult life studying the information in the data pad my grandfather left behind. I reviewed debates and read my grandfather's notes. He documented his time as ambassador. I would steal the device from my father and study his interaction with other worlds. You have a second chance Vincent. I suggest you seek council on matters that affect the mission and could potentially impact the Alliance. You must use restraint when necessary. Earth will not be saved in a single day," Maxis said.

"I appreciate your help. I'm in command and my orders are to be obeyed. However, the opinions of my crew will be given greater consideration in the future. In the end we all have the same goal. Set course for the Osarian System at maximum speed," Vincent ordered.

Chapter 15

Tony felt horrible. He knew he slept too long and didn't feel right. Someone was putting water in his mouth. He swallowed and sat up. After taking in his surroundings he found himself on a platform in one of the villages. The stranger from the cargo container was standing before him. He didn't know where he was, and he was tied down. The stranger held a translation device. "You have had a fever and are recovering. The sacred books were in your possession. You stole the most sacred documents in our history. Why are you here and what is your purpose?" the stranger demanded.

"How long have I been asleep?" Tony asked. "You've been fighting a fever for eleven days," the stranger responded. "Is the negotiation team from the Alliance still on the planet?" Tony asked. "The ship from the Alliance left seven days ago."

Tony was crushed. He failed and was now a prisoner on the planet. The sacred Nalis were gone and he would likely be killed. "No more questions; you must now answer mine," the stranger said. "I refuse to cooperate. Set me free or kill me. The choice is simple and it's yours," Tony said bluntly. "You don't understand Cardonia very well, my friend. There are those who choose to follow the words in the Nalis and there are those who believe the words within are designed to control people. You are not our prisoner. My people hide from those who believe in the Nalis. We are persecuted without valid moral reason. I hope we are on the same side. The only reason you have been restrained was for me to have a chance to speak with you. I will now remove the restraints. The Nalis are directly in front of you. You can choose to take them and run, or you can sit, and we can talk. My name is Salk."

Tony was still reeling from his failure when he sat up. He was hot, felt light headed and tried to focus his eyes. The Nalis was on the ground in front of him as Salk stated. "You have helped me. I am in your debt and grateful to be alive, but I don't understand. From what I was taught, there are only two factions on Cardonia. Both are loyal to the teachings of the Nalis. Who are you and what is your purpose?" he asked. "There are not many of us. It's impossible to defy religious rituals and live openly in Cardonian Society. Our singular purpose is to continue to exist and protect each other as best we can. Perhaps someday we will have enough members to mount a rebellion. "Why do you have the Nalis and where are you going?" Salk asked. Tony spent the next hour explaining who he was, where he came from and why he had the Nalis.

"Your abilities are unusual. We would be happy to accept you as a member of our small community. In time, we will find a way to return you to your people," Salk said. "There aren't many options for me right now. I gratefully accept your offer and I will use my skills to assist everyone in the community until I leave. Once I'm back on Rabanah, I will alert the council to your presence. It's possible the council might send some covert assistance in the future," Tony said.

Monique marveled at the planet of Osaria; it looked like paradise. The world consisted of thousands of islands surrounded by a bright yellow ocean. "Is there a mainland anywhere?" she asked. "The largest island is called Walzak and is located on the opposite side of the planet. The island is approximately the size of Greenland on Earth. The planet is ruled by a single individual known as Pivallu. He is the wealthiest man on Osaria and the de facto dictator. Azira conducted his illegal transactions with the leader. He reluctantly agreed to meet with us, but it's unlikely he will be very cooperative.

Maxis and I will be the only ones on the surface. Everyone else is to remain on the ship. Under no circumstances is anyone to set foot on this decadent planet. Vincent is in command on the ship and I'm in command on the ground," Dominic said.

"Captain, we are approaching the landing coordinates," Isabella reported. As the ship drew closer, local inhabitants pointed at the Santa Maria and many ran toward the landing location. "Holy shit. Most of those aliens aren't wearing clothes. There must be hundreds of them," Vincent said. "Some are carrying sacks and bottles," Monique said. "It's likely drugs and booze. The local population sells anything possible to off world species," Dominic cautioned. Osarians began banging on the hatches and the ship's exterior before it completely stopped moving.

"There's no way I'm going out into that madness," Maxis said. Security personnel quickly arrived and began clearing Osarians away from the primary hatch. "Vincent, return to orbit. We'll contact you when the meeting ends. Let's go Maxis," Dominic said as he opened the door. Everything within his field of vision was surreal. There were Osarians everywhere. Nearly all appeared to be under the influence of drugs or alcohol. The heights of the individuals ranged from two feet to thirty feet and body types varied drastically. All were somewhat humanoid in appearance. Dominic observed individuals with skin, scales, feathers and any number of combinations. Everyone in the area was trying to get their attention. He couldn't help but be fascinated with a pink skinned, short and sleek female. She had a tail, bright pink eyes and a painted body.

"Stay focused," Maxis said. "I'm trying, but there are quite a few distractions," Dominic replied. "I was talking to myself. It's good advice for both of us. The vast majority of these people are native to Osaria. They've been surgically modified to accommodate the taste of off-world species," Maxis replied.

After ten minutes, Dominic and Maxis were led into Pivallu's palatial estate. The leader was surrounded by security and a dozen unaltered Osarian females. Dominic closed his eyes and took a deep breath. "We are here to discuss matters of grave importance. If you are to take us seriously, please dismiss all personnel unessential to negotiations," he said. Pivallu waved a hand. The women exited immediately and only security guards remained.

"I've never been visited by two Alliance Ambassadors before. Let us share a drink," Pivallu said as he retrieved a bottle. "We appreciate the offer, but for the purpose of these negotiations we've brought our own water," Dominic said. "On Osaria it's disrespectful to refuse a drink from your host, but I will get to the point. What is your purpose here?" Pivallu asked. "In the past, you have negotiated transactions with Azira of Rabanah. The Alliance has declared all his transactions null and void. You corrupted the leader of the Alliance with gambling, sex, alcohol and drugs. After you cheated him at the gambling tables he owed you money. You used the debt to control him and your actions are immoral. We request the return of all materials and resources he provided to you. Our records indicate you made a few small payments to Azira," Dominic said.

"I did no such thing to Azira. He came here on his own accord. Many visitors on Osaria use poor judgment and I refuse to be held accountable for the bad decisions of one person," Pivallu said with disdain. Maxis didn't like the man. He was cocky and held too much power. "We have differences of opinion. You believe Azira made poor choices, but we believe he was intentionally targeted and corrupted by you, Pivallu. The Alliance has vast resources and an excellent space fleet. We wish to avoid a conflict if necessary," Maxis said. "Have you looked outside? Do you see what this planet has to offer? Azira was powerful and the leader of the Alliance. How many more leaders do you think visit this world? You are entering dangerous territory; I suggest you chose your words carefully," Pivallu replied. Dominic was about to respond when Maxis interrupted. "We appreciate your candor. I suggest we recess until tomorrow. You have given us much to consider. We made a long journey and are still adjusting to the conditions on this world. We respect your position as leader of Osaria. I believe we will eventually arrive at an agreement beneficial to both parties," he said. "We shall reconvene tomorrow, but remember, I have many powerful allies. Your position here is tenuous," Pivallu replied. Dominic transmitted a signal to the Santa Maria for retrieval.

The crowd was even larger the second time the Santa Maria landed. Vincent observed as security personnel slowly navigated through the crowd with Dominic and Maxis in tow. The two were disheveled as they entered the ship. "How did it go?" he asked. "It went as expected. Pivallu is reluctant to give up what he believes was legitimately procured, but we will meet with him again tomorrow. Please return to orbit," Dominic said. "Are you sure we can't stay down here for just one night? It's an excellent opportunity to study this species," Julia asked. "Absolutely not. We're in this mess because of what happened to Azira here," Dominic said.

Alixias recently began observing human males as part of her daily routine. She was having trouble selecting a possible candidate for the purpose of reproduction. She asked Mox why it was necessary with Vandi now free. Surely a Martian and a human would reproduce at some point in the near future. Mox stated the Vandi System was still at risk. There could be no guarantee that such a child would reach adulthood. Alixias enjoyed Dalton's company; he was intelligent, funny, and she considered selecting him. However, due to his advanced age, she decided he would likely die during the developmental years of their child.

She decided upon another. "Patrick, would you like to join me for a meal? I'd like to discuss some of the latest information I've translated," Alixias asked. "Sure, should I ask Dalton to join us?" he replied. "I have additional matters to discuss with Dalton and will meet with him separately tomorrow," Alixias responded.

Patrick normally enjoyed Alixias's company; she was a great problem solver who'd proven to be invaluable in her short time on Mars. She was confident and overbearing at times and she was now rehashing trivial matters that were already resolved. He had never seen her this way. She was talking incessantly. He didn't understand Martians but sensed something was wrong. "Is everything alright? You don't seem to be yourself tonight," he asked as he took a bite of his food. "Would you like to mate?" she asked.

Patrick turned his head just in time to avoid spitting food all over Alixias. He coughed and turned red. The translator must have made a mistake. "I think the translator is malfunctioning. Could you please repeat what you just said?" Patrick asked. "I asked if you would like to mate," Alixias replied. Patrick never felt more uncomfortable and awkward in his entire life. He wished to be anywhere else, but Alixias stared at him, waiting for an answer. "Your question is unusual. Why do you ask it?" he replied. Patrick listened for the next ten minutes as Alixias explained what she'd learned. He was fascinated by Salkex's discovery and saddened by what happened to the offspring of the Martians and humans on Vandi.

"The request Mox made is scientifically sound. There was a purpose in designing our species to eventually interbreed and the reason must be uncovered. Please understand I must take some time to consider what you've asked. You are prepared to be a mother to a child, but I need time to process all the information and understand what my role as father will be. Such a child will require parents who are united and able to cooperate," Patrick said. "I agree with you. Take the necessary time you require to process the information and find an answer. I'll be awaiting your response," Alixias said. "I will provide an answer as quickly as possible. I'm honored you've selected me as a possible mate," Patrick replied.

Mox was extremely uncomfortable physically but had never been more content. She instinctively felt at home on Mars. The comforts she enjoyed on Rabanah were not present on her ancestral home world and sorely missed. The humans were accommodating her as best as possible under the primitive conditions. It was now time to sleep. The bed would not heat and massage her failing muscles as she was accustomed to on Rabanah. A computer would not analyze her physical condition and administer medication. She knew sleep was necessary and would be difficult to attain. Her data pad indicated she had a new message. Alixias was requesting a meeting. Mox responded and instructed Alixias to report at midday tomorrow. She would finally share the knowledge hidden from the people of Sol at the meeting. The burden of the secret bothered her. She deactivated the data pad and prepared for a night of fitful rest.

Alixias spent her night thinking about Patrick's response to her request. It was rational, and she respected the human for taking the time to evaluate the situation. Her meeting with Mox was approaching and Alixias was comfortable with all the recent decisions she made. The situation was unique, and she required the wisdom of the wise ambassador.

Mox was a revered and distinguished leader for all those she represented and respected within the community and the Alliance. Alixias always gave the former ambassador great leeway knowing she was having difficulty resting, but Mox was now over an hour late. Alixias walked to her quarters intending to help Mox prepare for the day.

"Ambassador, I apologize for interrupting your sleep, but we had a meeting scheduled this afternoon," she said as she entered the sleeping chamber. Ambassador Mox didn't move. Alixias ran to the bed. She placed her hands on Mox's cold ears. She was gone. Alixias called the human in charge of operations on Mars. "Patrick, Mox is dead. We must make arrangements and honor her life," Alixias said. "I offer you my condolences; Ambassador Mox will be missed. She was a great leader," Patrick replied. "Please meet me in an hour. I will need your assistance to provide Ambassador Mox with a proper Martian service," Alixias said.

Alixias studied the ways of her ancestors. When Mars was alive and vibrant, the dead were launched into the sea on a sheet of ice. When the ice melted, the body of the deceased eventually descended to the sea floor. Aquatic life forms fed on the body and multiplied, perpetuating the cycle of life, but seas on Mars no longer existed. There wasn't a precedent to dispose the body of a native Martian on land, but Alixias was determined to honor Mox. Patrick sent medical personnel to assist with any requests. "The body of Ambassador Mox is to be preserved in its current condition as long as possible. Please see to my request. You have until sunset," Alixias said. "We will preserve the body to the best of our ability," one of the doctors responded.

"Is there anything else I can do to help?" Patrick asked as he entered the room. "Yes, as the human leader on Mars I request your assistance. I require ice. I need a single large block measuring ten by ten of your feet. I need volunteers to transport the ice and Ambassador Mox to the lowest point in the nearby valley. We will honor her at sunrise tomorrow," Alixias replied. "I will see to it immediately," Patrick responded.

The death of Mox caught him by surprise and Patrick was doing everything he could to accommodate Alixias' requests. He quickly assembled a work crew to make the required ice and sent a message to everyone requesting volunteers for the journey. After a brief consultation with the doctors, it was determined the best way to preserve Ambassador Mox's body was to freeze it.

Alixias requested much of Patrick and hoped there would be no delays. "What is the current status of my requests?" she asked. "I've been monitoring all aspects of your requirements and we are on schedule. We will be ready to depart for the valley at your command. The steel chamber will arrive shortly as will the ice sheet. Nearly every member of our community has volunteered to accompany the body of Mox to your indicated location. We will honor her life and accomplishments as you've requested. We have concluded the best way to preserve her body is to encase it in ice. Is the procedure satisfactory?" Patrick said. "Yes, ice is most efficient. This action will fulfill my wishes," Alixias stated.

"Have you reached a decision on my mating request?" Alixias asked. "If it's agreeable, we can meet late tonight after the ceremony. I would like to have some questions answered before I make a final decision," Patrick replied. "I understand. We will meet after the ceremony tomorrow in my quarters," Alixias replied.

Patrick gathered fifty people to assist in preparing for the ceremony. When the steel chamber arrived the body of Mox was placed gently inside. Water was carefully added until the chamber was full. "The steel is to be removed when the ice has solidified. Mox will be entombed in approximately eight thousand pounds of clear ice. Construct a rope and pulley system to lift the ice tomb onto the single sheet. Manufacture a sled to transport the ice," Patrick ordered. "When you move the sled, wet down the sand when necessary to reduce sliding friction, but don't use too much water. Use just enough to moisten the sand for binding purposes," Dalton added.

Under the shadow of the pyramid, Patrick and Dalton supervised all aspects of the operation. The men and women were using pulleys, sleds and sheer manpower to accomplish the work. "I imagine ancient Egypt looked very much like this," Dalton said. "I sincerely hope we aren't regressing as a species. Earth is in shambles and we're lucky to be alive," Patrick replied. "Mox has reached her final resting place. Sunrise is in about an hour. Let's clean up as best as possible before the ceremony," Dalton said.

Alixias didn't sleep well. The overwhelming responsibility of conducting Ambassador Mox's ceremony in a dignified manner was taking a toll. She was up early and needed to ensure everything was in place and ready. Patrick and Dalton were walking in her direction as she exited the pyramid. "The task has been completed as you requested. We will prepare ourselves for the ceremony and return shortly," Patrick said. "I will inspect the work immediately. Thank you for your quick preparations," she replied.

As she approached the site, Alixias became agitated. She wanted the opportunity to send Ambassador Mox out to sea in the traditional method. War transformed her ancestral home world into a wasteland. She was determined to see both Mars and Earth freed. The policies of the Alliance needed to be changed. Mars could be terraformed in just years with current Alliance technology.

Patrick fulfilled his obligation. The body of Ambassador Mox was prepared properly and placed where she requested. The sun crested the horizon and the human inhabitants of Mars began arriving.

Patrick took his place in front as Alixias began to speak. "I am not aware of all of Ambassador Mox's accomplishments, but I know she represented the citizens of Vandi and Sol with dignity and honor. In time we will learn the details of her life. Ambassador Mox did not have Alliance approval for her trip here. We are behind enemy lines and she endangered her own life to help us. Her sacrifice must not be in vain. It is our duty to continue her fight and do whatever is necessary to defeat our enemy.

Within my lifetime, I will make it my mission to see Mars terraformed and capable of hosting my species once again. The atmosphere will be restored, water will once again flow on the surface and native animal species will be reintroduced. The Alliance can reproduce any life form that inhabited Mars in the past. In time, Ambassador Mox will contribute to the life cycle of the planet as our ancestors did. I will become a soldier for Mars and am grateful to Mox for showing me what dedication really means. Prepare Ambassador Mox for her final task," Alixias said.

Patrick and Dalton approached and removed the steel plates. The Ambassador's body could be seen clearly through the ice. "Mox gave her life for the people of Sol and we must dedicate our lives to continuing her work. I invite everyone here to join me when the water arrives to take Mox on her final journey."

Patrick worked for thirty straight hours and was exhausted. He was having trouble thinking and needed sleep before meeting with Alixias. Her words during the ceremony were perfect under the circumstances. The crowd was dispersing and Alixias approached. "You did well Patrick and I appreciate your hard work. Are you ready to meet now?" she asked. "I will sleep for a brief time and meet with you……"

Alixias watched curiously as Patrick fell to the ground. Dalton quickly arrived and placed his hands on the human's neck. "What are you doing?" she asked. "Patrick is unconscious. His vital signs are strong, and he doesn't appear to be in imminent danger. He requires rest, water and food. I will see to it," Dalton said. "I will not allow it. You are more advanced in age and have worked just as hard as Patrick. You must rest and tend to your own health. I will ensure he makes a full recovery," Alixias said as she picked up Patrick. "He will be in my quarters recovering. Do not disturb us for eighteen hours unless an urgent situation arises," Alixias said. "I do need rest. Thank you for taking care of my friend. When I awake I will relieve you of your burden," he said. "Patrick is not a burden; he is important to me. Patrick will seek you out when he is fully recovered. Do you understand?" Alixias asked. Dalton wasn't sure if he understood. "I'm glad my friend is in such capable hands. Please tell him to find me when he wakes up," he said as Alixias walked away with his friend in her arms.

Patrick awoke confused and unsure of his whereabouts. "Welcome back. You overexerted yourself and must drink, eat and rest," Alixias said as she handed him a glass of water and a plate of food. Patrick was not only in her quarters, but also in her bed. He sat up to eat. "I apologize for disturbing you. I will return to my quarters," he said. "You will finish eating and you will sleep here. You should not be alone in your weakened condition. When you are fully rested, we will discuss our unique situation," Alixias replied.

"We must threaten Pivallu with invasion and negotiate from a position of power," Dominic said. "We have no power. The Alliance is in retreat. Vandi will be lost again and the capitol of the Alliance will be taken for the first time in history. We are stretched too thin already and an invasion is out of the question. Pivallu must be given the proper motivation to assist the Alliance. He is only interested in money and power. Greed and corruption are all he knows," Maxis replied.

"I have to agree with Maxis; we cannot create new hostilities," Vincent said.

"I have an idea. Vincent, you will accompany Maxis tomorrow. I will consult with a third party." Vincent and Maxis listened for the next hour as Dominic explained the plan. "It's definitely bold," Maxis said. "You've learned much from your father. If nothing else, it will prove interesting," Vincent said.

Pivallu had many duties which required his attention. Today's meeting with the Alliance Ambassadors would be his last. He would not give up any of the resources gained from Azira. Maxis entered, followed by a new representative. "Maxis, I agreed to meet with you and Dominic today. Who is this new human?" he asked. "I must apologize. Osaria has much to offer. Dominic is likely enjoying the pleasures of this world. I've been unable to contact him. When he failed to report, I was required to find a replacement according to Alliance regulations. My colleague today is Captain Vincent Moretti. He commands our ship and is quite capable of fulfilling Dominic's vacated position," Maxis said.

Pivallu was amused. Once again, an Alliance leader succumbed to the vices of Osaria. A new opportunity arrived and in time, Dominic might be persuaded to fulfill Azira's role. He would corrupt the new ambassador the same way he corrupted Azira. The meeting would end quicker than he thought. "I negotiated with Azira in good faith. He accepted the terms of our arrangement, so there is nothing left to discuss. The time has come for you to leave," he said.

"We will return to Rabanah when negotiations have concluded. Would you give up the resources Azira provided to you if we could guarantee a million visitors from Rabanah each cycle?" Maxis asked. Pivallu was done with negotiations and was ready for the Alliance representatives to leave. "Your offer is worthless. Osaria receives billions of visitors each cycle. You will be returned to your ship now and if you fail to depart you will become my prisoners," he said as his data pad alerted him to a message. His old adversary, Ardol, requested an immediate meeting. He regretted not killing the bitch earlier. She claimed to be his friend while in reality she was accumulating wealth. "Excuse me for a moment," he said.

Ardol's image appeared on his screen and as usual she was nude in her sleeping chambers. "Your interruption better be important. I'm in the middle of a meeting," he said. "Hello Pivallu. I've made a new friend. He wasn't satisfied with negotiations and decided to pay me a visit. I believe you know the human," Ardol said. The view widened and Pivallu was surprised to see Dominic lying in bed next to Ardol. "Good day to you, Pivallu. Your friend has been educating me. Perhaps it's time for new leadership on Osaria. I'm prepared to offer Ardol every resource the Alliance has to ensure she replaces you as leader of Osaria if we fail to reach an arrangement," Dominic said.

Pivallu was impressed. The human surprised him. Very few people were capable of doing so. "Very impressive, Ambassador Moretti. I will no longer wear the cloak of a politician. I rule Osaria completely and have many resources. "You will not exit Ardol's chamber alive. My forces will ensure you don't leave the area and a military ship will arrive shortly to obliterate you both."

"Your ground forces aren't very observant. Relocating Ardol was quite easy, but by all means send your people into her chambers. We're well-hidden and safe in orbit above Osaria. Consider your options carefully if you wish to remain the complete ruler of Osaria. I will now allow you to resume negotiations with my two associates," Dominic said.

Vincent watched as Pivallu threw a tantrum. The alien overturned two tables and began ranting. "Nobody treats me like this. The two of you and all the Alliance will pay a heavy price for treating me so disrespectfully. You will not be allowed to leave until Ardol is dead!" he shouted as he stormed out of the room. "What do we do now?" Vincent asked. "We let him cool down and come to terms with the situation. If he truly feels threatened, he will relent," Maxis replied.

After thirty minutes, Pivallu returned. "I want this situation concluded. What are your terms?" he asked. Maxis was pleased. "Our terms are simple. We will return your small payment for all military supplies and resources you obtained from Azira. I will leave an inventory list with you and once all provisions have been returned, you will receive payment," Maxis said. "Very well, I will negotiate with other parties from now on, but what of Ardol?" he asked. "She has requested asylum within the confines of the Alliance. You will not see her again," Maxis replied. "Our negotiations are concluded. I will ensure you receive transport to your ship, wherever it is," he replied.

Vincent knew all possible help would be necessary to save Earth and Rabanah. "There is another matter I'd like to discuss," he said. Maxis knew of no other matter. The mission was successful, and it was time to leave. He felt Vincent was complicating the situation unnecessarily, but it was crucial to maintain a unified front. He remained silent despite his wish to pull Vincent out of his chair toward the exit. "Our business is done. I have nothing left to discuss; negotiations are complete," Pivallu replied. "I would like discuss the relationship between the Alliance and

Osaria. There is a possibility for a new and profitable coalition," Vincent said.

"What do you propose?" Pivallu asked. "You previously negotiated with Azira. At the time you knew he wasn't operating in official capacity. You took advantage of the Chief Administrator and his weaknesses. We are representatives of the Alliance and wish to have an amicable relationship with all worlds we come into contact with. Our actions here are recorded and will be presented to the council. You and the previous leaders of Osaria have chosen to remain independent. I've reviewed your history and understand why you don't wish to be associated with the Alliance. As a representative of the Alliance, I have the authority to negotiate a new arrangement," Vincent said.

Maxis was surprised. Vincent was given no such authority from the Alliance and completely ignored his advice. The negotiations should have concluded, and the Santa Maria and her crew should have been on their way back to Rabanah. "I grow weary and request a short recess. The thin atmosphere is proving difficult and I'd appreciate some additional oxygen," he said. "Your request is granted. Oxygen will be provided. We will resume negotiations when you are sufficiently recovered," Pivallu responded.

Maxis waited for the Osarian leader to leave the room. "What are you doing?" he asked Vincent. "I'm attempting to assist Vandi, Earth and the Alliance. We need resources," he said. "This wasn't part of the plan. You are endangering the mission," Maxis replied urgently. "We have an opportunity and must make the most if it! Pivallu has quietly constructed a substantial military force. Osaria is defended quite well and only a major invasion could take the planet," Vincent replied. "You have overstepped your bounds, Captain. I will handle the remainder of the negotiations," Maxis said as Pivallu returned. "Please trust me, Maxis. You recently told me not to step down as captain; let me finish this," Vincent said.

"You've spoken in generalities. I require specific information if I'm to consider your request," Pivallu said. "Many wagers are made on this planet and I offer you a new one. If you commit your resources and military to the immediate crisis facing the Alliance, we will allow you to keep everything Azira provided. In addition, I'm prepared to offer you additional resources in the future. We can supply you with military assistance once the upcoming battle has been won," Vincent said.

"You still are unable to provide specific information. What conditions must be met for my deal with Azira to be declared valid?" Pivallu asked. "Vandi and Rabanah must be defended successfully against the Annunaki invasion and Earth must be liberated. If Rabanah is taken, Osaria will be invaded shortly thereafter. It's in your best interest to see the Annunaki defeated. Membership to the Alliance is not necessary for us to become allies," Vincent responded.

"I accept your wager and offer Osaria's assistance and resources. The council must provide a signed copy of the contract before I commit resources in this war," Pivallu said. "We are in agreement. Please ferry us to our vessel," Vincent replied.

Dominic was worried his plan failed. Maxis and Vincent should have returned by now. Pivallu either killed his friends or taken them hostage. "Ambassador, a ship is approaching and is requesting to dock. Vincent and Maxis are onboard and ready to disembark," Monique said. "Thank God. Initiate docking procedure; I'll meet them at the airlock," Dominic replied.

"What happened? What took you so long?" he asked as Vincent and Maxis entered the ship. "The plan worked perfectly. Our Captain decided to negotiate a new deal with the ruler of Osaria," Maxis replied. "What new deal? We didn't discuss any additional negotiations," Dominic asked. "I'll tell you all about it on the way back, but the council has a decision to make. I believe Vincent has helped the Alliance although I don't trust Pivallu. We will find out soon enough," Maxis replied.

Ekraq was as enraged as his counterpart. As the new leaders of Cardonia, it was their responsibility to deal with the most extreme act of terrorism ever committed. The Nalis was stolen and now off planet. "What do you propose we do?" he asked. "The note from the human, Vincent, stated the Nalis would be destroyed if we contacted the Alliance. If the Nalis are destroyed we will face chaos, mass suicide and anarchy. Cardonia will become ungovernable and unlivable. We have no choice but to assist in their war," Olube replied. "How do we know the Nalis will be returned when the war is over?" Ekraq asked. "It's a chance we'll have to take, so we must unite and prepare for battle. In the long term, we will plan retribution against the one who stole the Nalis. I have a contact inside the Alliance. If Vincent wasn't working alone, I'll find out. If the Alliance itself is involved, we will unite and declare war against them," Olube replied vehemently.

Tony did what he could to help Salk and the small community that welcomed him. He stole food and supplies from those who had excess. Salk began organizing his people in a remote, heavily forested area. The people were dirty and disheveled yet appeared happy. He took another drink from the crudely constructed goblet. The alcohol was strangely bitter. A small child played a stringed wooden instrument similar to a guitar.

Tony tried to clear his head and focus. A change occurred from the last time he visited the city. Military spacecraft on the ground were preparing for departure. The plan must have worked. The Cardonian leaders assumed he made it off planet. It was time to take his leave and say goodbye to his new friend. "I have a chance to leave Cardonia and I must make use of this opportunity and do everything I can to return to Rabanah. My mission is not yet complete. You have been a good companion to me and I've enjoyed the company of your people. I will do everything I can to help you in the future," he said. "I knew you would not be able to stay. You've helped more than you know. We will remain hidden and recruit carefully," Salk said. "Good luck. I believe you're doing everything you can under the circumstances and I think your plan is a good one," Tony said as he turned and ran toward the city. Salk was a good leader and Tony wouldn't forget about him.

It took three hours to reach the spaceport where ships were departing at regular intervals. A nearby craft was in the process of being loaded. Tony moved slowly and stayed in the shadows. He entered the cargo hold just as the last of the containers was loaded. The books grew heavy in his hands, but the ancient documents of Cardonia required the utmost respect. He climbed into one of the cargo containers hoping the ship was destined for Rabanah.

Every display in the cargo area changed. A solar system was displayed on each of the screens. The third planet from the star was blinking. The Cardonian ship was destined for Earth. Tony knew his destiny lay elsewhere. A rendezvous was scheduled with an Alliance ship for resupply. When the vessels docked, he would board the Alliance resupply ship and return to his friends.

Chapter 16

The Assembly was in heated debate and in session far longer than normal. "This is to be the last session on Rabanah. All issues must be resolved today or postponed. The Tactical Council has ordered all ambassadors to evacuate when this session is concluded," Dominic said. Vincent listened as the ambassadors discussed his negotiations with Pivallu on Osaria. Chief Administrator Kizak remained silent during the debate, but he now stood, and the chamber fell silent. "Captain Moretti didn't have the authority or approval to negotiate the agreement with the Osarians. We are retreating and facing annihilation. We have insufficient time to continue this debate. The Annunaki invasion will commence soon. The decision of the human wasn't authorized, but it was the correct course of action. Bold actions must be taken if we are to continue our existence. This debate is now closed. Voting will commence immediately on the Osarian issue," Kizak said.

The hole he dug was deep. The vote on his agreement with Osaria could go either way and he still hadn't heard from Tony. Even if he won the vote for his actions on Osaria, he would be vilified for whatever happened on Cardonia. The voting concluded. "Congratulations, Vincent. The Assembly has endorsed and approved your agreement with Pivallu. The vote was close, but the motion passed by three votes. The vote to restructure the Tactical Council was also approved. I think we are heading in the right direction," Dominic said.

Vincent breathed a sigh of relief. He received a brief reprieve from his eventual sentence. He observed as Chief Administrator Kizak proceeded through the formalities and prepared to end the last session on Rabanah. As he was about to adjourn the session, an aide approached and spoke with him quietly. Kizak became agitated as the aide spoke.

"We will not adjourn at this time. A new situation has arisen. The governments on Cardonia have united and are offering to assist the Alliance in the upcoming confrontation with the Annunaki. Another vote is required immediately. The preliminary recommendation from the Tactical Council is to approve the request. There will be no debate on the issue. Each representative will have ten minutes to review the data and voting will commence in fifteen minutes," he said.

"This information doesn't make any sense. Cardonia's civil war has been ongoing for centuries. I don't understand why the Cardonians would set aside their differences suddenly," Dominic said. "You are the Ambassador for Earth, Dominic. Whatever the reason, we must take advantage of the opportunity. Vote for what is in the best interest of Earth," Vincent said. The votes were cast. As the time for voting was coming to an end, Vincent couldn't help but look at the Vandi Ambassador. Maxis returned his look and smiled. He gave his brother from Sol a small nod and returned the smile.

"The vote is unanimous and the offer of assistance from Cardonia will be accepted. Evacuation plans remain unaffected by the latest development. The meeting is adjourned," Chief Administrator Kizak declared. "Why do I think you know something you're not telling me?" Dominic asked. "We all must do what is in the best interest of the Alliance and Earth. Certain questions must remain unanswered. Let's go tell the others and have one last drink before we leave Rabanah," Vincent replied.

"Why are we still evacuating if we are getting additional resources from Osaria and Cardonia?" Monique asked. "The Tactical Council is constantly crunching numbers as variables change. The latest summary indicates we cannot defend Vandi and Rabanah successfully right now. The added military strength may not arrive in time to assist against the invasion," Dominic said. A probe recently returned through the gate from the Annunaki System. The Annunaki Armada is massive, and the invading fleet will be larger than any ever encountered before. I agree with the Tactical Council's opinion," Dominic said. "What about the information Azira withheld from us? Do we have any idea what he was covering up and hiding from the species of Sol?" Monique asked. "I will ask the new Chief Administrator. If he won't tell me, I'll find out another way," Dominic replied.

Kizak monitored the evacuation. The enormity of the task made him feel uneasy. He would board one of the last ships leaving Rabanah. An aide asked if he could meet briefly with the Earth Ambassador. "Tell him to make it quick. I don't have much time to spare," he replied. Dominic entered a moment later. "I would never have imagined Rabanah would need to be evacuated. Have you ever seen such a sight?" Kizak asked as he gestured toward the window.

The scene was amazing. Ships of all kinds covered the sky, and most were leaving the surface. Dominic noticed a few larger ones returning and landing. "The pace of the evacuation is increasing as more craft return for second and third trips. Why did you ask to see me?" Kizak said. "Azira and the council are withholding information from my people. We are growing as a species and it's time to share the information," Dominic said. "I'm new to this position and am not aware of the situation or the information you speak of. I will inquire and find out what I can.

After the evacuation I will contact you and we will meet, but you must leave now. I have much to attend to," Kizak said.

Patrick was warm and comfortable. Alixias was asleep next to him. She insisted he sleep in her quarters due to his collapse. He felt rested and much better. When he returned from the bathroom, Alixias was awake and waiting for him. "You have some questions you wish to ask?" she said. "Yes, thank you for assisting me and allowing me to rest. If we are to bring a child into this world, we must have a plan. I insist in having a role in the educational and emotional development of our child," he said. "You are a being who cares for others and acts in a selfless manner. It's why I selected you," Alixias replied. "There isn't precedence for something like this. Should we live together as mates?" he asked. "It will take time to find out if we are compatible and comfortable with each other. I suggest we take it one step at a time, but I believe we agree on how to raise the child," Alixias said.

He promised Alixias an answer. He liked the Martian and felt at ease around her. "I accept your offer. When would you like to begin?" he asked. Alixias stood up and removed her robe. "As you humans say, there's no time like the present," she said. "Dalton was right. You're a fascinating specimen."

Under almost any circumstances Dalton could focus solely on his work, but Alixias's bizarre behavior disturbed him. The woman kidnapped Patrick for all intents and purposes. He was worried she might have snapped after Mox's death. Why would she want to harm Patrick or keep him secluded? He unraveled mysteries mankind was trying to solve for centuries, but this answer was elusive. Eighteen hours passed, and it was time to retrieve his friend.

Alixias thought she prepared herself physically and emotionally for the attempt of producing a child yet found herself unprepared. The human's passion caught her off guard and his passion ignited hers. She never thought herself capable of such intense reactions and emotions. He was intelligent, capable and understanding. She laid her head down on his chest. "Our relationship needs to be tested. We should share the same quarters. Such an arrangement would be a good first step," she said.

Alixias was a strong-willed female and knew what she wanted. She didn't speak in trivialities and Patrick was attracted to her. The lovemaking started awkwardly and ended spectacularly. "I enjoy your company and suggest we relocate to one of the empty chambers in the pyramid," Patrick replied. "You wish to leave the community?" Alixias asked. "I wish for privacy. Once the other humans learn what we are attempting, they will become curious. We can perform our work during the day and retreat to the privacy of the pyramid at night. Mox was wise. After the last few hours, I'm more convinced than ever that we were intended to reproduce. I've never had such an experience before," Patrick said as someone rattled the stone door.

"It's likely Dalton. He was confused when I picked you up and brought you to my quarters. I told him to check on you in eighteen hours. The time has arrived. Comfort your friend and consider what has occurred. We will meet later and arrange our new living quarters. The effort to produce a child must continue," Alixias said as the door rattled again.

His friend was in danger and Alixias was not answering the door. Dalton called Jose and requested security. As he transmitted the message, the door slid back, and Patrick appeared. "Good morning Dalton. It's good to see you," Patrick said. "It's not morning, it's damn near midnight! I've been worried sick about you. What the hell is going on?" Dalton asked as he cancelled his request for Jose. "Let's go for a walk. There's something we need to discuss," Patrick replied.

Patrick respected Dalton. The scientist possessed a sharp mind and good values. "Alixias and I are attempting to produce a child," he said as a look of astonishment materialized on Dalton's face. "Are you sure it's even scientifically possible?" he asked. "Mox said successful breeding occurred on Vandi. It is possible. As you are aware, the tablets state humans and Martians were designed to eventually interbreed," Patrick said. "If you're successful, the entire process must be documented. Please provide me all pertinent information as it relates to your breeding attempt with Alixias," Dalton said. "The first attempt was made a few hours ago. I'll keep you updated as the situation develops," Patrick said.

For the next twenty-three days, Patrick provided updates. Eighteen attempts were made without achieving conception. Each unsuccessful attempt reduced the odds of success. It was time for a new set of variables. He interrupted Alixias as she was repairing electrical equipment. "It's time to find a new human male. The attempts with Patrick are not producing results," he said. "Patrick and I are companions. I enjoy his company and he enjoys mine. For better or worse, Patrick is my companion. I'm growing annoyed with your interruptions and interference. I will no longer provide you updates of our intimacy and neither will Patrick. Perhaps we are incapable of breeding successfully, but it's no longer any of your concern. We are to be left alone," Alixias said. "I understand your position, but please understand mine and consider the request of Ambassador Mox. The birth of a child is of the utmost importance," Dalton replied.

Dominic said he trusted Chief Administrator Kizak and Vincent hoped the trust wasn't misplaced. The alien leader was very detail oriented. He would learn the secret that was being withheld from the people of Sol. Whether Kizak shared the information was another matter. Vincent took one last look at the shared quarters and picked up the case containing the few personal items he was taking to Valaxia. The rest of his crew was already aboard the Santa Maria preparing for departure.

"Are we going somewhere?" a voice said. Vincent quickly scanned the room. He didn't see anyone. "Goddamn it Tony, quit doing that. Where the hell have you been?" he asked. "I missed my flight and caught a later one. I have something for you," Tony said as he handed Vincent a sealed container. "Are the Nalis inside?" Vincent asked. "You will now be guardian of the books. It is an important responsibility. There is a third small faction on Cardonia unknown to the Alliance. One of their leaders helped me remain hidden during my time there. The faction is not beholden to the Nalis and operates outside the religious jurisdiction imposed on the rest of the populace. The Alliance must send a covert team of operatives to assist their cause.

The faction wishes to end the never-ending religious wars. They are small and slowly growing and their leader told me his followers only wish to be left alone and to survive," Tony said.

"I'll find a way to get the information to Kizak. Please provide as many details as possible. If the Alliance is to undertake such a mission, the operatives will need to know where to go. The intelligence can't appear to be coming from us. I must discuss what we've done with Dominic. He will need to figure out how to share the information without implicating us. I'd prefer if you kept the Nalis. If the books are found in my possession, I cannot claim deniability," Vincent said.

"The Nalis must remain with you, Captain. I cannot take them where I'm going. This will be our final conversation. It is unlikely I will survive the destination I've chosen," Tony said. "Where are you going?" Vincent asked. "I'm going to Vandi. In time I will travel through the gate to Tanas, the Annunaki home world," Tony said.

"Are you out of your mind? Vandi is almost completely evacuated. There is nothing left to do on the planet. What can you possibly accomplish by yourself against the Annunaki?" Vincent asked. "What I require is not on any Alliance world. I've researched the records of every Alliance planet. Very soon I will lose my sanity if I'm unable to satisfy my body's cravings. I need to continue my search and the only location remaining is in enemy territory. I've enjoyed my regained youth, but the price is too high. If I'm to lose my sanity and become violent, it's best for all concerned if I'm in the Annunaki System," Tony said. "You should stay with us; we are your friends and will help you in any way possible. Let the doctors perform more examinations. We will find a way to help you," Vincent said. "The doctors do not have a solution. More tests would be redundant and a waste of time. You've been a good friend. Goodbye Vincenzo," Tony said with a smile. "You've overcome a great deal Tony. I hope to see you again. This will not be our final conversation," Vincent said as he gave his friend a hug.

The Santa Maria was prepared and ready for departure. Vincent entered the command center and shared Tony's plan with the crew. "It's suicide. He's crazy and has become overconfident in his abilities," Julia said. "I don't think so. He is resigned to his fate and doesn't believe he will survive. There is no other option left for him. He must try to satisfy his addiction. I tried talking him out of it but knowing Tony he will create chaos before he's killed. It's likely he will accomplish much for the Alliance before he dies," Vincent said. "He was a good friend and will be missed," Monique said.

"Yes, he will. It's time for us to leave. Set course for Valaxia," Vincent commanded. "What about Isabella? Where is she?" Monique asked. "Isabella is with Azmune and the mathematicians. The missing tablet was found on Mars. Salkex was apparently on the verge of a great discovery. Isabella will depart on the last ship with the Chief Administrator, the remaining scientists and the mathematical team. She will catch up with us on Valaxia," Vincent said.

Azmune observed as everyone in the room processed the new data and attempted to solve Salkex's equation. "Isn't it about time to leave?" Isabella asked. "We still have a considerable amount of time. Kizak is being cautious. When the Vandi System is invaded, he will order our evacuation. "Has any progress been made? We received the new data from Mars days ago," Isabella asked. "The problem is with dark matter. It consists of particles which phase in and out of other dimensions. Dark matter continually changes and is not a constant. It is a significant mathematical problem," Azmune replied. An alarm sounded and one of the displays turned bright blue. "What does that mean?" Isabella asked. "It's a possible solution and a call to action. Everyone here will now discontinue their previous work and focus on proving or disproving the proposed solution," Azmune said excitedly.

Kizak was growing bored. The exhaustive evacuation effort was now complete. Vandi and Rabanah were evacuated. The stubborn species known as Volmer on Vandi refused to be evacuated and ceased communicating. Less than three hundred people remained on Rabanah. Every soul would successfully be evacuated to Valaxia. He reviewed his upcoming tasks. One of his first orders of business would be to speak with the Earth Ambassador. He researched all known information about the Sol System and as Chief Administrator, he could access every available piece of information. The information on the screen was stunning; it was a crime to withhold it from the Martians and humans.

"Captain we are receiving a high priority communication request. Chief Administrator Kizak is requesting an emergency conference with Dominic immediately," Julia said. "Can we still communicate directly?" Vincent asked. "We are not far from Rabanah. The communication delay will only be three seconds. Kizak is asking for you Dominic," Julia replied. "Activate the primary screen and accept the request," Dominic said as the image of Kizak appeared.

"I know you are busy, Chief Administrator. What can I do to help the Alliance?" Dominic asked. "I conducted research and have uncovered the information you seek. The Annunaki have a singular purpose in their attempt to claim the system known as Sol. Earth is abundant in resources and is very valuable. Feeding and maintaining a vast population is not easy and Earth provides enormous resources; however, a more ancient reason exists for the invasion.

The species you know as Martian are indigenous to the fourth planet of Sol. Martians weren't expected to survive due to sudden atmospheric changes on Mars. The air became poisonous and it appeared the species would be unlikely to endure. The species adapted early in their development, became advanced and thrived. Martians were not the first advanced species which inhabited the planet however. In its early history, Mars was vibrant and full of life much like Earth is today. There were oceans and water was abundant. The planet was a paradise. Martians were primitive at the time and able to adapt to the changing conditions. There was an advanced civilization on the planet that caused damage to the atmosphere and their species was unable to adapt. Modern day Martians weren't a threat at the time and were primitive mammals. The advanced species was intelligent and began to explore space. When the magnetosphere collapsed, the civilization evacuated Mars and eventually found a new home.

The species has advanced, grown and thrived since leaving Mars," Kizak said. "Is the species a member of the Alliance?" Dominic asked. "The first advanced civilization of Mars is not a member of the Alliance. The species is now known as the Annunaki. They have returned to claim and terraform their home world," Kizak said.

The command center was silent. Everyone on the Santa Maria was stunned. As Earth Ambassador, Dominic knew he was obligated to respond. "What about Earth? Why have the Annunaki ignored Mars and invaded Earth?" he asked. "Your home planet is rich in resources. The Annunaki must secure Earth's resources to terraform Mars quickly. When the time comes, the few humans on Mars will be killed or enslaved quickly. I'm not sure why it hasn't happened already. The Annunaki have ignored the planet completely thus far. The people on Mars are doomed; the invasion will be quick and overwhelming. There is little chance those on Mars will live long or recapture their freedom ever again. The process has already begun. The only reason people on Earth still remain is to work and provide food and resources to the Krace and Annunaki," Kizak said. "Thank you for the information, Chief Administrator," Dominic said. The command center of the Santa Maria remained eerily silent.

Dalton was tired, cranky and ready for sleep. He spent the last twelve hours on the surface retrieving buried artifacts. His door rattled. "Come in and make it quick," he said. Surprisingly, Alixias and Patrick entered his quarters. "I was about to sleep. What can I do for you?" he asked. "We have mated successfully. A child grows within me," Alixias said. "How do you know for certain?" Dalton asked. "We visited the doctor. The pregnancy is verified," Patrick replied. "When is the child expected to arrive? Will you give the doctor permission to release all medical records for historical purposes?" Dalton asked. "The situation is unique, and the doctor could not provide an exact estimate for the arrival of our child. We were given a rough estimate of a ten-month gestation period. I will instruct the doctor to release any records you request," Alixias replied.

"We must document all aspects of this pregnancy and birth. I would like for each of you to meet with me once a week to discuss how your relationship is progressing and your plan for the child," Dalton said. "Your request was expected. We are in agreement and will meet with you as requested. It has been a long day for me. I need my rest," Alixias said. "Get your rest. I'm very happy for the two of you."

The two lovers left his quarters. His friends were enduring enormous pressure. When crossbreeding was successfully achieved, Dalton was going to tell Patrick and Alixias what was deciphered on the golden walls. The ancient Martians planned on eventually interbreeding with humans and apparently knew why the two species were designed to interbreed. The walls were now fully translated, but the reason was never articulated. The societal process began in the distant past when Martians first visited Earth. He could find no reason to inform the couple now and add to their increasing level of stress.

"He is a unique human and quite correct in documenting the process," Alixias said as she entered their quarters and disrobed. "Dalton is very dedicated. He picks a project and doesn't let it go until he finds a solution. When he sets his mind to a task he can think of little else. We are a problem and he's determined to find an answer," Patrick replied.

"We've seen a native of Mars die for the first time in modern times and we'll see the birth of a child on Mars soon. We must begin considering a name," Alixias said. "Our child will be born on Mars and should have a Martian name," Patrick replied. "I will compile a list and we will decide together," Alixias said.

The invasion and occupation of Earth was proceeding exactly as planned. Bazor performed her duties honorably and would be known as a hero to her people. She was bored and decided to torment President Louis again. The President sat across the blackjack table inside the Bellagio Casino. She'd been spending her evenings with the human and enjoying the various beverages of Earth. The classical music of Mozart was playing as loud as possible. She particularly enjoyed Ode de Joy.

She was in the habit of enjoying alcohol recently while playing cards with the human. The guards often escorted her home. "The humans on Mars appear to be surviving. I didn't think they would survive this long," she said. "Why do you invade Earth, kill half the population and enslave the rest of us while ignoring Mars?" President Louis asked. "Our species originated on the fourth planet of Sol. Empress Zovad will be the first Annunaki to return. She will arrive on the planet and will remove the invasive species personally. I've been instructed to ignore Mars until she arrives unless Mars becomes a military threat. Hit me," Bazor said. President Louis gave her an ace of spades. She busted, and he won again. "I see why this city was so successful," Bazor said.

President Louis waited long enough. The lone guard left for the bathroom. Bazor wasn't threatened by his presence whatsoever. "You're right, the house never loses," he said as he pulled out Sandy's gun and shot Bazor through her forehead. He used the second bullet and shot her in the chest. The alien leader fell to the floor. President Louis wanted to run. There was a chance for freedom and the clock was ticking. Bazor could be revived for up to ten minutes. If he was going to help his people, Bazor must die. He quickly picked up the alien and put her back in the chair at the blackjack table. He feigned playing blackjack with the dying leader as the guard returned from the bathroom. "I think it's time to bring her home," the guard said from across the room. "Give her a few more minutes. She's on a roll," President Louis responded. The guard sat in a chair and waited. President Louis continued to deal cards and distribute chips.

Empress Zovad reviewed the most recent report. The armada was finally ready, and victory was mathematically guaranteed. The time for invasion arrived. "Begin sending the armada through the gate. It's time to go home," she said. When she arrived on Mars, she would destroy all Alliance forces and would eventually enslave every remaining Alliance world. The defeated enemy would quickly provide the resources necessary for her to rule the entire galaxy. She watched with satisfaction as the first ships of the armada traversed the gate.

"Kizak, the invasion has begun. The gate leading to Vandi has been breached. The Annunaki have reclaimed the Vandi System and are on their way to Rabanah," his aide said. "Issue mandatory evacuation orders for remaining personnel. Anyone left on Rabanah is to evacuate immediately," Kizak ordered.

Isabella observed as the various mathematicians and scientists consulted and verified the solution. "Why does it take so long?" she asked Azmune as the evacuation alarm sounded. "I don't know, but the question will have to wait. We've been ordered to evacuate at once," Azmune said as the verified equation was finally displayed on every screen in the room. "I'm tired of this exercise in futility anyway," Isabella said as the information officer appeared.

"Agreement has been reached. The equation has been deciphered and verified. A summary of all information relating to the equation and the astounding implications have been forwarded to everyone. According to our analysis, we can now affect the transitive properties of any gate with the deciphered manipulation of dark matter. The Tactical Council is in the process of analyzing the situation and determining a course of action. Based on their recommendation, it is possible the evacuation order may be rescinded," the communications officer said. "What is he talking about? Why would we halt the evacuations?" Isabella asked. "Because Salkex was a genius. His discovery has given the Alliance a new tool that might turn the tide in the forthcoming battle. The information officer just stated it's possible to disrupt the gate. We will be able to stop the Annunaki from entering the Rabanah System if the discovery can be implemented quickly enough. It's too late for the Vandi System," Azmune replied.

The room was in chaos. Tony watched as the most experienced mathematicians and scientists attempted to solve the complex equation. Nobody could see him or knew he was present. Before his transformation, he wouldn't have understood anything on the various displays throughout the room, but when the verified equation was displayed, Tony surprisingly understood how and why it would work. He would take the knowledge with him and try to find a way to use it against the Annunaki.

The sky was filled with spacecraft. Tony went to the busy supply station and the line was long. Most of the crews waited inside the station and enjoyed a meal as the automated system resupplied fuel, water and food. The automated system sent the next craft in line into a holding space. The crew was still inside the station enjoying their meal when Tony entered the craft and set a course for Vandi. The spaceship quickly left the atmosphere and accelerated toward the gate. He passed thousands of ships evacuating Vandi citizens. The plan was very simple. He would land the ship on Vandi and wait for the Annunaki to arrive.

The command center on the Santa Maria was silent. Vincent couldn't help but think Azira might have been right. Knowing Mars was the original home of the Annunaki completely demoralized himself and his crew. Isabella finally interrupted the silence. "Captain we've received a change in operational orders. All military vessels have been ordered to return and defend the Rabanah gate against the Annunaki invasion. The Cardonian and Osarian fleets have also been instructed to protect the gate. Evacuations remain in place for civilians. A battle plan and specific orders will be transmitted shortly. We are to rendezvous with a civilian ship and transfer Dominic. All ambassadors are to arrive on Valaxia as scheduled. The rendezvous is scheduled to take place in fifty-seven minutes," Isabella reported.

"Why would the Alliance strategy suddenly change?" Monique asked. "For reasons we haven't been told, the conditions of battle have changed. I wasn't informed of any new developments prior to departure. The solitary issue that was still unknown when we left was the Salkex equation. The Tactical Council was pursuing the correct course of action, but something major must have occurred," Dominic said.

Vincent didn't want to evacuate or retreat and was suddenly reenergized and ready for battle. "I'd rather fight than run. The Annunaki were the first intelligent species in our solar system. We're no longer primitive and will now meet them on equal terms. The atrocious and immoral race of Sol will regret not killing us while we were on Vandi. It's time to retake Earth and exact our revenge. The entire species must be annihilated for slaughtering the people of Sol. It's time for us to go home."

Book three of the Lost Sols Trilogy is now available! The final book "The Awakening" and all other work by the author can be found here:

http://JamesKirkBisceglia.com

Follow the Lost Sols Trilogy on Facebook at:

https://www.facebook.com/thelostsolstrilogy

Made in the USA
Columbia, SC
13 March 2019